ALL THE LIVING
AND
THE DEAD

Joseph Kenyon

Mill City Press

Minneapolis, MN

The Library of Congress has cataloged this Mill City Press edition as follows:

ISBN: 978-1-63505-042-4

LCCN: 2016902779

Interior design and layout by Daniel Snyder

Cover design by Brian Fell

Cover photographs:
"Field and Road" by Jennifer Terranella. All rights reserved.
"Piano" by PhotoSpin

Publisher website: www.millcitypublishing.com

Author website: www.bookmakersediting.com

Published in the United States of America

For Barbara,

First and foremost

And

For the two Johns,

Gibbs and Adair,

who have taught and given so much.

September

1999

≈ 1 ≈

D usk. Mist. Perfect for this night. The way the fog haloed the streetlights, diffusing their beams, sending them drifting to the sidewalk like feathers. The union of mist and dusk gave everything a gritty intensity, blurring the edges between the light and the darkness. The coarse, damp, swirling air. The decrepit neighborhood. Anticipation. All whisked together into the moment. It was the kind of night Autumn would choose to bring a society into the world.

For as long as she could remember, she wanted to feel at the center of something, at the heart of a thing larger than life, and from the moment last spring when Gaston and Lyle first suggested forming a society, she latched onto the idea as that thing. This was the night to carve out a niche: the six of them moving forward into the unknown with only artistic skill to cut the way. Too romantic or dreamy a thought? Well, screw realism. The world was too coldly realistic. Let passion hold sway.

She walked past the shrouded houses and the vacant lots that divided the residential section of Prue from "The Roughie": a three block strip of bars, dingy diners, and sagging buildings rented out to art students as studios by college-town landlords. The area had become a student haven almost from the moment the North American University of Fine Arts — or NAUFA — opened its doors. Here the air was always intense, the byproduct of ruin and rot.

Signs had no reason for being here, another plus in Autumn's mind. If you didn't know where you were going, you didn't belong here. Like the Lick and Poke. Just a plain brown door set a yard inside a plum-colored stone façade with blurred neon signs burning behind glass blocks. Autumn went in and steered past the bar and its huddled crowd of drinkers, heading down the corridor to the back room. Chet, Lyle, and Mary occupied a table to the side of the empty stage, and when she sat down, Chet tossed a copy of the Artisan, the campus newspaper, onto the middle of the table. Hands outstretched, beer foaming over the lip of his mug, he said, "If we're raising a *secret* society, why is word of the initiation rite splashed about in this rag?"

Autumn picked up the paper.

"Third item from the top, second column," said Chet.

"The initiation rite of Société de l'Esprit Artistique will be held on Friday, 21 September 1999, nine o'clock p.m. Nothing's splashed. It's a quiet announcement. So people know we exist."

"Why do we want them to know?"

"What good would it do to form a society that no one knows exists?" Autumn caught the eye of a waitress and lifted Lyle's mug.

"I may only be an illiterate painter, and Mary, as our writer-in-residence, may correct me if I'm wrong, but 'secret' means something no one else knows about, doesn't it?"

"Not in this case," said Lyle. "We're not talking about forming an order like the Golden Dawn. We want an artistic society in the German Romantic mold. They were called "secret societies" because not anyone could join, and the works created by the members went public first under the name of the society, not the individual. Only later, when the societies disbanded or the members reached a certain level of recognition, did the works get individual attention. Groups of that sort were known all over Europe. Anyhow, patrons of the day were aware of them. We're going to want people to know us in the same way, and, for that to happen, they have to know we exist. Pique their curiosity."

Chet grunted and gulped at his beer. "Where the hell's Gaston? What's his take on all this?"

"He was going to Montreal earlier today," Lyle said. "Maybe he got held up. He wanted to do a little research on the rituals and things that societies performed."

"So, there are five of us, right?" Chet asked. "The four of us and Gaston?"

"Don't forget Patrick," Mary said, picking up the paper and re-reading the announcement. "He can't shut up about this Society; he's so excited."

"And you're not?" Autumn asked.

Mary shrugged. "I don't get the same charge out of it that all of you seem to, but it's okay."

Autumn felt the anger rise up through her chest to her throat. So, Mary wasn't excited about the Society. No surprise there. Mary Han was like the good part of Prue and the University: she had to project the appropriate image; she was attending an art school, so she had to be an artist of some sort. Mary only comprehended the beauty of the surface because that was her plane of existence, what she valued: a delicate-as-scrimshaw posture; two brown, Chinese-American shaped dollops for eyes; and skin, as well as poetry, that was as soft and powdery as flour. She wasn't like others in the group, not made of the same artistic stuff, bred from the same artistic bones. They were, to borrow Lyle's term, Romantics – in different ways: Gaston — genius in its purest form; Lyle — the living incarnation of the *Peanuts* character Schroeder; Chet — stoutly devoted to his paints and his pints. Then there was this Patrick Mallard person. Who the hell was he other than Mary's lover?

Chet and Lyle turned the conversation into a debate over what the Society's rituals should be, and Mary waved them into a pause. "All this talk about rites and dark rooms and stuff sounds so weird and cliche-ish," she said. "It doesn't have feeling."

"But that's what we're trying to get," Lyle said. "A feeling, a sense that we belong to a bonded group. All societies had ritual."

"Maybe back in the Middle Ages, but not today. All that stuff just gets in the way of creating."

"How so?" Chet asked.

"Well, look. You say you want us to work on things, write and paint things. Well, if we spend all our time doing this hocus-pocus kind of stuff, then we have to get back in a creative frame of mind afterward. The rituals just take us out of the mood we have to be in to create."

Lyle pointed his finger at Mary. "That's it, right there. That's why we're debating. We want to come up with a ritual to enhance that mood, not destroy it."

"I just don't see the point of it. If you want to create a mood, put on a song. This occult stuff just isn't real. I like to write about real things, things that make a person feel something, an emotion, like ... love for instance."

"Then," said Autumn, "maybe you should write about being in love with yourself. Call it 'To Stroking — An Ode.'" She gave the comment time to settle in on everyone at the table. "Oh, I'm sorry. You said you wanted to write about something that would make you feel. My mistake."

Mary went stiff, and Chet wagged his finger toward Autumn. "Temper, temper, Autumn-girl. Let's keep our tongues a bit more dull, shall we? This is an important meeting."

"Yeah, so damn important that Gaston can't even show up. And where's this gung-ho Patrick I keep hearing about? If he's so excited, why hasn't he hauled his golden ass down here? In his place we have Mary Poppins who doesn't even know what a society is let alone want to be a part of one." She gulped the rest of the beer and slammed the glass down on the table. "Forget it. We can't do this until we're all here and we're all into it, and it pisses me off that we're not. I'm going home."

"Autumn ..." Lyle started.

"No, don't 'Autumn' me. When everyone's ready to do this thing right, when everyone's serious about what's going on, you let me know!"

The anger followed her out of the bar and nagged her all the way up Bloom Street to the apartment. She went in, undressed, and got into bed. Why was Mary with the group if she hated what societies involved? Why did everyone put up with such casual attitudes? Didn't anyone else see what this Society could be? Didn't they care as much as she did? Why did she care so much about any of it? And how did she get like this? The questions circled around her brain until the anger spun away. She dozed off into an uneasy sleep until a tapping from across the room snapped her out of it. She raised her head off the pillow as the bedroom door creaked open, and Lyle's head appeared in the dim crack of light. "Is it safe?"

"Yeah."

He stepped inside and closed the door quietly. "You're in bed? At least you'll be rested for the first day of classes."

"Dammit! I forgot to set my alarm."

"What time's your first class?"

"Eleven."

"I see. And you forgot to set your alarm because you were riddled with guilt about the way you acted tonight, right? You made Mary cry, you know."

"Good. She's damn lucky I didn't tear what passes for her tacky heart right out of her chest. 'Writer-in-residence.' What a load of crap."

Lyle took a seat on the corner of the bed. "So, she's not Wordsworth, but she's not bad. She had some suggestions about a libretto I'm working on, and the stuff she wrote is pretty good."

"I'll be sure to get her autograph when it's performed."

"The point is we better all try to get along. In a little more than two weeks we'll be Society fellows. Speaking of which, you should've hung around a little bit longer and saved yourself — and all of us — a taste of your rage. Gaston showed up about a half an hour after you left, and we got some things settled."

"You want to climb on in under the covers and tell me?"

"Please! You're speaking to the monk of the group, appointed by Gaston to be the keeper of the instrument of initiation for Société de l'Esprit Artistique."

"What the hell are you talking about?"

"Ah, that's privileged information, not to be discussed with every harlot who invites you into her bed. Anyway Gaston drove me over here to pick up some piano string he got for me, and I thought I'd see if you'd calmed down any."

"I have."

"Well then, since my mission's accomplished, I'll go."

"You're sure you wouldn't rather stay with me?"

"My first class is at nine tomorrow, sorry."

He went, but Autumn couldn't go back to sleep. She focused on the shaft of light coming into the room through the thin space between the door and the doorpost, then on the steady stream of aimless guitar chords. She got up, threw on a man's extra-large, flannel shirt and traced the sound to the living room.

Gaston sat on the wide wooden bench built into the bay window, one foot braced against the far frame, the other leg swaying like a metronome. The washed out light from the street lamp brushed across him, occasionally flashing off the bobbing tuning knobs. He managed to gather the random notes into something coherent, and the sound changed, becoming Irish and light, like a fairy dance. Autumn took a seat on the couch and listened as he repeated the complex passage more smoothly.

"What's that you're playing?"

"It's called *Epona*. Patrick showed it to me one night while you were back in Pittsburgh."

"Over the summer?"

He nodded. "Probably about a month ago. I'd forgotten about it 'til now."

"You're playing a song filled with sub-rhythms and quick changes after only hearing it once a month ago?"

"Yeah."

"You suck."

"It's not as hard as it sounds. Get your guitar and try it."

"It's not hard for you, but I'll try it for an hour and not get the opening bars right. Then I'll get so pissed off I'll end up pushing you out the window, and I can't afford the rent for this place by myself. No thanks."

He shrugged and retreated back into his space – this state that only he knew how to reach. When they first met, Autumn suspected him of retreating there to get beyond the reach of everyone. But he insisted that he didn't "go" anywhere, that his level of concentration didn't differ from the concentration every good musician employed. He had always been that sort of man: a genius of creativity who was truly convinced that he was average and that everyone could do what he did. But he had never been average. She remembered listening to him play in the clubs and bars on Pittsburgh's Southside, watching him take requests for an hour — everything from jazz to blues to rock — and play each one flawlessly. Then later, when she first came to stay with him, they worked out this game of musical Bonnie and Clyde: she would cajole club-goers into betting her that Gaston could play any song they named. Classical pieces, show tunes, dusty big band songs poured out of his guitar. They never lost. They ate with that money. He was nineteen; she, eighteen.

No wonder she had fallen in love with him then, this genius whose music she heard in her head while they made love. Five years later she was still in love with him, maybe more so because he had the good sense even that young, to end the affair. She winced at that word; it really wasn't right. "Affair" made their relationship sound equal when their coupling had all the equality of a 72-0 football score. She had been more like his number-one groupie. Once the relationship ended and the friendship began, the gap between them narrowed, and she gladly settled for that. She had too much ego to take another crack at a relationship with a genius.

Gaston never batted an eye when Lyle brought up the idea about going to NAUFA. She hesitated, not having exactly been an academic genius in high school. But Gaston simply said, "Sounds cool," and came along. While she attended the university, he pulled in the money by playing in clubs, sometimes locally, but most often in Montreal.

Despite their history together, she never quite made it into his space. She understood that place to be a perfect pocket of deep passion for him, a place that he searched for in bits and pieces in the real world. Within a month of coming to upstate New York, he found a chunk of that place in Montreal. Within a year he had mastered Canadian French, mastered the musical styles of the Québécois, and fled to the city as often as he could. When he couldn't be there, he brought the nexus of Montreal back to Prue in little ways, such as insisting that the Society be known by the French version of its name. That intermingling of his space and his world served as a conduit and a governor for the incredible passion that lay like an aquifer in the man. He remained the only person, place or thing in the world that made her feel wide-eyed and in awe.

"You hungry?" she asked.

"Yeah."

"Okay, so what'll it be? Do I make a midnight breakfast for two or push you out that window?"

"Eggs'll be cool, if you're up to it."

"Good choice."

~ 2 „

The fall term began on a day as fine as Quinn Gravesend could hope for in early September: a crisp blue sky and a steady breeze that had the trees shaking their leaves like they were laughing in places. The air moving into the classroom through the window had lost the wilted, sense-dulling feel that comes with the sultriness of summer, and, instead, it marched in with a fresh snap. This was the way the first day of the term should be: a day of no surprises, the kind of day where one could find excitement in the anticipation of knowing that what is expected is right on schedule.

Gravesend stood at the window near the head of the class, his back to the door. Students filed in behind him, and he felt first their eyes and then their thoughts probing the fact that he was not expected to be standing at the window ten minutes before the start of class. They'll grow accustomed to it. He smiled and amended his previous thought: the first day of the term should not hold surprises for a member of the faculty. Students, however, should find surprise in ready quantities.

There came the last burst of commotion as the stragglers and the fashionably-late took their seats. Still, Gravesend didn't move from the window; he waited until the room became quiet. Nothing measures the mettle of a class as the length of time it takes them to notice the professor is waiting for them to hush. It was an old-fashioned method, and granted, in this day and age when collegiate manners and protocol had gone the way of the turntable and the record album, perhaps the method wasn't quite as accurate as it once had been. Still, it worked.

This class settled rather quickly. With an expected rush of anticipation, Gravesend left the window and the waving trees and strolled to the lectern resting on the front desk. There he raised his head for his first view of the group. There were twelve: fresh student faces like eggs in a carton awaiting painting for Easter before being laid out for the hunt. Every semester they came to be made in this way, their faces holding the same expression. Only their clothes changed. This group consisted of tie-dyes, rugby shirts, jeans, a ruffled blouse, and three unkempt fashions lumped, Gravesend supposed, in the modern style he still thought of as "grunge." Standard wrapping for standard packages, the products of two years of a good undergraduate education in the rudiments and technology of composing music.

Gravesend leaned forward, elbows resting on the chipped, wood veneer box and smiled an expectant smile. A colleague once defended the practice of lecturing with his eyes closed by saying that after twenty years very little remained to be seen. Gravesend saw it another way: a professor is poorer for sailing through the first day of the term blind. The best part of the semester is that first day, cracking and freeing those eggs made from the shelled conformity of their earlier education. No, the first class of the term was the one class that was too good to miss.

He took a deep breath. "The composition of music is a hunt for a mythical beast. Therefore, I want you to tell me all that you know about hunting mythical beasts."

The first cracks appeared in several egg faces. Two of the more anal students made worried checks of their schedules to be sure they were in the correct classroom. Gravesend looked directly into the eyes of the sole student in the front row, the young woman in the pristine ruffled blouse with the starched brown eyes to match.

"Ms ...?"

"Green. Charlotte Green."

"Ms. Green, what do you know about hunting mythical beasts?"

"Well, you'd have to be pretty imaginative for one thing." Her answer drew laughs from several people in the room. Gravesend was impressed. Perhaps this group wasn't as dull as it looked.

"Very well said, Ms. Green, and correct. But please, add to that answer that one must also be prepared — for anything."

As if on cue, every student opened a notebook and jotted down a note. The note. If anything were to doom education specifically and thinking in general it would be this endless fascination with note taking. Jotters, Gravesend called them, diseased to the point of delusion. As if they could transcribe meaning by scribbling. More often than not, the jotters missed the whole tenor of the lecture. He wasn't about to let this group stain with ink the keen edge Ms. Green just showed. He came out from behind the lectern and leaned against the edge of the desk, not a yard from the first row of seats.

"Be prepared. The motto of the Boy Scouts and the most useful advice a person can take to heart. You have all come up through the ranks of the music program. How many of you feel prepared for this class?"

Several students raised their hands. Others, sensing the trap, remained still.

"Prepared for what? The ancient hunter, about to embark on the chase after his not-so-mythical beast, certainly had his tools ready: weapons, butchery utensils, supplies, water. Much like that hunter from ancient times, you sit here before me today, *prepared*. You are armed with your knowledge, your skill, and your endless hours of practice on various instruments. You no doubt could pass an exam on the compositional techniques of composers ranging from Mozart to McCartney with flying colors. But is that all it takes?

"The ancient hunter's preparation was not limited to the gathering of tools, but it included the ritual to gather the spirit. A hunt was more than a search for food; it was a spiritual undertaking, and every step in that hunt had a higher meaning that carried nearly impossible stakes. 'All well and good,' you are saying to yourselves right now. 'I'll remember that, Mr. Gravesend, if I have to answer an anthropology question on *Jeopardy* tonight.' If words to that effect have passed through your head in the last five minutes," a sweeping glance revealed some startled faces, "then I suggest you think with a bit more depth.

"No doubt, your compositional theory courses have supplied you with all the physical tools you will need to engage in your own personal hunt for that mythical beast we call music. But in this course, Philosophy of Composition, we will explore the spiritual side of the hunt. The ritual."

Gravesend was making some headway against the jotters. Two particularly dogged students were still writing; most, however, had given up. A few even looked interested. He left the desk and plunged into the middle of the room, coming to a halt between the two jotters. Ms. Green and another student near the front turned their heads to follow him with their eyes. Everyone else, including the two pillars of note taking, froze.

"The first question becomes, then, what is meant by these metaphors: mythical beast? spiritual side? ritual? Mythical beast, I have already defined for you; it is your music, your own creations, the *anima* alive inside your breast, usually forced into the more common appellation: potential. You are at once the hunter and the beast. The beast must be flushed out before it can be slain. So too, the music must be wrenched out of you before it can be composed. Thus, the metaphor. Now, what is meant by the metaphor implied by the word ritual?"

Tapered fingers appeared at the head of the row, waving like a flag of torn flesh on the corner of the lectern.

"Yes, Ms. Green."

"Ritual would be how we call out the beast, how we get the music out."

"In order to ...?"

Her fingers fluttered in mid-air, groping for the answer not coming into her head. Gravesend made his way back to the front of the class and turned to her with deliberate confidence that the correct answer would be forthcoming. He held her in his gaze until the muscles in her face began to quiver. The mind is a muscle as well, Gravesend thought; it must be broken down in order to rebuild it as a stronger and wiser mass.

"Much of what we do is ritual, yet to what end?" He resumed his posture against the edge of the desk and gazed up at the ceiling, stroking the short white bristles of beard on his chin, beginning his mental count to thirty ... his allotment of time for the class to dwell on any question before receiving another prod.

But a voice from the back of the room broke his count at nine. "The end would be unlocking the soul, which is what ritual does. So, the metaphor states that in order to search for the music inside us and to bring it out, we need to look into our souls, or our spiritual side, as you called it."

Gravesend stopped mid-stroke and directed his gaze toward the back of the room. "Mr. ...?"

"Lyle Glasser."

"Mr. Glasser," he repeated, making a mental note to be aware of this fellow; he was a sharp one, more so because Gravesend hadn't marked him as sharp in his opening estimate of the class. Sleepers appear not to be sharp, but more often than not Gravesend picked them out. But he had passed over this student, one of the rugby-shirters. He returned Gravesend's gaze with an impassive expression but an intensity that was magnified by round, wire-rimmed glasses.

"Excellent, Mr. Glasser. That's exactly what we will be doing in this class: probing our souls and discovering what beasts lurk therein. And, if we're lucky, we may discover a few ways to lure the beast out into the open where it can be handled through music. At any rate, we'll be taking our first steps on that hunt. When you come to class on Thursday, I want each of you to submit a cassette tape on which you'll have recorded a musical interpretation of your soul."

There was a long silence, then a flurry of questions:

"How long?"

"What instruments?"

"What specific type of music?"

Gravesend fended off the blows with upraised hands. "Far be it for me to put limitations on your soul-searching. That's the province of your minds and hearts, not mine. All I ask is that you put your name on your tape, purely for reasons of return. That's all. Good day to you!"

He swept out of the room, letting the door swish shut behind him. An exhilarated breath escaped his lips. The first class of the semester was always the peak of the mountain, especially as he got older. And Gravesend felt old indeed. It would be a long descent toward Christmas, but now he looked forward to his office and a cup of tea.

Mrs. Bourgione, the Music faculty secretary, handed Gravesend a note as soon as he came through the door. "Dean Oughterard called a moment ago. He wants to see you as soon as you can make it, so don't get comfortable."

"Did he mention what he wanted?"

"No, but he made the call himself, and he had a sweet sound in his voice."

Gravesend groaned, and he kept at it inwardly as he made his way down to the first floor and the office marked *Dean of the School of Music*. After the requisite delay by the secretary, he was ushered into the spacious office wrapped in glass on two sides for the view, then covered with insipid plastic blinds to obstruct the same view.

Dean Oughterard was a slight man whose attempts at informality consisted of wearing plaid ties rather than solids with his conservative suits. He doled out his Deanship from behind his desk with the traditional range of expressions: from corporate-firm in debate to piously apologetic when in need of a favor. Gravesend knew the university chain of command well enough to understand that deans were often caught in the verbal crossfire between senior administrators and faculty. Deans fell in the middle, having to endure the complaints of both sides, and the result was a group of ear-strained, academic orphans. For this visit, Oughterard assumed an apologetic expression with a hint of desperation, and it was the latter that Gravesend feared most.

"I took a call this morning that concerned you, Quinn."

"A student or parent is complaining already?"

"Nothing that easily dismissed. The call came from Antoinette D'Abonne. It seems the Home Society is gearing up for its visiting season, and your house is on the top of the list. Congratulations." The Dean lowered his head and raised his hand. "Before you say anything, let me state that I did everything in my power to get you off the hook again. But Madame D'Abonne has had your house marked for the past few years, and I've somehow managed to steer her away from you. This time she just wouldn't be deterred. At the first sign of resistance from me, she played her trump card, dropping dark hints about slamming the lid of her late husband's substantial coffer on the hand of the School of Music."

"What possible reason does that woman have to be interested in my house of all places? There isn't anything spectacular about it."

"On the contrary. It's a beautiful home. And, even if it were a two-room box, it contains a mystery."

"What mystery?"

"An article about you that mentioned a room you haven't entered since you composed your last piece."

"That article was published in 1980! Julia had died just a few years before that. Does Madame D'Abonne think people's lives don't change? That a person would stay out of any room in his own home for nineteen years?"

"So, you do use that room? It'll open for the tour?"

Gravesend shifted his jaw back and forth. "That's beside the point."

"No, Quinn, that's exactly the point. It's that kind of trivial mystery that would keep Madame D'Abonne's interest fired for nearly two decades. And finally, if your home didn't have a mystery room, if it didn't have anything else, it has you, Quinn. And in a town of so many successful artists who teach here, you are the crown jewel."

"Spare me your flattery, please."

"That isn't flattery; it's truth. Modesty aside, you're the most influential composer of classical music in the last half of the century. Period."

"I haven't composed a piece of music since the 1970s."

"That makes no difference. In the eyes of the Antoinette D'Abonnes of the world, you rank supreme."

"Eyes! You don't know how right you are! The last thing I want or need is to host a dinner party for a group of pseudo-social voyeurs who get their jollies by pushing their noses into other people's closets and discussing what they see for an age afterward! How could you agree to setting such people on me? They want a mystery? Why not investigate what happened to that art professor, Shero Bosellini, when he disappeared back in the 70s?"

The desperation in the Dean's expression became more pronounced. "They'll never find an answer to that and besides, Bosellini kept a lousy house. Look, I agreed because the whole affair will endear the School of Music to this University's most generous benefactor, and that endears the School of Music to the Chancellor."

"This all belongs in the School of Dance, you know." Gravesend rose. "Of one thing you can be sure: neither D'Abonne nor any of her social chippies are getting a look at any room I wish to keep closed. I won't have my private life open to public debate."

"There's no reason why you should. Here's the guest list she faxed over." He handed Gravesend a piece of paper.

"Your name is here."

"Yes, at my insistence. It's the least I could do. You shouldn't be stuck with shouldering the burden of hosting this alone." His voice dropped to the level of an undertaker. "If I may touch on a sensitive subject for a moment, will this be the first gathering at your home since Julia passed away?"

Gravesend nodded. "With all good luck, it will also be the last."

"Drinks at six then, on Friday the 21st, followed by dinner and a tour of the house. It won't be so bad, Quinn."

That phrase — "It won't be so bad, Quinn" — skipped around his brain throughout the day, tagging along on his evening walk. He reached the mid-point — a grassy hillock crowned by a stone nearly twice his height and set in the center of the summit —

and stepped around the stone. The St. Lawrence River came into view. As a rule, he only paused here for a quick view and a breather, but the Dean's words had changed to music: two different musical sequences bending together to meet, harmonize, and create a perfect circle. Notes gathered to the theme of completion and emptiness in his head, swirling and then dying, like the lonely silence in a recently deserted ballroom.

He leaned against the monolith, warm with the heat of the afternoon sun. The notes slowed in tempo and became regal. Images followed, images of the stone as an ancient boundary mark and the river as the border of unknown lands beyond. Quite a metaphor for life, thought Gravesend, even his own life. If he turned and looked back at his life, what would he see? A good life, one that afforded him a place at the top by any measurement one would care to use: age, accomplishment, stature, money. Indeed, his was a tall life.

The notes changed with the last thought, becoming dirge-like, as if playing for all the dying things he saw giving way at the moment. The day. His summer routine. His life, so much closer to its coda than its overture. And yet, somewhere behind the somber and funereal notes, he discerned another sound, a very faint but pervasive note of joy. It was jarring and off-kilter, like laughter in a funeral home filled with mourners. Laughter that was entirely inappropriate and socially embarrassing, and yet, beneath that, refreshing and relieving.

The sense of completion stayed a steady course through the fleeting musical notes and unbidden images. The sense of being inside a circle around this time and place in his life intrigued him. What enabled this walk, such a routine act in his day, to trigger the sense of being on the brink of a critical point in life? Never before had he heard the epiphanic voices that seem to make occasional visits to everyone's ears and whisper that life was about to radically change course. When he composed the first notes of *The Julia Suite* — indeed, when he first talked with Julia — he heard no notes to clue him into how that composition and that woman would grip and frame his life. When he first read the newspaper accounts of the plans to construct the North American University of Fine Arts, he sensed nothing that would have given him an inkling to how linked he was to become to the school. He did realize that his life would change at the moment the doctor announced that Julia's cancer was beyond cure, but only a fool wouldn't recognize such a life-shifting event as that.

The notes in his head faded off one by one until only a single sound remained: a B note played very high up on the scale, tapped out consistently in mezzo piano. He knew the note, recognized it from two decades ago when one of his composition students suggested he listen to a Pink Floyd piece entitled *Echoes*. The work opened on that note and in the very same way he felt it playing in his head now, unwavering, like a lighthouse. A perfect beginning, he had thought. That's what he told the student, adding that the note remained the only worthwhile thing he found in that backwash of noise the student had called "musical composition at its most innovative."

"Good," Gravesend thought, "I recognize the note and have a feeling that I'm headed for a radical change in life. Bloody well wonderful. But why now? And what does the sensation demand I do about it? Seek a major life change? Ridiculous. One cannot go about *making* a life change. Laying that aside for a moment, I went through an irrevocable life change when Julia died. No sensation, no matter how strong, will change that."

He watched the river flow by, thinking that he could retire. Every spring he decided to retire, then changed his mind sometime around the end of term. This early in September the thought became appealing again as he spied out the school year from the long end, but a sense of duty always suppressed the notion. Although the thought of rocking Oughterard's this-is-best-because-I-know-best expression with a retirement announcement effective January 1 brought Gravesend a moment of delicious enjoyment, the Canadian in him vetoed such an act. It would not be fair or appropriate.

He could compose again. Perhaps begin a new work to fit this new feeling or time? No. He was done with that, or rather, composing was done with him. A twenty-three-year-old iron is too cold to strike. The notes in his head had nothing to do with actual compositions. They were the same notes that he had always heard and felt in response to everything he perceived from the time he was a boy: a sort of sixth sense, interpreting both the seen and the intuitive world via music. Random notes came to him in his younger days as the musical potential in every animate and inanimate facet of life. They remained, aged like him, until they sounded like mocking shadows, ghosts of notes that could have, at one time, perhaps been collected and collated into a composition but now would never see a score.

The best course of action, Gravesend decided, was to let the note and the sounds be. He had no idea what purpose they intended, if they had any purpose at all, and he wasn't likely to reach home before dark if he didn't start walking very soon.

He disengaged himself from the stone with a lurch, causing a sharp pain to shoot up his back. Sixty-three was not a pliable, stone-leaning age, but thank God it wasn't a macho one either. He didn't have to care what others thought of his manhood. He could hobble if he liked, and so he did, down the hill toward home, thinking of dinner and an early bedtime with a good book. B notes be dammed.

ॐ 3 ॐ

Night on the 21st came late with the sun bleeding in pink, orange and red hues all along the horizon. Wind moved in off the river in wavy rushes rattling by the window of Lyle's studio apartment, a third floor attic in an old house. The decor inside stood in counterpoint to the changing weather outside. Four candelabra with six candles each threw out the majority of the light from their perches around the room: atop the grand piano, on the shelf below the window, on the wire and blotter rack that served as a night stand,

and on the stove in the kitchenette. Inside and outside, Autumn approved.

Everyone had dressed with some sort of distinction. Behind the piano sat Lyle in formal wear, complete with white gloves and tails, his face moving in and out of shadows so that it never was completely revealed or hidden. He tinkered with the piano keys, mixing together ethereal sounds. Beside him stood Gaston in a long brown robe with a monstrous hood that covered the whole of his head and shaded all of his face but his chin. He had come in character: Gaston the father-confessor, the shaman-priest. Chet rested on the page-turner's seat to Lyle's right, his burly frame slung with paint-spattered jeans and sweater; even his canvas sneakers were globbed with paint dribbles. Mary and a tall, wiry man with an English accent and a cloth bag stood beside the piano. Both of them were dressed in black turtlenecks and jeans.

And Autumn, standing apart from the group at the piano caught a glimpse of herself in the room's only mirror and declared herself in sync with the spirit and the sense of the room. The effect she wanted was sylvan: a draping, cape-like top of hunter green, edged in lace that hung like leaves from her sleeves. Tight green leggings ran up beneath the cape and down into black, high-heeled boots. The curls of her hair spilled down between her shoulder blades and under the influence of the guttering golden glow of the candles, the auburn shade deepened to the color of wine.

She moved in closer to the piano as Chet said to Mary, "You and your friend chose the right color for the occasion. This place looks like a morgue on Halloween."

The man offered his hand. "Patrick Mallard."

"Chet Kunzler. And if there's a bottle in that bag, you'll be my friend, too." He nooked open a corner of the bag and peered in. "Champagne? Ah! May I call you Pat?"

Lyle kept repeating the phrase he was playing in an attempt to find an exit. Unable to do so, he softened the bars with each run, hoping to fade them out of existence. Finally at a signal from Gaston, he just stopped and swiveled around. "Okay. So, what's next?"

Gaston set the candelabrum on the piano beside several note cards and a gold-plated paten. "Time to start. I'll conduct. Lyle, you'll assist. Could all of you move around to form a half circle in front of me?"

When they were in position, Gaston took up the pile of cards and consulted the first one. "I'll begin with a quote from C. Kerenyi's essay entitled *Prolegomena*: If cosmos is understood in the Greek sense that everything spiritual, and our compulsion towards the spiritual, are an essential part of the cosmos, then here," he paused and made eye contact with each person in front of him, "we have the cosmos meeting with itself."

Gaston shuffled to the next card. "Now, I'll read a description of our purpose, as written by candidate for membership, Lyle Glasser: All of us came to this university to learn and advance our skills in our chosen arts. That's what the studies, professors, and performances are meant to do. But there's another quality to art that seems to have been lost to the mechanics of education. It goes beyond our physical talents to an awareness of and marriage to the spirit behind art, the mystical presence attending the creation of every composition. The Romantics, because of their very nature, were keenly aware of this presence, and they formed societies to draw the spirit of art closer to the surface so that it was there beside them as they composed and critiqued what each of them was striving to create. That is our purpose, to bring our artistic selves into closer contact with the spirit of art and assist in each other's creations. Rituals, such as this initiation rite, do that. We share a communion with the past and the future, a communion of who we are and what we have committed ourselves to doing."

Gaston raised his hand with the palm outward. "Therefore, here in this room, on the 21st of September, in the year 1999, I declare the formation of Société de l'Esprit Artistique: to advance the growth of each member in the art of his or her choice, to encourage and draw from each other's raw inspirations and ideas in order to mold and create living works, and to realize our artistic role as the bridge between the unseen and the visible."

Gaston flipped to the next card. "The next step is the recitation of the litany to reaffirm the principles that will guide the Society. Respond 'Aye' to each phrase. Do you wish to be initiated into Société de l'Esprit Artistique?"

"Aye."

"You are then charged with advancing each member's work through the sharing of thought and spirit. Do you make such an oath by seeking initiation still?"

"Aye."

"You are charged with sharing yourself and your work with the Société and promoting those works under its name during membership. Do you make such an oath by seeking initiation still?"

"Aye."

"You are charged with not revealing the membership, the inner workings of the Société and its members' discussions, works in progress, or ideas to any who have not been initiated. Do you make such an oath by seeking initiation still?"

"Aye."

"As all present have sworn themselves to the principles of the Société, let the initiation passage begin."

Gaston placed the note cards on the piano and motioned for Lyle to take up the candle as he lifted the paten and stamp. He pulled back his hood, revealing his face for the first time. "As the Ovate of Société de l'Esprit Artistique, I declare that I seek initiation still and accept the sign of the Society and creativity." Lyle poured some of the wax onto the paten. Gaston dipped the stamp in the wax and immediately applied it to his forehead. He removed the stamp, leaving a wax impression of the crescent moon on his skin. Then he pulled the hood forward, and his face disappeared in its folds.

"Lyle Thomas Glasser." Lyle moved in front of him. "Seek you initiation still?"

"Aye."

"Then accept the sign of the Society and creativity." The wax poured, Gaston set the stamp to Lyle's forehead, after which, Lyle resumed his place beside Gaston, who called the rest of them forward:

"Autumn Seanna Gilhain."

"Chester Kunzler."

"Mary Han."

"Patrick Stuart Mallard."

Patrick stood nearly six inches taller than Gaston, and when he bent to accept the mark, Autumn did a double-take. Was it her imagination or did he genuflect on one knee rather than bend? That was not a gesture she expected from Mary's lover, and she stared after him as he resumed his place in the semi-circle.

"The purpose has been read," Gaston said, "the oaths sworn, the initiation rite completed. Let the work of the Société begin."

"I call for a toast," said Chet. "A round of the best stuff befitting this occasion."

Patrick opened his bottle of champagne first, followed by Chet's bottle. By the time the group dipped into Autumn's wine, midnight was approaching, and the rites took on a mellower, less inhibited air. Chet, who had brought an easel and canvas, declared it too constraining and began to paint the wall on one side of the window. Mary, who had been sitting upright on the corner of the bed, peeled off her turtleneck and laid back, her skin aglow in the candlelight, offset by a black bra. She continued to write in the notebook. Lyle sat at the piano, Gaston had his guitar, and Patrick worked with his pennywhistle as the three of them tried to pull together an original arrangement.

Autumn had her guitar as well, but she didn't join them. She sat in a far corner, trying out a melody of her own, but the room had grown hot. The fumes of Chet's paints, Mary's unexpected exhibition, and the tinkerings of the group at the piano became agitating, and the magic she felt in the early part of the night began to fade. She tried the tune once more, but when she misplayed a phrase near the middle, she rose without a word and went out into the night.

ֆ 4 ֆ

Gravesend hated pettiness. There should be no place for it in a life too short for most of the good things. Why waste precious time on the irrelevant bad? But even he had to admit at this moment, as the Home Society seated themselves around his dining room table to indulge in dinner, pettiness had a place.

He did all that Oughterard could ask. Throughout cocktails, he played the gracious host, putting forward his best effort to be accommodating and charming at the same time. Not an easy task by any means in the face of the fifteen members of the decor Gestapo, spearheaded by the inimitable Antoinette D'Abonne.

"Inimitable" was the first word that sprang to Gravesend's mind, followed closely by "swooping." After that, the mental descriptions went downhill. D'Abonne had a relentless habit of answering the simplest questions with what she called "pearled words." Earlier in the evening, when asked by a new member in the Home Society why she began the group, D'Abonne replied, with complete sobriety, "I felt my hand must contribute at least a minor stitch to the ever-spinning loom that produces the tapestry of our university and community." Gravesend recalled her commenting after her husband's funeral that not enough people used pearled words anymore, a social deficit for which Gravesend felt truly thankful.

And there didn't seem to be enough linguistic oysters in the world to produce the string of words D'Abonne could let fly when describing the Home Society. Members devoted themselves to the joys of the decorated house. To that end they toured houses "in season" — that is to say in the spring and the fall as well as a special to-do at Christmastime — on both sides of the river. The tours consisted of drinks, a room-by-room viewing guided by the owner, a catered dinner (paid for by the Society) and then an after-dinner review at a less-organized, more informal pace. This last segment often proved to be the most torturous for the owner. He or she may be called upon repeatedly to explain why a certain piece of art came to be displayed as it was or why a chair had been placed in a corner instead of around a table, and so forth. Now in its fifteenth year, the Home Society had become something of an institution. And like all institutions, it was tolerated with good cheer, usually forced, and would remain so for as long as the late Monsieur Emile D'Abonne continued to be more generous to the university dead than all other living benefactors combined.

By dinner, the tour had severely taxed Gravesend's patience and graciousness. Twice, D'Abonne asked about the locked door on the second floor. Both times Gravesend pretended not to hear her, and when she suggested in a more enunciated and shrill voice that they had missed a room, Gravesend promptly replied, "Not at all, Madame; the dining room will be our final stop." The comment drew a laugh and temporarily silenced D'Abonne, but Gravesend's whole attitude became porcupinish.

Revenge, however, awaited him at table. The Home Society graciously allowed the host to choose the menu, although that honor came heavily seasoned with hints that Madame D'Abonne's French blood and bias were strongest in matters of food and drink. With that in mind, Gravesend smiled as the potato and leek soup was followed by grilled duck in plum sauce. The side dish was corn, and English tarts comprised dessert. Drinks consisted of the finest Burgundy and Chardonnay wines New York's Finger Lakes region could produce.

D'Abonne, who sat to the right of Gravesend, had regained the use of her tongue and was holding forth on the subject of the painting on the north wall of the dining room. The avid attention the two women to Gravesend's left and the man on D'Abonne's right were paying her, marked them as either new to the area or candidates for full membership in the Home Society, perhaps both. The painting depicted two men standing en garde with a writing quill and a paint brush across a river. Above them floated a host of seraphim with horns and lyre, and a ribbon coming from the mouth of the middle angel bore the legend *Jette la chose maudite dans la milieu de la rivière, et c'est tout pour ca.*

"Magnifique!" cried D'Abonne. "The entire painting, but especially the statement, is a wonderful tribute to the wife of Mortimer Howell, one of the University's founders of course. It is art with just the right amount of good-natured mischievousness. Do you not agree, Mr. Williams?"

The man blushed and replied in a low voice, "The soul of the painting is beyond me, I'm afraid, Madame. I don't speak much French."

The corners of the lady's mouth turned southward, and her expression told the world that Mr. Williams had just sealed his exclusion from the Home Society. "Mr. Gravesend, perhaps you would be good enough to explain?"

"Certainly, Madame. The North American University of Fine Arts was founded by Mr. Russell Moss, an American poet and literary critic, seen holding the quill on the right, and Mr. Mortimer Howell, a Canadian art patron and musical manuscript collector who holds the brush. Both men wanted to found a college specifically for students in pursuit of a degree in the fine arts, but they quarreled incessantly over where that university should be located; Mr. Moss wanted it in New York and Mr. Howell argued for Montreal. After one meeting, both gentlemen carried their argument outside to the car that had arrived to pick up Mr. Howell. While the driver opened the back door and waited as the two gentlemen continued to argue, Mrs. Howell reportedly leaned across the seat and called out, 'Put the damn thing in the middle of the river and be done with it.' That is the translation of the phrase from the angel, and the genesis of the idea to put the university in both countries. The Schools of Music, Writing, and Sculpture are here in Prue, and the Schools of Painting, Theatre, and Dance are across the St. Lawrence River in Newtown, Ontario. On the island in the river are the library, dormitories, student center and faculty and student dining halls. Only footbridges connect the island with both banks of the river. The bridges were donated by the U.S. and Canadian governments and can be crossed without customs checks. As far as we know, our university is unique in this arrangement."

"As it is in other ways ..." D'Abonne's attention wandered and alighted on a storm brewing at the center of the table concerning the rose upholstery patterns on the chairs in the adjoining sitting room. Now that he was paying attention, Gravesend heard four or five mini-debates popping up around the table. Somewhere along the course of the debates, the participants threw glances in Gravesend's direction, eager glances of the seeker to the guru. The final push toward the after-dinner inquisition had begun, and Gravesend, suddenly, couldn't face it. Excusing himself to take care of a problem arising in the kitchen, he left the table, plucked an old jacket and a battered tweed cap from hooks on the basement door and went out through the cellar entrance into the night.

He walked to no place in particular, allowing the wind to wrap him up in arms of damp silk and soothe his jangling nerves. Some things never change; he couldn't remember a single party in his life from which he hadn't "fled," as Julia used to call it. He hated crowds in close quarters. Crowds were so intense, growing into entities unto themselves like tornadoes, sweeping up individuals and gaining force until they dominated the room, whipping at people who only preferred a bit of solitude and quiet conversation. It was a trait he picked up from his father. Gravesend could take crowds as long as he could separate himself via a classroom desk or stage piano. The Home Society, however, made separation impossible. He shrugged as he walked. Let Oughterard handle them.

He had no idea how long or how far he had walked until a steel column rose up in front of him, twisting with switchback angles. The piece, entitled *The Beginnings of Creativity,* stood beside the entrance gate to the University, bringing Gravesend to a halt. The gate was two miles from his house. He was calm but tired. Instead of turning around and trudging home, he decided to go to his office and call a cab.

He passed beneath the arches of the gate and started down the path leading to the Music building. The wind carried distant sounds, adding them to the echo of his own footfalls, and one of the sounds Gravesend recognized as an acoustic guitar. He didn't know the music, but immediately he noted that the guitarist was using a heavy hand to play a song that demanded a light and delicate touch.

The sound broke off, followed by a single-word outburst: "Shit!"

Gravesend kept walking, and ten yards on a young woman materialized seated on a bench, one leg tucked beneath her, the other planted firmly on the ground. For a moment, she reminded him of the fairytales he read as a child in which woodland elves would step out from the forest dressed in flowing clothes the color of trees and flowing hair decorated with leaves and flowers. So she appeared to have done, even though no forests were about, and Gravesend could not recall ever reading about an elf that cursed its own music. She bent over the guitar in such a way that her face was obscured from view.

The song broke down near the middle again, and she let out what sounded like a growl. She tossed her head with enough force to dislodge two leaves, which promptly skittered away into the darkness. Gravesend noted how pale her face was, and before he could judge whether she was pretty or not, she spotted him standing on the path. If it were possible for a person sitting in her position to jump, she did.

"My apologies", said Gravesend. "I didn't intend to startle you."

Instead of replying, she turned back to the guitar and made another attempt at playing the song.

"If you don't mind my asking, what's the name of the piece you're playing?"

"*Epona.*"

"Are you learning it for a class?"

"No." This time the song broke down only a few bars in.

"Was the piece originally done on guitar?"

She lifted her head again. "Look, what the hell is this? If you're looking for sex, try the apartments on Chaucer Street. Or is it your job to prowl the college annoying the shit out of people trying to play some music?"

"I'm sorry, no. I'm questioning you out of habit, I suppose. I'm Quinn Gravesend, Professor of Music, and I was thinking that the difficulty you're having with that song might be the result of the instrument you're playing."

"No, my difficulty is the result of the fact that I suck." She closed her eyes. "Sorry. I'm frustrated."

"Indeed. But don't judge yourself too quickly. Do you know what instrument the original song was written for, Miss ...?"

"Autumn Gilhain. Dulcimer, I think."

"In that case, Miss Gilhain, a piano may serve you better than a guitar. The tone would be closer to the original. Hearing the song in a similar tone will help you to learn it."

"Maybe, but I didn't have a piano on me when I came out here tonight."

"Quite right. Still, there is the piano lab in the music building and a good piano in the student practice studio. You could also ask one of your music professors. Many of us have pianos in our offices."

"Um-hmm." She fingered the guitar slowly, working her way through the sequence of notes.

"Well then, good evening and good luck," said Gravesend, but she didn't reply. He continued on down the path.

– 5 –

The first tangible result of Société de l'Esprit Artistique is evident in Lyle's apartment, 25½ Davis Street. A cassette demo, roughly taped with two microphones, holds close to eleven minutes of music written and recorded by Lyle (piano), Gaston (guitar) and Patrick (pennywhistle and some sort of percussion, perhaps a pot?). There are places where they play together and breaks for individual instrumentation. What's surprising is that the finest moments in the work are all parts they play together. Despite the fact that Gaston and Lyle have played together often, neither has ever played with Patrick, whose style and approach is so very different. I would think the shining moments would have been the individual sections. But there it is: the musical version of a fried egg in a salad. Somehow, it works.

But the most impressive effort tonight is the mural Chet painted on the far wall of the room. The first half from the south wall to the window is done in black, red and copper tones against the whitewashed block: a hunt scene, primitive in the way that all raw art is primitive; the bulky coat that hides the svelte form. The painting seems like a cross between the Bayeux Tapestry and animal paintings found on the walls inside of European caves. On the window, which is surrounded by a misty swirl of grey, like fog, he painted a poem by Mary:

Through this shifting world's maze
we race, but stop—
The sound of the horn delays
the chase. To crops
we're called, our dreams to raise.

On the other side is a lush growth of vines in soft greens and black earth under an azure sky. The work steals emotion from the viewer but gives back more than it takes. Whether or not this adds or detracts from the work, Chet is sound asleep on the floor in front of it, having given his all. Lyle is on his bed talking softly to Gaston. Mary and Patrick are gone.

And what contribution did Autumn make to the Society's first night? She tried and failed to learn Epona, and swore at a complete stranger. In other words, about what she contributes to art every night. In lieu of few artistic achievements, this record will be my contribution, but a silent one since I can't tell anyone about it because of that oath of silence, but more than anything I want to record all that happens here. This group of people, at the very least Gaston, Lyle and Chet, will one future day mean quite a lot to the artistic world. That is when I will make my contribution to the group. A Society member, not some half-assed critic or student looking for a doctoral dissertation, will give a first-hand account of their growth, of who they were and how they came to their recognition. But for now, this record of a secret Society will remain the secret seed buried within me.

October

❧ 1 ❧

"I came to use your piano."

Gravesend shifted his attention from a student's score book to Autumn, framed in the doorway, a passing nod to the tradition of waiting to be invited into a professor's office. The top half of her was already in. She leaned forward with one hand gripping the door frame for balance. Gravesend didn't respond, watching her disengage from the doorframe and enter his office with bold-faced steps. She stopped short of the desk and rocked forward, bouncing her thighs lightly off the front edge, giving the room a critical once-over.

"Nice place."

"Thank you. When you teach at one institution for nearly a third of a century, you earn a few benefits."

Autumn pointed at the overhead lights. "Too bright though. Those things wash out all the atmosphere. You should have lamps to give the place a softer look."

"I'll mention that to the interior decorator."

She shrugged, tossing her knapsack of books onto an unoccupied chair, and made her way to the piano in the corner. She studied the keys with intent, as if they were arranged in code.

"You came to use my piano?"

"Yeah. You invited me."

"Did I now?"

"You said most professors had pianos in their offices, and I should see about using one. Here I am." She sat down on the bench and began to play.

Throughout his career, Gravesend had observed literally thousands of students at work behind the piano, but he never recalled anyone approach a piece like Autumn went after *Epona*. Predatorial was the nearest description that came to his mind. She padded around the first part, circling the melody, moving in a slow weave, her eyes glued to the keys. At every change of tempo or key, she lunged forward, her fingers bounding after the notes she wanted, running the melody down, teasing it with a game of cat and mouse, wearing it out. Finally, she moved in for the kill on the parts of the song that brought out the most passion in her playing: jabbing at the keys not just with her fingers but with her hands, arms, and shoulders to boot. Her body heaved, her back arched, and her elbows swung madly. The end result was nothing short of butchery. All the timing and touch of the song were lost. Nevertheless, Gravesend was intrigued. The teacher in him cringed at her form, but the musician found her passion riveting.

"That stunk," she announced, pounding out an unrelated note and swerving around on the bench. "I thought you said it'd be easier on piano?"

"I never used the word 'easier'. I said the piano may give you a more true sound, one that would be closer to the original because the notes in your head and the notes that you play will be closer in quality, pitch, and tone. That can help you get a more honest sense of your progress. But easier? I'm afraid that depends on how skilled you are with the piano."

Autumn pointed her thumb toward the piano. "Not very. Obviously."

"Then you should spend more time with it. The keyboard is literally the 'key board'. It's the key to all forms. If you master the piano, you open the gateway to the mastery of all music."

"I didn't say I couldn't play it. I just don't, not that often."

"Perhaps try warming up first to get reacquainted. Get comfortable. Play something you're familiar with instead of throwing yourself straight into the unknown."

She swung around and fiddled with a few keys. Gravesend left his seat and assumed his teacher's stance: positioning himself to her right, one foot on the piano bench to afford him a view of her hand movements. She tinkered with several sounds, started something and stopped, and then made an abrupt entrance into *Ode to Joy*. This time, however, the hound-on-the-hunt contortions didn't follow. The spirit and the passion that she put into her performance of *Epona* remained, but her body remained calm. Her fingers struck the keys in smooth, easy time and with flair. Only her lower lip caught in the grasp of her upper front teeth displayed any sign of intensity.

Gravesend's concentration shifted from her playing to the music itself and the wafts of jasmine drifting up from her swaying wrists. Smell and sound lingered and mingled in his brain waking a deep memory. He let it come to him rather than trying to grab for it. Something about the jasmine scent Autumn was wearing. The idea of a club came to him, but whether that was part of the memory or some puzzle piece his mind created to try to bridge the gap, Gravesend couldn't tell. The memory got stuck just below his conscious horizon but sufficiently near and powerful enough to send a chill through him. Autumn closed the piece, and the memory sank back into the depths. The chill lingered.

"Getting comfortable, you mean, like that?" she asked.

"That was beautiful. Absolutely beautiful! How is it that you can play *Ode to Joy* with such perfection and yet have so much trouble performing a lyrical song like *Epona*?"

Autumn shrugged. "I've been playing *Ode to Joy* since I was ten. It was my mother's favorite piece."

"I see. Well then, onto the next step. What I would like you to do now is to sit with your eyes closed and hear *Epona* in your head. Play it in your mind exactly. Keep it in tempo. Concentrate. Listen to everything: the pattern of the notes, the variations, and the stresses. Don't do anything else. Don't try to visualize the music or any of that nonsense. Just replay it note for note in your brain."

She responded with a queer look but complied, sitting quietly and motionless except for one foot that tapped to the invisible sound of the song in her mind. Gravesend, meanwhile, went after the hint of the memory. Was it the music or the smell of the jasmine that had summoned it? Both together? But they were contradictory, were they not? Beethoven rough-and-tumbled the senses with a raucous, spirited lift, while jasmine caressed subtly and sweetly. Then there was the club idea. He searched his mind for a connection between place, sound and scent, but found none. He hung out and played in many clubs up through the end of the '70s. *Ode to Joy* he had heard an incalculable number of times. Jasmine was more of a rarity. No. The club was a red-herring, and he was certain that the other two things never met before this moment in this room. He took a deep breath to close that door and clear his mind, but another thought slipped through: Was the chill in response to false memory or a living emotion?

Autumn opened her eyes. "Okay, I've done it."

"Good. Now, replay the song in your head just as you did, only this time let it run out your fingers — but slowly. That's important. You want to feel the flow of the music; you want to feel for the keys, not think about them or how they sound. As each note comes into your mind simply react and reach for a key. Remember to keep the song playing in your head in its proper time, but don't worry about hitting every note or hitting the wrong note. In other words, concentrate on the note in your head, not how you're playing that note."

Her fingers tapped along the keyboard calmly, without the accompanying body gyrations. The rhythm and timing of the song remained uneven, and after striking several incorrect notes, she banged her hand down on the keys. "I just can't play this damn thing! I've been practicing for three weeks now, and I still play like my hands are covered with glue!"

"Patience. You have to let the music come out of you, and that can be difficult work. You can't force it out. And getting angry will only make it worse."

"It can't get any worse! And don't tell me not to get angry. I've had this song in my head ever since Gaston first played it, and I still can't learn it!"

"You may find it helpful to work on something else for a bit and allow your subconscious time to mull over the song."

"I just told you I can't play it."

"Then why bother? Is this an assignment for a class?"

"No! It's because Gaston Gunn is a genius." She scowled at the keys, swiping a piece of lint from the board. "There's nothing he can't play and play well. He heard this song once, just once, and without thinking about it, let alone practicing, he was playing the freaking thing on the guitar like he wrote it."

"This Mr. Gunn is a student?"

"I said he's a musical *genius*. He doesn't need teachers. Any song he's heard once, he can play. It's like people who can remember names after meeting a person one time or people who remember every bit of trivia they hear. Only he does it with music. And like a fool, I try to keep up with him because I don't want to admit that I'm not a genius."

Gravesend took his leg off the bench and straightened up. "Can this Mr. Gunn play your piece on the piano?"

"Piano, dulcimer, bongos, you name it; he plays them all. It's like he can just visualize a song and — poof! — he plays it. The instrument's irrelevant."

"Well then, Ms. Gilhain, I'm afraid you've come to the wrong place for help. You should consult your friend. I make no claims to being a musical genius."

She threw him a look of pathetic disgust, a look Gravesend knew so well that he took an involuntary step back from the piano bench. He used it often enough to jab students who fell short of their potential because they had given up or had not tried hard enough.

"You know," she said slowly, "I came here because a friend of mine said you were a cool teacher who wouldn't mind helping me out. So don't give me attitude. Sorry if I bruised your delicate professor's ego, but the truth is geniuses don't need teachers. Only the marginally talented like me need teachers. And if you don't believe Gaston's a genius, come down to the Lick and Poke one night and hear him play."

"The Lick and Poke?"

She waved her hand in some vague direction. "A bar near the end of Bloom Street, The Liquor in the Front, Poker in the Rear. There's a room in the back where people just take the stage and play what they feel like playing: rock, jazz, blues, classical, ethnic stuff, whatever. It's a cool place with some great music. Gaston plays on Sunday and Thursday nights. Come and hear him for yourself, and you'll find out just how great he is. Drinks are cheap."

Gravesend smiled. "Thank you, but no. It sounds like a place more for the student set than for me."

"We get a mixed crowd. And I've seen faculty in there lots of times. Sarah Xydon from the School of Art plays a set on the flute every once in a while. Anyway, it's not a drink-'til-you-drop kind of place if that's what you're thinking. People come to talk and hear good music."

"And do you ever perform?"

"Sometimes I play accompaniment for Gaston. But most of the time I just go to listen. You'll know a lot of the people there. Lyle for one."

"Lyle?"

"Lyle Glasser, from your Philosophy of Composition class. He's the one who first told me to come here and ask for your help." She looked at her watch. "Shit! I'm late." She was off the bench and brushing by Gravesend before he could move. Grabbing her bag off the chair with one hand, she swung it onto her shoulder as she headed for the door. Then she stopped, turned, and tossed her hair, flashing a smile at him. "Thanks."

"You're very welcome, Ms. Gilhain."

She walked backward through the door. "See you at the Lick and Poke soon?"

"I won't make any promises."

She nodded as if he had, and then she was gone.

ఏ 2 ⊷

Autumn stayed curled in the leather armchair that Gaston found in a second-hand store, a copy of Barthes' *Image/Music/Text* open in front of her. From that vantage point, she tracked Gaston's rustling and humming as he gathered up what he needed. With a quick "later," he went out the door, but Autumn still didn't move, keeping the book open, and listening. Gaston was forever forgetting this or that, but she knew he had a one-block window in which he would turn around and come back to the apartment to retrieve the forgotten item. If he were more than a block away when he remembered, he went on without it. She let enough time elapse until she was sure he was further than a block away, then got up, checked that Gaston had locked the door, and went into her bedroom. She tossed the book into her knapsack and grabbed an ordinary spiral-bound notebook down from the shelf above her bed. Settling back against her pillows, she began to write.

Society Meeting #3, October 8, 1999 ... 7:30 p.m. - 12:10 a.m. ... Lyle's Apartment.

The session opened with a long discussion about what the Society's first tangible production should be. There were two possibilities: a recording of the works the musicians and Mary had composed, or an exhibition by Chet of thematic works done with oils, which was almost complete. Everyone had an opinion and while no one got out of hand, there was a lot of tension. More of a sense of urgency about producing something that could be shown or performed in public. Lyle was wound pretty tight. Mary didn't look bored. Patrick and Gaston spoke in clipped sentences. Chet didn't drink. Once word of the Society got spread around the campus, the level of curiosity about who the members were and what we were doing took all of us by surprise. Before the campus lost interest, something had to go out. Up until now, some of the compositions in rough form had been performed at the Lick and Poke, without fanfare or any announcement that the pieces were composed by and for the members of the Society, so they were useless. Good decisions couldn't be made in that kind of an atmosphere, and everyone knew it, so in order to do <u>something</u>, everyone agreed to make a rough demo on Lyle's reel-to-reel machine of the songs we had been practicing and go from there.

The recording began around 8:45. The first piece we got down was called *The Grammar Snippet* composed by Lyle, with the following line-up: Lyle on piano, Gaston and me on guitar, Patrick on recorder, Chet on drums, Mary on tambourine. It took three takes with the third being the only complete version. Patrick sneezed eight bars into the intro of the first one, and Chet lost the beat halfway through the second take. No one got pissed, but no one joked about the breakdowns either. After the third take went smoothly, it was clear everyone felt relieved. Gaston is a guy in constant motion, but until that third take was done, he stood perfectly still. Once finished, he started to nod. Chet just continued to keep the beat to the song on his head.

Next, a Gaston composition, entitled *Summer with the Swans*, was recorded with the same line-up, except Gaston played a portable organ, and Patrick used a flute. This piece was much more complex, and we made nine attempts. Six were complete. We stopped to have some pizza and listen to all the takes, all of us, except Mary, agreeing on take seven. She liked nine.

The recording session ended with a strange, jazz-like piece that Patrick composed and only Lyle and Gaston had worked on, so the rest of us went to the other side of the room and tried to stay as quiet as we could. There were some interesting musical things being done that showed just how talented this group is, such as Lyle and Gaston breaking into a spontaneous, improvised duet in the middle of the music.

G: *If you like water / L: I don't prefer wine*

G: *Settle for something hotter? / L: How's about some moonshine?*

G: *Got a taste for the hills / L: Never liked the street*

G: *Run, darling, run / L: Mama's got quick feet*

G and L: *There's no way out of here! Hmm-hmm-hmm-hmm-hmm-hmm-hmm-hmm.*

Gaston began that last line, and Lyle jumped in on the "no" in perfect sync, and they even hummed in unison. After the recording was finished, Patrick and Mary, looking stunned, applauded, but Chet and I accused them of planning the duet ahead of time. They looked at each other. Lyle explained that they hadn't, but when they both realized that the music veered a little close to an old David Gilmour song, Gaston sang "there," and Lyle went with it. They didn't want to wreck Patrick's piece by continuing with the Gilmour lyrics, so they hummed themselves back into place and carried on the rest of the song. Now we were all stunned.

Lyle volunteered to take the tapes to the studio in the Music building and transfer the "best" versions. Then we renewed the discussion of what should be the first public works of the Society. *Ritual,* the piece composed on the initiation night, still needed to be put on tape, and music also had to be worked out to accompany Mary's recital of three poems. Gaston was all for reserving studio time and working out everything on real tape. Lyle and Patrick both weren't sure. It was Patrick who came up with the final argument against recording now, saying any recording would sound amateurish until they knew the works inside and out. Gaston might be ready, but we all needed more time.

I hadn't marked Patrick as being as serious or as much of a perfectionist as the other two. But, he's really turning out to be quite a match for them, although much different in style than either Lyle or Gaston, who are much more traditional in their compositions and instrumentation. The duet aside, Gaston's experiments are for his private retreats and rarely shared with the group or suggested for recording. Lyle is straight classical music and traditional forms. He even admitted to Quinn Gravesend that he didn't care much for Gravesend's works! Patrick has this way of suddenly going on some wild tangent — for instance this jazz piece — which is so totally different and off-the-wall that it's almost shocking. Yet when he does this, he seems more in his element, more natural. He brings the color and variety to the music that Gaston and Lyle won't.

By putting the musical angle on hold, we were still in need of an introductory work, so the conversation turned back to Chet and his oil paintings. He said that a series of thematic paintings concerning time could be ready for viewing by Halloween. That's all we needed to hear. The decision was unanimous. Chet said he would make the proper arrangements with the University gallery.

❧ 3 ❦

From his car, Gravesend watched young men and women — all dressed in flannel shirts and jeans — pass by and disappear into the wind-blown drizzle and darkness. They moved with the ease and confidence of youth: that protective sheen that allows young people to think the time in which they live is virgin clay, theirs to mold.

There had been a time when he walked this sidewalk with the same belief and much the same swagger. These crusty old buildings looked better then, too, although not new by any means. By the time a young Quinn Gravesend claimed these streets, they had already been over a hundred years old. There were sounds back then, sounds that had gone silent now: Workers calling back and forth, whistles blowing time, trucks moving raw materials in and finished products out. Music had to elbow its way into The Roughie and fight for some space. That's what made the place so raw, so intense. This was captured ground where bodies once lay. That night when a promising, young saxophonist, Alston Kamp, was pulled into a service alley and beaten to death because a gang of whites held different views about a black man having a white woman on his arm than the students who came to listen to the music play.

He smiled at how Autumn Gilhain felt compelled to explain the open-mike forum at the Liquor in the Front, Poker in the Rear as if her generation created that format, that stage, and that place. She can be forgiven. Doesn't every generation assume their way of doing things was born of their own genius? Yet, there was something sad in what got lost over time. That club got its strange name because of an incident that was just beginning to grow into colorful legend when he arrived in Prue. As the story goes, the tavern used to be called The Mill Race, and the back room was a dining area, not a stage. It stood a block away from the old Prue lumberyard and came to fame in 1919 under the ownership of Roland Siegel, an ex-lumberman who lost his arm in a planer. Prohibition changed The

Mill Race, and most other bars along Mill Street (as Bloom Street was known then), from a drinking establishment to a card club that specialized in poker. But unlike his competitors, Siegel used the cards to front a more profitable enterprise: the smuggling of whiskey and wine from Canada into the States.

When Congress repealed Prohibition in 1933, Siegel sat in the enviable position as the sole provider of alcoholic beverages to mill workers with a fourteen-year thirst. On the day drinking became legal, Siegel's helper, fondly remembered in the legend as a dim-witted young fellow, came to work and nearly died of fright when he found cases of alcohol scattered around the front of the room. He was hurriedly hauling the goods to the back when Siegel walked in, saw what he was doing, and reportedly yelled, "For chrissakes, boy, don't you read the papers? Prohibition's been repealed, and the Governor's cracking down on illegal gambling! You know what that means? It means liquor in the front, boy, poker in the rear!"

Ages upon ages ago.

How many old mill workers watched their time disappear into crowds of young artists — his crowd — who flocked to this section of the town once the university had been built to write their chapter of history? Personal history, such as the Friday night after his first week teaching at NAUFA when the other members of the music department hauled him down to the bar and made him take that stage and perform *a capella* as a rite of initiation into the faculty. Or town history, such as the night in 1968 when, sitting at a side table with some colleagues, he looked up to see Miles Davis strolling, unannounced, onto the stage. Over the next hour, Davis performed a tribute to John Coltrane that still made Gravesend's blood tingle, thirty years removed.

Now, these kids on the sidewalk, not his own white-haired generation, continued that history. In his era the bar's name was shortened to the Liquor and Poker. What did Ms. Gilhain call it? The Lick and Poke? "Crude" was the first thought that came to his mind, but he checked that line of thinking. Looking down on the young is the first and most obvious sign of getting old. While he found some modern music distasteful and a lot of the habits of modern students lazy, he knew too that jealousy underpinned a lot of both feelings. The fact was that when he thought about himself at all, he thought of himself as a young man. So whenever he caught a glimpse of his face, or even its shadowy reflection in the rear-view mirror, it startled him. His face had aged like these buildings, but was far, far less solid, less recognizable. He still felt like the man he was in his youth, but there was no getting away from it: He was more timid, more introverted (if that was possible), less willing to take risks. Less willing, even, to enter the door of a club he had walked through countless times before. Souls doomed to Hell, he concluded, did not burn in unflagging fires; they became eternal spectators.

The last thought drove him out of his seat and down the sidewalk. He felt self-conscious in his tweed jacket and tie, found himself wishing he hadn't come. But he kept walking. Take a deep breath. Grab the brass door handle of the Liquor and Poker — so familiar, like the hand of a lover. Go in.

After ordering a whiskey and water at the bar, Gravesend went down the corridor past the rest rooms and into the back. The room had changed, but there were still familiar touches that he remembered: The stage front made from wood slats of varying sizes, The Mill Race sign above the doorway leading to the basement, the worn currant-colored velvet curtain that covered the corridor to the kitchen. Gravesend surveyed the people in the room; not another tie and jacket in sight. On the stage, a fellow in a hooded sweatshirt and shorts pounded out a rhythm on steel drums. At a table to the right of the stage, he spotted Autumn Gilhain with a companion who was wearing sunglasses and nodding as he listened.

The percussionist finished to loud applause and deep-throated chants of "Ar-tee! Ar-tee! Ar-tee!" Tossing his dreadlocks, he sauntered off stage, and Autumn's companion took his place, guitar in hand. He began with a rendition of Stephen Stills' *Love The One You're With* and his voice was double-edged — partly sweet and partly rough, the kind of voice that allows the singer to perform love ballads and throat-ripping rock and roll with the same ease. He finished the Stills song with a flourish on the guitar, acknowledged the response of the crowd with a soft "Thank you" and moved on to a blues melody.

"Am I privileged to be hearing the famous Gaston Gunn?" Gravesend asked arriving at Autumn's side.

"Hey! Have a seat. Isn't he great?"

"Very good."

Gunn ran the gamut of styles in his set. After the blues piece, he played a jazz tune, a fiery rendition of *Blue Suede Shoes*, two pieces of contemporary music categorized as alternative, and finished with a long guitar version of Mike Oldfield's *Tubular Bells*. When the applause began to fade, he leaned toward the microphone and announced that he would take requests.

"*Green Grow the Rushes*," someone called out from the back of the room.

Gunn nodded and started into the song.

"As many times as I've seen him do this, it still amazes me," Autumn said.

"Play this song?"

"No, take requests. I've never known him to get stumped."

"That's not surprising," said Gravesend, "considering the sort of audience a place like this draws."

"What's that supposed to mean?"

"Well, the people here are all roughly the same age. Most likely they have the same interests and musical tastes as Mr. Gunn. As long as he knows what body of work is currently popular or fashionable among the students, he should be able to handle whatever is requested."

"You just don't get it, do you? He can play anything as long as he's heard it once! This isn't some average college crowd, you know. You heard his set. The people here appreciate all forms of music, not just pop stuff."

"Agreed. But if you surveyed the room, you would find most of the patrons prefer a similar type of music or a list of songs from all genres. Also, judging by the response he was given, I'd say Mr.

Gunn is more or less the house act so the people know what he can do, and they request songs within his range. Nobody in this room is going to ask him to play, for example, the Rondo-Allegro movement from Mozart's *Concerto for Flute and Harp*."

"Ask him."

"Pardon me?"

"Ask him to play the Mozart piece. Or any classical work for that matter."

"Don't be ridiculous."

"He'll play it, I'm telling you."

"First of all, I don't see a flute or harp up there. Secondly, I'm not going to embarrass the young man."

"Embarrass my ass. If he's heard it, and he's heard a lot of music in a lot of forms, he can play it. Go ahead."

"Listen, I didn't mean to insult your friend or take away from his talent in any measure. I can see that he's an incredibly gifted musician, and I understand your defending him, but that is no reason—"

"I don't have to stick up for him. He's capable of doing that for himself. Request something."

"I will not."

"Afraid you'll look like an ass when he knows how to play it?"

"I won't even dignify that comment with a response."

"Then go ahead. We can bet."

"Bet?"

"Yeah. If he can't play what you request, I'll buy you a bottle of your favorite. What is it, whiskey? wine? a case of beer?"

"I'm not much of a drinker anymore."

"Okay, then you name your winnings. Anything you like. Your call, any price."

"And if I lose?"

"Then you'll have to give me something I like ... to be named later."

Her head fell to one side, and Gravesend found her smile to be too coquettish for comfort. He felt his face grow hot. "I'm not sure I like the sound of that."

"Well, you don't have to worry about how it sounds, right? I mean, you're so sure that he's going to blow it. But he won't, as long as you don't pick some obscure, 5th century Belgian madrigal or something."

She was smiling at him cat-like, and it made him feel like the mouse at the edge of its hole contemplating the crumb of cheese just beyond its reach. There was an intensity about her that put him off-balance, an intensity that told him she desperately wanted him to play along. And he was still blushing; he could feel the heat coming off his face like thermals rising from the pavement in the summer. He always was an easy blusher, whether he was embarrassed or not, and he hated it. Even more, he hated the idea that a student thought she had him just where she wanted him, especially about music. Julia used to call it his "closet competitiveness." For good or bad, Autumn Gilhain had just wrenched open the closet door.

"Very well. I'll choose something that he should have heard if he is as well versed in music as you insist."

Gunn was sailing through the final chorus of *Swinging on a Star*, capturing the song's jaunty, hat-tilted sound. When he finished, he wiped his face with a towel and said in that same soft voice, "One more I think."

"*The Promenade* from Mussorgsky's *Pictures at an Exhibition*," Gravesend called out.

A look of uncertainty flashed across Autumn's face, but without missing a beat, Gunn unstrapped the guitar and laid it aside. He stepped over to the piano, seated himself, and then off he went. The piano needed tuning, Gravesend noted, but Gunn managed to give as much justice to the piece as the instrument would allow. At the end, the crowd rewarded him with another blast of applause. He stood, nodded slightly, and went to retrieve his guitar and towel.

"He did it. Ha!" said Autumn, "and he did it damn well if you ask me."

"So he did."

Gunn came off the stage and joined them. Autumn waved a hand toward Gravesend "Gaston, this is Mr. … Doctor? … Quinn Gravesend, Professor of Music and pomposity."

Gunn removed his sunglasses, a gesture Gravesend recognized as a sign of respect. His eyes were naturally wide, showing white completely surrounding the brown iris, making him appear to be in a state of permanent wonder. Much to Gravesend's surprise, the wonder appeared to be genuine. "No kidding, Quinn

Gravesend? Wow! I know your work. Cool stuff." He coughed. "My throat's all dry, you know?"

"I'll get some beer," said Autumn.

Gunn took the seat across from Gravesend. "*Symphony Number 1976* was simply awesome."

"Thank you. It's always flattering to meet someone who knows my work."

"Know it? Man, I studied it. I mean, everything was so perfectly balanced even though the tempo kept changing. And some of the heights! Listening to it sounded like being on top of the world, you know? And then coming down, it was like falling fast into nowhere. How'd you manage to come up with that?"

Gravesend lifted his chin and stroked his beard. "To tell you the truth, I don't remember. I haven't thought about composing *1976* in a long, long time. That was ... a chaotic time period for me. I really couldn't say for sure how I managed to keep anything in balance then. I don't mind telling you, however, that the effect you described as 'falling into nowhere' pleases me. I suppose I was trying for something rather apocalyptic."

"You got it! Boy, you got it! But, it wasn't like the whole piece was depressing or anything. You had sub-rhythms going through the down parts that were good, I mean happier, you know? And the high parts always were balanced by some more ominous sounds. Balance! Everything was in perfect balance."

Autumn returned with the drinks. "What're you talking about?"

"Mr. Gunn was just boosting my ego with his flattery."

"Not flattery. It's the truth. Man, *Symphony Number 1976* was something. I also loved *Symphony Number 1967*. Another one that blew me away. I told Autumn that she should find some of your stuff, and we should listen to all of it. You've never heard the symphonies, have you, Autumn?"

"Uh-uh," she replied brusquely then looked at her watch. "I wonder where Chet and Patrick and Mary are? They should've been here by now. You don't think they thought we meant we'd meet them at the party, do you?"

Gunn shrugged. "We can go see if they're there. If they come here and don't find us, they'll go on to Donner's place."

"You have plans," said Gravesend pushing back his chair, "so I won't keep you. I came to hear you play, Mr. Gunn, and I must say that I'm impressed."

"Hold it, Mister! You're not going anywhere!" said Autumn." We're not leaving right away, and you owe me something."

"You said that was to be named later."

"Well, I'm naming it now. I think Gaston's right; I should hear your works. So, Gaston, what're you in the mood to hear now? *Symphony Number 1976?*"

"You want me to play from one of my symphonies?" asked Gravesend.

"Yeah."

"*1976* would be cool, but it couldn't be done on that piano," said Gunn. "It could handle one of the slower movements from *The Julia Suite*, though."

"Great," said Autumn. "A movement from *The Julia Suite* it is."

"I'm sorry, but I couldn't possibly play right now."

"What kind of a teacher tries to slide out of a bet?" asked Autumn. "A musical genius would never do that."

Gravesend raised both hands, palms outward. "I'm not trying to get out of making good on my bet, I assure you. It's just that I can't play now, here. Especially not from my symphonies."

"Why not?" asked Autumn.

"For starters, I haven't played one of my pieces in twenty-some years."

"Jesus Christ, I'm not asking for a whole symphony! Just a selection or two won't kill you."

"I promise, I'll return and play something – soon. But not tonight. Thank you both. Mr. Gunn, I'll say it again, you're an excellent musician."

"Fine. Leave," said Autumn kicking at the leg of an unoccupied chair. "But, I'm not going to let you forget about this."

"Nor will I forget. Goodnight." He nodded to both of them and moved away from the table, making a conscious effort to appear like he was simply leaving the room and not fleeing. But once he was beyond the door, he hurried down the corridor and out into the cool night as fast as he could. He drove erratically all the way home.

§ 4 §

The air had turned cold and smelled of snow on the way. But Autumn was grateful for the heavy, low-slung clouds; they cut off the moonlight. The wind, too, subdued all fainter sounds. What boldness made her come this far, she didn't know. Still, when Gravesend froze in the act of raising his glass to his lips and looked alert, as if he heard something, she ducked behind a tall grave marker, crouching in its shadow. At the same time she heard the sound of a car moving in reverse. Headlights appeared, arcing away from where she sat and pointed back toward the main road. That was Gaston pulling away from the cemetery entrance; she had no other choice now but to stay.

She stood. The stone she had been hiding behind was topped by a statue of the archangel Michael slaying the serpent. Gravesend sat only a few yards away.

She moved to the edge of the monument.

Gravesend finished his sip of wine.

"I favored Halloween above any other day in the year as a child," he said holding up the bottle and refilling his glass. "I bet I never told you that. Or perhaps I did and forgot mentioning it. Anyway, Peter, Ingrid, and I would leave the farm at dusk and try our best to flit down the country roads, pretending to be invisible, carried along by the stiff winds blowing off the Manitoban plains. We were spirits haunting the paths of the world because for that one magical evening our farm, and all the others surrounding it, formed the entire world, and we were the spirits loosed upon that world. If the winds howled through the trees, they did so at our bidding. We called for moonlight to shine, or if clouds cut out the light then our spells caused it to happen. We commanded the rain and snow, or, if we wished, the sky would remain clear and cold and the lingering light of sunset could not fall beneath the horizon until we gave the sign. The roads were empty for fear of us, for the door of the underworld stood open, and all the people barred their own doors against our terrible faces.

"Because, you see, we took corporeal form in order to demand offerings from the living, our tithe, to ensure that we would remain in the formless underworld for another year. Their doors would open slowly in response to our deadly hollow knocks, and the warm air from inside their houses would come pouring out to soothe our cold faces. The neighbors passed out their goods with looks of feigned horror poorly covering genuine amusement. This would go on until eleven when we were called back along the dark road to Erebus. Actually, home, where we delivered all the goodies we had gathered and changed into pajamas to await our transformation. We were imaginative kids, weren't we?

"Our transformation came at midnight. Then the haunters became the haunted. We would gather around the fires of hell – the living room fireplace, the only light allowed in the house on Halloween – and suck on lollipops as mother, whom we referred to on this night as *Mor Mephistopheles*, spun Danish ghost stories. Her spells were far more powerful than our own. As she spoke, the wind became the cries of the dead approaching from the graveyard two miles away; the crackle and snap of the fire became echoes of their laughter and footsteps, drawing closer, lured toward us by the sound of her voice and the spidery piano accompaniments played by father.

"How I'd love to go back to that time, to recapture the feeling of being innocent and wide-eyed again. To experience Halloween one more time as I did fifty years ago, or even twenty-five. I know you don't like it when I say I hate something, but I do hate Halloween now and have hated it for two decades." He took a deep breath. "I know, I know. You wouldn't like me talking this way. Forgive me. More wine?"

Gravesend filled a second glass with the Pinot Noir and poured the contents slowly into the grass that covered the grave. After topping off his own glass, he settled back against the headstone and took another drink.

"Okay!" He blew out a deep breath. "How am I? I don't know. I know I cannot hide anything from you now that you have solved the final mystery. Like I could hide anything from you when we were married! But I'm good at hiding things from myself. So, take this with a grain of salt when I say that I am not being swept away. I'm too old for that sort of nonsense." He snorted. "I would have thought I was too old for any of this. Let's see. What's happening?

"You know what this feels like? Victoria Day, 1956, in the Ornsby Ballroom. Only I was much more full of myself then. I had so many people telling me at twenty that I was sure to be a genius by thirty, and I believed every word of it. Into the room walks this exotic Indian woman with a soft face and a very shapely dress, and Ryan tells me she is a freshman at the University of Toronto, not yet a year in Canada. Knowing that, I knew that getting her to bed would simply be a formality; after all, any young, Manitoban lad worth his stripes in my day knew immigrant girls were less uptight about sex than native Canadians. So I strutted over to her, and in return I got such a slap that my cheek carried the bruise from her hand for several days.

"Just as well, wasn't it? Had she accepted my proposition that night, I surely wouldn't be here now. Her slap sent me off on a chase that led right to you, didn't it? You tried to convince me for years that you planned it that way, planned on me even before you met me. Well, my love, I have little doubt now that you did."

Gravesend poured another round of wine: one on the grave and one for himself. "Anyway, that's how I feel: as if I am at the beginning of something much like I was at the beginning of my work and love when I first saw Teema, and that romance led me to marry the greatest woman in the world. I cannot envision ending up quite as well the second time around.

"So, where was I? Yes, these feelings. I'd brush the whole thing off as self-indulgent rubbish, but I'm having that recurring dream about composing again, the same one I had right after you died. It begins with me in the auditorium of the Conservatory watching old Heinstadt, but instead of lecturing, he is writing out a musical score on a large chalkboard at the side of the room. Each time I have the dream, the score grows, becomes a bit more complete. And each time, I raise my hand and comment that I'm not familiar with the piece. He gives me the how-stupid-can-students-be look and yells in that terrible German accent he had, 'I am noting vat you are tinking because it's damn goot!'

"When did I first start dreaming this again? Sometime around the beginning of the term. Actually, I think the dream is rooted in vibrations I first sensed on the day the term began, when I took my walk and stood watching the river. I had it again during the night of that stupid Home Society Party. Then I had it again two nights ago when I went to the Liquor and Poker to see that guy I was telling you about play and his friend Ms. Gilhain. When she asked me to perform, I panicked. There is no other word for it. The vibrations at the river, the dream, the unknown sensation I told you about earlier when Ms. Gilhain came to use my piano: what's the connection?"

Gravesend stopped talking to take a sip of wine and stare up at the sky for a minute.

"Of course, it's entirely possible that I'm asking the wrong question to evade the truth. What do you think, Julia? You always waited for me to ask for your help, and you never failed to be helpful in your own aggravatingly mysterious way — and that's when you were alive. So, I'm asking now, and I'm going to shut up, close my eyes and listen for your reply, if, indeed, you haven't nodded off into spiritual sleep. I hope not, my love. I always want to hear from you, but now, I fear, I need to."

Autumn watched him shift, settle against the headstone, and close his eyes. What the hell was he doing? Was he going to sleep? No, no one could sleep in this cold and wind, with snow on the way, but as long as he sat that still, she couldn't move, unless she wanted to jump out and say "Boo!" She hunkered down beside the stone, huddling in her own arms, to wait for whatever was to come.

✍ 5 ✍

Gravesend awoke with a start and a fierce chill, disoriented and with pockets of snow in the folds of his jacket. Driven by the wind, the flakes continued to prickle his face. He shook his head at his stupidity. He was going to be frightfully sore in the morning if not downright sick. Stiffly, he turned and used the headstone to get to his knees. Keeping both hands on the stone, he pressed his lips to the top of the cold marble. Then, he pushed himself slowly upward, checking to be sure everything was in working order. After gathering up the glasses and empty wine bottle, he lumbered forward in the general direction of his car.

"Hey," said a soft voice from the shadows.

The bottle and glasses fell from his hands; Autumn Gilhain stepped out into the dim light of a half moon.

"What? What in God's name are *you* doing here?"

"It's an accident ... really ... well ... sort of. Gaston and I were on our way back to NAUFA from Kingston when he took a turn that he thought was a road but was the driveway to the cemetery. When I recognized your car, I got curious. I didn't think you were going to make a night of it here." She held her arms close to her side and shivered.

"So to satisfy your curiosity and amuse yourself you turned to eavesdropping."

"That's not true! I did listen, but only to see what was up. I was worried for a moment; I really thought you lost it when I heard you talking to a tombstone. Then, I figured out it was your wife, and I didn't want to interfere, so I hung out over here."

"You 'hung out.' No doubt within hearing distance."

"Well, it's all pretty bizarre, isn't it? I mean, why did you do all this?"

She pointed at the glasses and the bottle. Gravesend bent, slowly, and picked them up from the grass.

"It's late and cold, and I don't feel especially bound to stand here and explain anything to you."

"Would you explain it to me on the way home then?"

"Pardon me?"

"Well, one of the reasons I hung out was because I need a lift back into town."

Gravesend paused, trying to think of a way to not take her with him. The wind kicked up again, a single gust, and whether it hit some tree or his mind the wrong way, he thought he heard in that gust a passing echo of Julia's laughter. He grunted and started off toward the car. "Come along then."

Gravesend kept quiet, waiting for Autumn to speak, but she had nothing to say until the car was turned about and heading for the road.

"I know I shouldn't have done this. And if it's too personal to talk about I'll understand, but I'm curious about what you were doing. And why this." She leaned down and picked up the empty bottle of wine from the floor in front of her seat.

Gravesend shrugged. "It's October 31st, at least it was when I arrived at the cemetery. Nearly every culture in the world believed at one time or another that on one night of the year the dead could come in contact with the living. Usually they celebrated it with a feast of some sort. And since my wife died on Halloween, you could say I feel especially linked to this night and that ritual."

"So you do this every Halloween?"

"That's right. The first year, I brought two bottles, one for each of us. I learned my lesson then, so every year afterward, we share a bottle."

"What happened that first year? Did you pass out?"

"Face down."

"On her grave? For how long?"

"Until a grave digger arrived to start work in the morning. Poor fellow thought I was his next customer."

"So you were busted?"

"No. He brought me over to the toolshed and gave me coffee from his thermos. In fact, he gave me most of his coffee. Quite a sacrifice, really. Did you ever hear the expression 'cold as a gravedigger's ankle?' A hot drink would almost seem to be required to get through the day. Even given modern methods, digging graves is cold, nasty business in November. Much like spying. Out with it. What did you hear?"

"Not much, honest. I heard you talking about some girl who slapped you in a Toronto ballroom. But I missed the connection between that and your wife."

"That's a long story."

They went on in silence.

"Of course," she said, "to get back to the American side, we'll have to go up to Cornwall and cross the bridge there."

"True."

"And that can be a long ride."

"Yes."

"Well? Longer than the story?"

"I see no reason to tell you the rest. Furthermore, I don't understand why you would want to hear it. There's nothing lurid about any of it."

"Hey! I don't get off listening to other people's sex stories. You know you want to tell the whole tale to someone, so I'm letting you know I want to hear the rest of it."

"Why?"

"Because I'm interested in it, in you, in this whole damn bizarre thing I just saw."

Gravesend wished he had followed up on his initial response to finding her in that cemetery: Telling her to hoof her way back through Newtown to Prue, but at the same time, he was glad for the company. Also, technically, he was at fault; he had asked for Julia's help, and this sort of coincidence bore her mark. It seemed ungracious to second-guess that now.

"Julia and I met in 1957. I was a third-year music student looking to leave the University of Toronto for a conservatory where I could devote myself completely to music. Julia was a third-year mathematics student. The whole twisted process that brought us together really was as natural as breathing, even to a blind Romantic such as I was in those days. Actually, Romantic might be too generous a label. I was a naive, cocky, over-ripe adolescent, much too sure of myself for my own damn good. Quite like you are now, I might add.

"Anyway, at the time I met Julia, I was pining away for the woman you heard me speak of in the cemetery, the woman from India. Her name was Teema, Teema Bhudartashinti, the most exotic woman I ever knew. We would go places on purely platonic terms — her terms not mine. But I was certain those terms would change as soon as I began to seriously compose. I ached over having to wait, something of a Romantic self-flagellation. You see, suffering was what we young Romantics did best: the more angst, the more Romance. I saw my pain as real, as the price exacted by destiny for blessing my future with Teema. I would make up scenarios in my head: she would run off with someone else to Europe, and I would carry on alone in Canada, composing stunning pieces inspired by her memory and a single photograph. Then one day she would realize she did not love the man she married, or some terrible event would send her — and a child, of course — fleeing back to me. By that time, I would be wealthy and famous. I would take her in, adopt her child, and we would live out our pre-ordained lives together in absolutely blissful love. What rubbish."

"And Julia straightened you out?"

"Not at first. She couldn't have been any less like me or Teema or the Romantics. She was independent, fiery, with a mathematical assuredness to her and an eye that cut to the heart of all matters. We met in a physics course. After one class, we started talking, and, since it was getting on toward noon and we didn't have another class until two, we decided to have lunch. The next thing we knew, the waiter came around setting the empty tables for dinner. It was four-thirty."

"You blew off your class for her?"

"No, nothing so grand as that. We simply got lost in conversation every time we talked. I would ask a physics question that she would answer in the first five minutes, but then we would end up talking for two hours. It got to where we would have to make a conscious effort to watch the time to be sure we didn't get into trouble."

"And that's when you realized you were falling in love with her."

"I don't believe anyone can say exactly when he falls in love, and certainly I couldn't pinpoint when it happened with Julia. Love had always been something of a lightning bolt, striking me with such a force that all other thoughts burned away in its aftermath. That's how I reacted to Teema, so while whatever was happening to me with Julia was happening, I was not aware of it. I still believed that Teema was the only woman in the world for me. I noticed, of course, that Julia was kind and sensory and brilliant, and all that was fine. But somewhere in that time, I began to notice she was beautiful, and that's when I panicked."

"Panicked?"

"Jumped right off the cliff. She was no Teema. Julia didn't have an exotic bone in her body. But every woman has her own beauty, and once that beauty reveals itself to a man, he can't ever understand how he didn't see it straight away. And then if he notices a woman's beauty without looking, it scares him. It felt like going on stage to rehearse and suddenly realizing that this was the performance."

"So, what did you do?"

"I muddled about, making a total mess of everything. Fate loves to tease fools. As it turned out, for such an analytical woman, Julia loved flowers, pretty things, pretty words. She hated the Romantics, and Romantic-era notions, but she loved to be romanced. But she got none of those things from me early on because I was so far out of my league. I was acting the way I thought she would want me to act. And although I wasn't aware of it at the time, in retrospect I could see that while I groped my way toward her, there was always something completely natural about us, some guiding hand that either made sure I didn't go too far overboard or supported Julia's humor when I did. Years later, I realized all that naturalness that held us together stemmed from our talks."

As Gravesend drove and talked, he kept using his peripheral vision to observe Autumn, who was sitting with her arms folded and staring straight ahead out the windshield. He guessed that since the heater had the car warmed up to the point where both of them had loosened their jackets, she was trying not to look at him, her crossed arms holding her back. Now, however, she couldn't help herself. Her arms went down to her lap, palms upward, her head swiveled toward him, her expression rearranging itself into a look of disbelief.

"Your talks?"

"Yes. Our talks."

"Not you doing stuff together? Holding hands? Or Being together? You know, your intimacy?"

"Talking *is* a form of intimacy. Learn that. I didn't know it back then, either, but from the very beginning, we took time every night to talk, be it about trivial matters or debates over issues. Talking was how we bonded: the communication and intimacy of sharing voices and thoughts. From the time we began to date, I can't remember a night ever going by when we didn't have a good talk, even if most of them started out, 'Hello, how are you, what's new?' We walked around the campus to talk, and when I went to the Conservatory in Montreal, we talked by phone and letters. After we were married, we always held our talks either on the porch or in the sitting room. Right up until the end. The week before Julia died, she demanded that she be released from the hospital. I tried to tell her that it wasn't wise, but she just shook her head and said she wanted to go out on her terms, and her mind had set on the fact that we would sit on our porch and have our last talks. I had to carry her out to the porch swing, and she lay there swaddled in so many blankets she looked more like a cocoon than a person. Her voice had gotten wispy, but we talked. We finished our last conversation of her life around six o'clock on Halloween, just before the children began to make their rounds. She died at nine-thirty. So that's why every Halloween I come out and talk to her. Now you're up-to-date, and we're coming up to Prue, so where do you want to be delivered?"

"Mendelssohn Avenue."

Gravesend swung the car in alongside the curb in front of number 127. Autumn's hand was on the door, but she made no move to open it.

"I really am sorry for eavesdropping tonight. That wasn't a cool thing to do."

"I repaid you by burying you alive under my story. I still don't believe for a moment that you wanted to hear it. Perhaps you were trying to blunt the edge of my anger for finding you at the cemetery?"

"Maybe. Or perhaps I was just trying to be a friend? Sometimes you just have to talk to people who can still hear you."

"I have no doubt that Julia hears me. But thank you for that."

She looked away and fidgeted. Gravesend sensed she was caught in the middle of something, swinging in the wind and uncomfortable. He was enjoying her discomfort until she reached for his hand resting on top of the gear shift and closed her own hand over his, giving it a gentle squeeze. His conscious reaction was to pull his hand out from under her grasp, but instead, his fingers curled around the top of the gearshift and stayed put.

"Goodnight," said she, cool as ice, smoothly disengaging her hand from his and sliding out the door.

He watched her walk up to the entrance of the house and disappear inside. Although he listened all the way home, Julia never made a sound.

November

&~ 1 ~&

"I'm looking for recordings by Quinn Gravesend," Autumn said. "Symphonies."

The clerk, who looked to be about sixteen, shook his head and said "I am sorry, but we do not carry very much classical music in this store."

"You know he's a Canadian composer, right?" Autumn asked. "That he studied in Montreal? Has a huge international reputation as probably the best living classical composer?"

The boy shrugged. "I am sorry. We carry only the very popular styles of music." He picked up a CD case of Roch Voisine's *Chaque Feu...* pointed, and shrugged again.

"So, you don't have anything by Quinn Gravesend?"

The boy shook the case, shook his head, and said "Non."

"Nothing? This is the fourth music store I've been to, and none of you sells *The Julia Suite*. This is Montreal, and he's Canadian for God's sake! One of the greatest composers of symphonies, and you people don't think you could have one damn CD lying around? I mean, really? Nothing?"

The boy's face shifted from apologetic to startled and then to angry. "What is the matter? Do you not speak English well? We do not carry classical music, not for Quinn Gravesend, not for Amadeus Mozart."

"Screw it!" She slammed her palms down on the counter, making the boy jump. She covered the space to the door in three steps. With one hard shove, she was out into the twilight gathering around the edges of Montreal.

People whirled by her, talking in a cacophony of a language she couldn't comprehend. The sounds pressed in on her from all sides, nudging her anger higher. Fuck the other members of the Society for not offering to go along with her. But that wasn't true; Patrick offered, and she turned him down. Well, fuck him for not going anyway. If they wanted to leave her alone in this strange country to fend for herself, it wouldn't be the first time. She turned around completely looking for a street sign, and seeing none, she just started walking. What was pissing her off? It really wasn't the members of the Society. Or the store clerk. It wasn't because she couldn't find a Gravesend CD. So what was it? She had no idea.

She spotted a street sign on a corner: Av du Parc and Rue Milton. She turned down Milton. What was getting under her skin was this country. Everyone talks about Canada like it's the nice, unassuming guy who always gets stuck sitting next to the loudmouth U.S. on the plane. Sure, she gave the kid in the music store reason to think of her as another ugly American tourist, but from what she saw, Canada was no great place. What did Gaston see in this city? What did her father see in this country? Just a place to be left alone.

If that's all Canada seemed to be good for, then fine. She was more than willing to leave it alone.

She continued down Milton, past Durocher, past Aylmer. She didn't realize she had wandered so far. As best she could, she shut out the passing conversations. She didn't want the chaos of unintelligible talk, the exclusion of not understanding. What did she want? To get drunk. Roaring drunk. To drink a bottle of good, French red wine in a cafe by candlelight and watch the people and light and sound all blur together. She wanted to feel that slow descent into the nexus where inhibition and appetite meet. There, all of these voices speaking words she didn't know would become just another part of the mix. Drunkenness – the great equalizer. Once the language barrier was gone, she would be free to dance in a place where the music would be loud and fast and the faces of men would whip by her. And before the night ended, before she climbed back up to sobriety and the unreal reality, she wanted to be kissed. Not as a prelude or an ending to something else, but truly kissed, solely and entirely for the kiss itself. She wanted a kiss that became an entity, blacking out sounds and sights and smells: a kiss that, for the moment it lasts, is the only reason for living and being.

But first she had to find a way to cork the disappointment with herself that the anger had left behind. And that was no easy task. Since no one was with her, the devil turned inward. Cutting away from the rest of the group to go trudging through a foreign city late in the afternoon was a pretty stupid thing to do. And for what? What made her think that four small stores around McGill

University, not a hotbed of musical composition, would have a copy of *The Julia Suite*? Especially when the large store in Prue had no copies, and the clerk said it couldn't be ordered? Just because Gravesend was Canadian didn't mean every record shop in the country carried a complete catalog of his works.

But why get so upset over it? Because she hadn't planned on going. Because her reason for wanting the CD wasn't for herself but curiosity about Quinn Gravesend. What other reason could there be for even taking the time out to look for the work? Well, Quinn Gravesend can give her a copy, or he can go to hell. She had more important things to do. Automatically, she squeezed the outside of her bag until she traced the outline of the steno pad and pen inside. The notebook she used to record the doings of the Society would have been too big to carry along, and not knowing where she might be staying tonight, she didn't want to risk having one of the others accidentally discover it. She would transfer what she wrote later.

She looked up to see she had missed Lorne, so she went on until she came to University. She could get to Prince Arthur from there, so she turned toward the McGill University campus. Rue University was blissfully empty of both people and cars; she walked out into the middle of the street and looked both ways. Nothing. She shrugged and headed west toward Mount Royal Park. What would normally have struck her as eerie and even dangerous anywhere else didn't register in her brain beyond the thought that the street must be shut down for some reason. More than anything, she was thankful for the quiet. She strolled along, reveling in the silence until it was broken by the sound of multiple footsteps running toward her. She turned and saw three people gaining on her. She couldn't tell if they were men or women, and the sight of them made her stop and stand where she was. The leader wore a mask of the sun, its rays like golden spikes sticking out on the sides and the top. One of the companions sported a goat's head, complete with horns, and the other had on a sheep's head. The trio reached her and raced past going straight down the center of the street. Autumn watched them barrel ahead and then stop, grabbing each other's arms and pointing. She looked beyond them.

A wall of people was coming down the street toward them and her. More were pouring in from the sides. They carried torches and lights of all sorts until the street became a river of flame flowing with people in masks and costumes on parade. Before she could move, they had swallowed her. Whooping and hollering, dancing or strutting or walking, characters of all shades and styles, all contortions of face and color of body, swam past her. A man with a golden headdress and gold-painted hands grabbed Autumn's arms and twirled her as he danced by, leaving her with a passing phrase in French. A man on stilts brushed by her, followed by a woman carrying a battery powered strobe ball. Instruments spoke and answered without pattern or score, creating a surreal voice that, despite its lack of order, sounded far more harmonious to her ears than the normal course of the native language had only moments before. Autumn tried to move out of the center of the street toward the sidewalk, but she wasn't making much headway until strong hands grabbed her arms.

"Not a good night for a stroll down University, Autumn-girl," said a familiar voice plowing a path for her through the mayhem. "This is some group out here."

"Chet!"

"And his mate," said Patrick. "Two white knights coming to rescue a lady ... of sorts."

"What the hell's going on?"

"You've been Chet-mated," said Patrick, hauling her out of the crush of people and up onto the sidewalk. Chet reached up and slapped him on the side of the head. Patrick chuckled, turned toward the streaming crowd and spread his arms wide. In an emcee tone, he bellowed, "I give you *La Mascarade Rouge!*"

"Jesus Christ, what's that?"

"*La Mascarade Rouge* means The Red Masque," Patrick said, "a holdover tradition from the European universities in the Middle Ages. Simply put, it's a student carnival. The closest thing I can think to compare it to in the United States is your Mardi Gras, although the Red Masque is not on so grand a scale as that. Students dress in masks and costumes and parade through the streets of the university and the city at dusk. In medieval times, the paraders carried torches, and it would appear this group decided to carry on that tradition. This is the lead group. The streets of the University behind us are lousy with others. They'll circle around and end up in the Park."

"Why are you two out here? Weren't you going to Gaston's gig?"

"Not the best choice tonight, I'm sorry to say," Patrick said. "He's playing a rather dull set to an audience consisting of one couple in a corner holding hands and a fellow sweeping the floor."

"It seems," said Chet, "that the owner of the place wants to draw in the love-birds and leave the frenzied masses out here, so he has Gaston playing all slow stuff until midnight. Patrick and I opted to check out this Red Masque and keep an eye out for you."

Autumn looked around and noted Chet's easel standing against the wall of one of the buildings. Patrick held a flute in one of his hands.

"So, we drove 84 miles for this?" Autumn asked.

"Do you know of any better entertainment in Prue?" Chet said.

"No. I guess not. Where's Lyle?"

"He stayed on at the club to accompany Gaston on the piano," Patrick answered. A section of people dressed in monk's robes came by humming a dirge that grew louder as they went. "Here's for it!" With a wave, he plunged in and began piping out the melody, moving with the group, swallowed up by the revelers.

Chet retrieved his easel, placed it under a streetlight, and opened the case that held his paints and sketching nibs. Grabbing an outcast crate from in front of one of the buildings, he sat and began to sketch. Autumn, looking for a more secure vantage point than the curb, settled herself a short distance away on the steps of an apartment building. She watched Chet become absorbed in the masque, and when she felt sure he would stay put, she took out her steno pad and began to write.

November 12, 1999 ... 7:10 pm ... Montreal on the night of the Red Mask, McGill University. All members of the Society are in the city except for Mary. Gaston and Lyle are performing; Chet and Patrick and I have come to see the event.

Patrick has gone on ahead with a group of imitation monks. Chet sits below me sketching the crowd passing by him. Music is everywhere. The torches throw a red cast over it all, hence the name, I guess. The costumes are bizarre — at this moment walking past me are a man with an elephant trunk hanging from his face, a woman with bottles tied to her clothing, and two men in suits bearing a third dressed as a knight on a wooden plank. On the knight is a broadsword, the hilt extending off the edge of the bier in such a way that the edge of the blade runs along the middle of the man's body. The point nearly touches his chin.

The door to the apartment behind Autumn opened and two girls stepped out. They were dressed in street clothes rather than costumes, and Autumn stared at them as they whispered and giggled, clutching at each other's arms. Then one of them pointed to Chet and said in English, "Oh look, he's painting. I want to be painted."

"Marisse, you don't."

"I do. Look at us, out-of-place, dressed so nice. I want to get wild."

"But painted?"

"Yes! I bet the touch of it lasts all night."

"Or as long as the wine does," said the girl, frowning.

Marisse straightened herself and nodded. "I'm going to do it. But, what if he charges. Are you carrying any money?"

"Only four dollars."

"Excuse me," said Autumn. "But I could get him to paint you for free ... or, well, almost free."

"What do you mean by 'almost free'?" asked Marisse.

"Maybe we can work out a deal? How about I get him to paint you for no charge in exchange for some wine?"

"That's fair," said the other girl, and Marisse nodded.

Autumn led them down to Chet, leaning in close to his ear. "These girls are going to give us some wine, if you paint them. How about it?"

"But I was only going to draw tonight, to use for a later painting. This isn't just some college carnival, Autumn-girl! It's artistic fodder!" He looked past Autumn at the pair fidgeting behind her, and a smile crept across his face. "However, I suppose I could use these beautiful ladies as warm up exercises." He waved Autumn aside to address the girls. "Now, ladies, what if I draw you?"

"No! I want to be painted!" said Marisse moving her hands in circles before the trunk of her body.

"But I brought only paper, no canvas."

"You do not understand. I want you to paint on me." She crossed her arms and tugged her shirt halfway up her torso, baring her stomach. "Paint me here to start."

Chet simply waved Marisse closer.

"The wine," said the other girl to Autumn, "is inside the apartment on the kitchen table. Go through the door and down the hallway."

Autumn nodded and retreated back to the steps of the house. Inside, a dim light burned in the corridor, and she followed it into a tiny kitchen where six bottles of wine stood on the table. She moved toward the bottles, then a noise startled her. She looked to her right and saw a woman in her early thirties sitting on a kitchen chair in the corner, near the entrance to the basement. She wore a dress hiked up to mid-thigh and was slowly rolling a stocking up and down her leg, staring dreamily at the movement.

"Hi," Autumn said. "Marisse told me to come in for a bottle of wine."

The girl said nothing until Autumn began to squint at the labels to see which were French and which were full.

"Do you want love?" asked the girl.

"Excuse me?"

"I want love. Tonight is a night for love."

Autumn didn't answer her. She found a bottle of unopened Beaujolais and looked around for a corkscrew.

"Do you want love?" repeated the girl.

"Right now, I want a corkscrew."

The girl giggled, putting a hand to her mouth. "I think you would like a man. A certain man."

Autumn nodded, looking around in the dim light to see if a corkscrew were laying around.

"An older man, perhaps?"

Autumn focused again on the young woman. "Let me see your face."

The girl looked up and the dim light of the kitchen fell on her round face. A wayward, brown curl swung before her right eye. The rest of her face looked very dreamy, very drunk. "You want an experienced man, one who will sweep you up and make your life a mystery. You want a man with history and passion and secrets. That's what I want. You want secrets? We all want secrets. We all have secrets, but they aren't enough."

"Uh-huh." Autumn went over to the sink and looked over the counter. "Mind if I look in the drawer for the corkscrew?"

"Corkscrew! Bah, corkscrews. You don't have a chance with a man of mystery if you only are interested in corkscrews, you know. You are too real. You are not enough aware of the secrets of a man. The deep secrets. You need to grip the mystery. To show him mystery. Do you want to be just kissed? Or kissed by him?"

Autumn whirled around. "Who the fuck *are* you?"

"I am called ..." She raised her arms above her head and twirled her hands, "Helene."

"Helene the damn psychic or what?"

"Helene ... the lover." She giggled and wagged a finger at Autumn. "Secrets and mystery" she said in a sing-song voice, "or you will never understand a single kiss."

Autumn put down the Beaujolais, grabbed a nearly full, opened bottle of burgundy, and left the kitchen, retracing her steps down the corridor to the stoop. She took several deep pulls at the wine bottle to chase Helene out of her head. She opened her steno pad and focused on the scene playing out beneath the street lamp.

Marisse is her name, this beautiful, petite girl, probably eighteen. She stands with her arms raised, her hands behind her head holding and feathering her hair. She is naked from the waist up and is leaning slightly backward so that her stomach is thrust forward. Chet dips his brush into the paints before finishing a pattern on the bare skin by circling her navel. At a word from her, he cleans the brush, takes more paint on the tip and moves it toward her chest. He paints a thick line from the notch at the base of her throat down through her cleavage to the pattern below. Next, two branching lines extending around the inner swell of each breast up to her shoulder.

She turns now, facing away from me, and the painting resumes on her back. Each stroke of Chet's brush may as well be his fingers for the reaction it draws from Marisse. Her head is turned to the side toward me, and her eyes are closed. Her fingers are caressing her hair, and her face is nearly dripping with delight and erotic pleasure. But it's Chet who is the curious one. He's all artist, giving the same attention to Marisse's skin as he would give to any canvas. He told me one time that personality plays better in the trenches than looks, that looks get you in the door, but they aren't the best for sealing the deal with a woman. From what I've seen of the angles he's worked with several girls in the Lick and Poke, I'd say he may be right. But this is different. Marisse is stunning in her build, and I can't see Chet in the darkness, but I'd like to see if he's got a bulge in his pants. If I had to bet I'd say no. I'll say it again: The members of this group are extraordinary in the way they focus on their art, but they are human beings. When I recount this scene to Chet tomorrow, he'll throw an adorable fit.

Right now, he leans in and is saying something to Marisse, then dips his brush in a small jar of turpentine and wipes it, stowing it in his case. Marisse moves under the light and twirls for her friend, displaying Chet's work proudly. Tying her top around her waist, they step into the street and are swallowed by the crowd.

Chet picks up his pen but draws nothing. The people still swarm by coming and going. The parade seems to be thinning out in this section of the street, and people are drifting in and out in a more social way. Chet's still not drawing anything. Maybe I was wrong. He's looking into the crowd like it's a lake and he's a fisherman. The big one has just gotten away. I don't blame him if his artistic concentration has dimmed. I'd be a little relieved, actually. It's good to know that these artists are still human and can be thrown off track by the right human incentive. Like attraction. Appetite. Love.

She watched the parade, pen poised to jot down notes and descriptions, but her mood started to sink again, sucking up her interest in the writing. The wine bottle lay empty beside her. The words "secret" and "mystery" bounced around inside her head, but she ignored them. Instead, she understood what Marisse had said to her friend; she felt like such a deadweight sitting on these steps while the party passed her by. The sight of Marisse being painted brought back the feeling she had had earlier on her walk from the record shop. She put the pad in her purse and went over to where Chet sat contemplating.

"I'm going to mingle," said Autumn. "I guess we'll all meet at the club around midnight, when Gaston's done?"

"At midnight if the crowd thins or before if I overdose on all this. My God, what fine stuff!"

She nodded. Four men set up Congo drums a half block down the street and began to lay down a beat, around which several drifting musicians began to play. Autumn wandered toward them, at first on the fringe of the crowd, then moving tentatively out toward the middle, looking at the faces and the costumes. A young woman handed her a balloon. Autumn smiled at it and then promptly let it go, watching it float up into the darkness. "That's all it takes," she thought. "Just let go." She looked around at several people who had started to dance to the rhythms bouncing around her, and she began to dance along with them, swirling in the street. She was on her way; the faces were beginning to blur with the sounds. She twirled again, and as she slowed, she spotted Lyle and another man heading along the far sidewalk, walking against the route of the parade toward the park. Lyle, in plain clothes, was in the lead, about five yards ahead of the other man, who was in a fool's costume.

Autumn's suspicions went into overdrive. What was Lyle doing here when he was supposed to be at the club with Gaston? Hadn't Gaston mentioned something over the summer about trouble in Lyle's family, something to do with his father, who was in the Senate? Then in September, Lyle said he thought someone had been following him in Prue. Now, some joker, literally, was following him.

Autumn tagged after them. Intrigued and just drunk enough not to care, she intended to catch up to the joker and put him in his place, but something in the way Lyle moved told her he didn't want to be caught. So she shadowed them, using the crowd as a screen, all the way down to the park. It felt like hundreds of people milling around, all the early paraders having completed the route. Autumn recognized several costumes, including a short fellow holding a sheep's head tucked under his arm talking to a woman juggling apples. For the first time, she noticed police mingling among the revelers. She toyed with alerting one of them, but when she momentarily lost the pair, she nixed that idea and plowed ahead. She picked them up again as they weaved their way through the revelers, and, leaving them behind, Lyle moved deeper in among the trees. The fool followed, and so did Autumn.

The crowd sounds faded into the jumbled hubbub of background noise from the city itself, and the clash of white noise and dark woods tilted her senses. Everything seemed to be suspended. The pair had melted into the darkness, so she went forward carefully, listening. Voices came from the trees off the path to her right. Lyle's quiet voice and another man's, gruffer but indistinct. She was about to step forward into the grove and see what was going on, when Lyle said clearly, and with anguish, "But I love you, Jacques-Yves."

Autumn stopped cold with one foot off the path and one foot on. Jacques-Yves response was too low for her to hear, but slightly drunk as she was, she realized this was a place she shouldn't be, hearing something she shouldn't be hearing, and seeing something she shouldn't see. With even greater stealth than she used in following the two men, she backed away. When she thought she was far enough out of earshot, she turned to leave but checked herself again when Lyle yelled out, "What do you mean 'just politics and money?'" Her original thought about catching up to the joker and kicking his ass came back to her, but for a second time she vetoed the idea. If this was some sort of relationship bust-up moment, Lyle would be hurt enough. He didn't need to be humiliated on top of it.

Autumn hurried back toward the remains of the Masque not stopping to mingle this time, making her way out of the park. She skirted the reservoir and made her way back to Rue University but further west than the area where she had left Chet. She found Prince Arthur Street and then the club and went inside. Twelve couples sat scattered around the room, and Gaston sat perched on a high, three-legged stool behind a microphone. Autumn fell into a seat at a table in the back. She had descended too far and not far enough. She was drunk, and she was stunned. Retrieving the pad and pen, she started writing a description of what she'd witnessed, but she changed her mind, ripping out the page and tearing it up into tiny bits.

A waiter brought her a glass of wine. Merci. No, she didn't want the candle lit; she preferred to be in the shadows.

The man withdrew, and she sat, glass in hand, listening to Gaston's melodies and words, letting her mind cast about for something to write that would be independent of her control and direction. Rational thought was impossible anyway. So she wrote, letting the pen ride across the page, lassoing as many of the random thoughts as it could catch, weaving all the feelings the night had inspired between the subtle sounds of Gaston's guitar. Pride, anger, promises, secrets, trouble, love – but didn't those last two always go together? She looked around the room again. How different this scene was from the Red Masque winding down a couple of blocks away.

Patrick arrived around eleven-thirty, and Autumn smoothly closed the steno pad and slipped it into her bag before he sat down at her table. Chet and Lyle came in together near midnight. Chet was rumbling on about the Masque, and Lyle was nodding as if listening, but Autumn noticed that he was light-years away. Gaston finished his set, coming over to the table and announcing he wanted to see what was left of the Masque. Autumn felt content to sit in the cafe, but she said nothing and followed the group outside. They wandered down through the McGill campus and over to Mount Royal Park, but the crowds had gone. There was a little action around the apartments on University, but without the energy of the parade, these gatherings felt like any other college party, only with costumes. Autumn suggested heading back to Prue; however, the others voted to camp out in the room Gaston was using for the night.

Within an hour, everyone was asleep but Autumn. She lay on the bed with Gaston snoring lightly beside her, unable to close her eyes. Sometime near dawn, she took her bag into the bathroom and locked the door. She leaned against the sink, feeling like she was going to cry and not knowing why. No, that was a lie. Of course she knew why. She left the sink and cracked open the bathroom door. Just enough light from the street made its way into the room for Autumn to see the sleeping group. Chet sat propped up in one corner, his head on his chest. Patrick's boots extended past the end of the foot of the bed where he was stretched out on the floor. Lyle was asleep on the sofa, his arm thrown over his forehead as if fending off blows. Surely, she was putting her own spin on the way he was sleeping, but her heart ached nonetheless. She wanted to go out and take him in her arms, enfold him as a mother would. It wasn't possible, not in a room full of the other Society members, but even if she and Lyle had been alone, it couldn't happen. She had no idea how to do that, to embrace someone with maternal care. Add one more item to the list of things she wasn't good enough to achieve.

Was that why she missed, or ignored, the fact that despite Lyle's outward appearance of normality his essence was slowly being leeched away? Chet and Patrick didn't know Lyle as well as she did. Gaston knew him better, but the single-minded focus that he had toward music would have dulled him to the changes in Lyle the same way that she was blinded by her own self-concerns and deficiencies. They both had failed him, she concluded. She would talk with Gaston, and she'd be more watchful herself.

She closed the door again and snapped on the light. After pulling the steno pad out of her bag, she read over the jumble of thoughts that she'd written at the café up to where the words ended mid-flow when Patrick arrived. All of it was trivial and meaningless now, but she stopped herself from tearing out the pages. She was in an emotional whirl and that wasn't the time to make decisions about quality. Instead, she flipped the page and began to write.

We all know things that we don't realize we know until something happens to knock what we sense or feel or ignore into the forefront of our brains. And when that happens, whether something is said or seen or both, those things we sense surface unbidden and become part of our conscious knowing, and they make us feel like we should have known them all along. I knew about Lyle. Not what was specifically wrong, I still don't know that, but that there was something wrong. Then came the confirmation in that tortured cry, "But I love you Jacques-Yves!" What I can't figure out was the "Just politics!" said with angry disbelief. It's clear he was repeating something Jacques-Yves said, something that surprised Lyle, something that wounded him, mortally. Something to do with Lyle's father being a politician? But why would some guy in Montreal care enough about the politics of an American senator to ditch his son? And a step-son at that?

We never know when those moments will come. When we just get blindsided by something that tears into us, and then we suddenly find ourselves into something deeper than we can know. Those depths are dark, but wisdom is being able to plumb that darkness before the moment happens. But I'm not wise. I'm not even good with conscious knowing. Because with all that's happened tonight, all the concern I'm now feeling for Lyle, I don't know how or why at the same time, the name of Quinn Gravesend is still in my head. Love and trouble go together. Well, I don't love him, but trouble is coming. It's probably the "secrets and mystery." Damn you, Helene. Damn myself.

❧ 2 ❦

Gravesend woke feeling out of kilter, like a piece of music slightly out of time. The remains of his dreams lingered in the form of a knot lodged between his ribs although he couldn't remember dreaming at all. He chewed at the knot along with his breakfast, trying to recall dream plots and how they could have spawned this feeling of being misaligned. But the answer, like the dreams, lay just beyond the rim of his conscious memory, like the eyes of an animal peering from the underbrush at people around the campfire: simultaneously present and out of reach. By the time he left for the university, he gave up searching, content to let the knot remain. Surely in time something would see fit to dislodge or untie it.

That time came when he opened his office door. Autumn, comfortably ensconced in his desk chair, glanced up from her study of his gradebook with a look of innocence on her face.

"What do you think you're doing?" Gravesend asked.

"Waiting for you."

"Close that book!"

"I'm not doing anything to it."

"Other than thumbing through it, you mean?" Striding to the desk, he reached over and snatched the book out of her hands. "This is confidential; you can't look at other people's grades."

"I wasn't 'thumbing' through anything! I was checking on Lyle, seeing if he really was getting a B+ in your class. And if the gradebook is so damn private, you shouldn't leave it out in the middle of your desk."

"My desk is private as well. I don't expect students to be in my office when I'm not."

"Then tell your secretary. She let me in." Autumn leaned back in his chair, her lower lip curling in a pout. "Anyway, it serves you right. You're late you know. What did you expect me to do while you took your time getting here?"

"You could wait in the reception area for one thing. That is where students are supposed to wait for their professors."

She returned the remark with a cold stare, then lifted herself out of the chair with a slink that was more sexual than apologetic.

Quite an expressionist she was, thought Gravesend, a woman of so many faces and postures, a stage talent that would be lost in the world of musical performance. She wandered over to his bookshelf before sitting down on the piano bench and stretching out her legs. Gravesend regained his chair, and sorted papers, business-like.

"You don't have any pictures in here," said Autumn.

"Should I?"

"Everyone else does."

"I have the print."

Autumn flicked an eye over Dali's *La Persistance de la Mémoire.* "Yeah, but so do hundreds of other people. It's not personal."

"This is not a personal office; it's my place of public business. Many people come through here, and I don't see any reason to have my personal things hanging like flags around the room."

"You just don't like people to know you, right?"

"I like my privacy. That may not be popular in this age when everyone is expected to be so open and public, but there it is."

Autumn lifted her legs and swiveled on the bench, jumping up and strolling over to the state-of-the-art shelf stereo unit on a side table. She lingered in front of the unit for a moment before moving on to the Dali painting, facing away from him, observing the print with her hands clasped behind her back. "Your colleagues know you, though, don't they?"

"The ones who have worked with me for many years do."

"But Dr. Spire, my music instructor at the moment, doesn't know you. I asked him a question about *Symphony Number 1967* — my favorite of yours by the way — and he got all flustered. He hemmed and hawed around and went on with his lecture without answering my question. What's the problem between you two?"

"Dr. Spire and I differ in our opinions about music." Gravesend chanced a glance in her direction. She still had her back to him, examining the painting or pretending to do so. But her posture had taken on a predatory form, like she was gauging him, testing his movements with the air of one who has the advantage.

He picked up a pen and began marking off assignments in his gradebook. "I infer from your remark that you have listened to my symphonies since the night we spoke at the bar."

"All of them except *The Julia Suite*. I haven't been able to find it. Do you have a copy?"

"Not in the office, no."

"It's at home, I suppose, with your personal self."

"Correct. If the question you put to Dr. Spire concerned whether or not he had a copy of *The Julia Suite*, I can assure you he doesn't."

"That wasn't it. The question wasn't important, really. I was only asking it to see how he reacted to your name being brought up in class."

"And why would you do that?"

Autumn shrugged. "To see if his opinion of your work matched mine."

Gravesend smiled to himself. So the game was chess, and she was working a gamut to bait him into asking for her opinion of his symphonies. Fine. He was once an aggressive chess player. "And as a student of music in this modern time, what do you think of my symphonies?"

She spun on her heels, and the movement reminded Gravesend of a griffin spreading its wings and opening its talons before striking. The thought was unsettling. People think mythical beasts only live in legends and fairy tales, but Gravesend begged to differ. They live inside us as aspects of our personality, and he had seen enough of the griffin in Julia and other women to be fully fearful in the face of it. Where an animal attacks to devour the surface, the griffin rips the body to expose the soul. A woman bent to such a purpose is at her most powerful and her most dangerous. All the more so when the griffin appears in a young woman who doesn't have complete grip on the reins. Mrs. Bourgione, his secretary, was no easy touch or simpleton. If Autumn got past her defenses, she was good. Put that together with a rising griffin, and he better tread lightly; this one could wreak havoc.

"I thought you would get around to asking that," she said. "Do you really want to know what I think?"

"I like hearing the views of all types of listeners; so yes, I value your opinion."

"Well, I'd love to tell you, but ... I think it's just a little bit too personal."

"We are alone."

"Yeah, but I don't know." She shook her head and clasped her hands behind her back once more, giving the office a perfunctory inspection. "I think this office is just a bit too public for what I have to say."

"Spare me your sarcasm and come to the point."

"Okay. I'll make a deal with you. I'll tell you exactly what your music made me think and feel — because it made me do both — but I'll only tell you at your house."

"My house?"

"Your house."

"What is this obsession you have with seeing my personal things?"

"It's not an obsession. As a critic I couldn't give you a credible analysis without having heard all of your music. Where do you keep a copy of *The Julia Suite*? At your house. So, that's where I'll have to go in order to form my complete opinion."

Gravesend didn't immediately respond. Instead, he watched the triumph radiate from her face; no doubt she could feel his soul in her talons. She must be a woman used to winning, thought Gravesend. Pity, she would not be winning today.

"You're right, of course," he said aloud. "How inconsiderate of me to not help you in your search for my music." He scribbled on a pad and tore off the sheet, laying it at the edge of the desk. "It just so happens that the assignment in my compositional theory class for next week is to get to the library and hear all of my symphonies, including *The Julia Suite*. One of the first class sessions following the Thanksgiving break will be devoted to an open discussion of the works. I'd be more than happy to let you know the exact date before the break, so you can make plans to attend that class. This note will enable you to gain access to the pieces, which are on reserve for only my students."

"I said I'd only tell you what I think at your house."

"Then I regret the fact that I will not have the pleasure of hearing your opinion."

He watched her watch him, eyes locked and the moment tense, much more tense than putting a forward student in her proper place should be.

"Shall I take back the pass?" he said reaching out toward it.

"No," said Autumn beating him to the note and stuffing it in her pocket with her triumph. Watching her go, Gravesend felt much less joy in beating back the griffin than he expected. The dream knot swelled in his ribs.

❧ 3 ❦

Autumn found what she was looking for on the eve of Thanksgiving, an hour before the University library closed for the holiday break. She carried the volume of *Contemporary Composers* to a desk in a hidden corner of the room and took a long look at the picture on the page. The photograph staring back at her showed a clean-shaven man looking up and away from the camera through thick, black, horn-rimmed glasses. His hair lay on top of his head, parted to the side, affording a more subtle view of the familiar, strong bone lines that stood out in that forehead now. The nose had the same Scandinavian, ruggedly-puttied shape to it, but she was surprised to find that his chin did as well. And a handsome chin it was, although it changed the whole complexion of the face, rendering it almost unrecognizable. In her mind, she superimposed the present-day, close-cropped, gray beard on that face and tossed out the offending glasses. A more familiar Quinn Gravesend appeared.

She turned her attention from the photograph to the text wrapping around it.

Alquin (Quinn) Samuel Gravesend (1936 —): At a time when the composition of classical music was moving into an era of experimentation, Gravesend refused to turn his back on the traditionalists. His compositions, while employing some startling innovations, remained rooted in many traditional structures. The result is a body of work that forms a bridge between traditional and modern theories and instrumentation and provides a springboard for the composers of the latter part of the twentieth century. Despite a relatively small number of completed works, Gravesend's compositions carved out a place for him in the ranks of classical music's elite composers.

Gravesend was born near Winnipeg, Manitoba, Canada, on June 26, 1936, to musical parents. His father, Samuel Gravesend, was a well-known amateur violinist in the Winnipeg area. His mother, Birgitte Kirkegaard Gravesend, first cousin once removed to the Danish philosopher Søren Kirkegaard, tutored students in piano and harp and taught music in several local schools.

Birgitte Gravesend found an eager and gifted student in her youngest child. At the age of seven, Gravesend gave his first public performance: a piano piece he composed to commemorate his parent's 15th wedding anniversary. Gravesend's interest in and study of music increased with age. He first enrolled in the University of Toronto, where he met Julia Robertson, whom he married in 1962, but Gravesend left the University without taking a degree. He moved on to Les Conservatoire du Montreal, where he devoted himself to the full-time study and composition of music.

Gravesend's innovative style of blending non-traditional instruments and movement structures with traditional instruments and techniques was showcased in his first symphonic composition, The Julia Suite, a work in four movements for piano, dulcimer and bells. The piece was first performed by the Toronto Symphony Orchestra in 1961, and while conservatively hailed as "promising" by both classicists and modern performers, *The Julia Suite* has become the least known and most rarely performed of Gravesend's works.

After accepting a teaching post at the University of Ottawa, Gravesend composed *Symphony Number 1964* and *Symphony Number 1967*. Both works continued Gravesend's exploration of traditional thematic structures woven through a host of unconventional time changes, and both pieces were instant critical and performance successes. Hal Galbreath called Gravesend, "a musical alchemist, who is able to blend tradition and experimentation to create compositions of pure gold."

In 1967, Gravesend resigned his teaching position in Ottawa to accept an invitation to join the music faculty at the North American University of Fine Arts. The change of scenery bore fruit in the guise of Gravesend's master works: *Symphony Number 1970, Symphony Number 1973* and *Symphony Number 1976*. The three pieces employed such rare symphonic instruments as the sitar and Uilleann pipes and were put through diverse and heretofore untried time changes. Argonne Papaté was the first to identify the three works as a linked trilogy. Since then, the symphonies have been analyzed and exalted as the most important and influential classical masterpieces in the latter half of the twentieth century.

Despite this success and the promise for more to come, Gravesend turned away from the composer's pen, and since 1978 he has refused to appear in public to perform or conduct. His last public appearance came at the Royal Command Performance in London, during which he performed *Symphony Number 1970* on piano. Gravesend continues to hold his post on the music faculty at the North American University of Fine Arts, and, in the past two decades, he has published sixteen scholarly papers on modern classical music and compositional theory.

Leaving the library, Autumn walked through the snowy afternoon along the road that circled the island. The name "Argonne Papaté" brought a gripping but risky thought to mind. It took two passes around the island to ponder it, but once she made up her mind, she hurried across the footbridge to the American side of campus and through the whitening streets to Lyle's apartment. Gaining the metal stairs, she heard the sound of his piano from the landing outside, so she opened and closed the door as quietly as she could, sinking to the floor next to it. The music seemed to dovetail into her mood and the mood of the day: a late-autumn afternoon fading to winter, fading to night, escorted by flying snow. Lyle ended with a flourish and stretched. He never turned around.

"Hi, Autumn."

"Either I made too much noise, or you're getting psychic."

"Neither. I think my senses get better when I play."

"That was beautiful."

"*The Kanon* always is beautiful. Bach is beautiful."

"You're beautiful. I don't tell you often enough what a magnificent, sensitive musician you are."

Lyle removed his glasses and wiped his face with a towel. "Am I as good as Gaston?"

"You both touch people but in different ways."

He bent forward and brushed the top of one of the keys, shyly, almost timidly. "Now that's a compliment. Thank you."

There it was again, Autumn thought. His movements, his body, seemed to be both in the room and far away like they always did when he was playing, but there was more, or rather less, to him. His entire self seemed to be shrinking. She had seen this once before when she was about ten. Mrs. Olsavsky, the neighbor who used to make her cookies, died in March, and shortly after the funeral, Mr. Olsavsky started to shrivel. Not physically, but inwardly. She couldn't have put it in those terms back then as she watched him putter around the yard and rock on his front porch, occasionally reaching out with his foot to lightly tap Mrs. Olsavsky's rocking chair and set it in motion. In September, he collapsed while mowing the lawn, and two days later, he was dead. "A broken heart never mends," her mother said at the time. But was Lyle's heart really broken? He had had relationships in the past, but they were always discreet because of his step-father, Mitchell Kroft. Lyle had described Kroft as a moderate Republican, not well liked by the more radical members of his party. She remembered when Lyle told her that — how he said it with disbelief — as if he couldn't understand how anyone could not like his dad. When his mother married his step-father, Lyle was six, and he adored the man. So, was Lyle really suffering from a broken heart? Or something less painful and more damaging?

"I sure you didn't drop by just to hear Bach," Lyle asked. "So, what do you want?"

"Because I give you a compliment, do I have to want something?"

"No, but you're sitting on my floor unannounced and as tense as one of these piano wires. So, what's up?"

"How do you know I'm tense? You haven't even looked at me since I came in."

"Heightened senses while playing, remember?" His voice was slow and thoughtful as if the words were traveling from some great distance to get out of his mouth. She watched him turn on the bench. Even his turn was slow, as was the blinking of his eyes behind those wire-rims, like shutters on an abandoned house moving in the breeze. "Okay. Now I'm looking at you, and I see a girl who wants something."

"I want to know if I can help you in any way."

Lyle shrugged. "Help me? I'm fine."

"No, you're not. I don't know what's going on, but it doesn't feel good. Ever since the night of the Masque. Are you ready to tell me about it?"

"There's nothing to tell."

"When there is, do you promise to tell me? Or Gaston? Or Chet, Patrick or Mary?"

Lyle smiled. "You want me to tell Mary?"

"Strike that. Me, Gaston, Chet or Patrick. Got it?"

"Got it."

"And make it soon. I'm asking now, but I won't be asking later."

"Got it. Now, what do you really want?"

"Yeah, Mr. Heightened Senses, I want something. I remember when you were doing some work for Dr. Brahl earlier in the semester, you mentioned using a master key that Mrs. Bourgione keeps hidden in her desk. I need to know where that key is."

"Why?"

"I'm not going to tell you."

He fingered the towel beside him. "If you get caught—"

"You don't have to lecture me about consequences."

Lyle turned back to the piano and started playing another song — more modern and rockish. In the place of lyrics, he hummed, and when he finished, he said, "Could you at least tell me what you're looking for in Gravesend's office?"

"Who said anything about Gravesend?"

"Autumn. Come on."

"Look, you're the one with the heightened senses. You tell me."

"I just know you mean Gravesend. Am I wrong?"

She got off the floor and sat beside Lyle on the piano bench, fiddling with two keys. "I have a hunch about something, and I need to see if I'm right. It'd take too long to explain, and I don't know if I could explain it anyway."

"The key is in the bottom right-hand drawer of Mrs. Bourgione's desk, inside the margarine container."

Autumn nodded, and gave him a kiss on the cheek. "I'm serious about telling someone about what you're going through. It feels dangerous to me."

"I could say the same about you."

She heard him start into the rock song again as she slipped out the door.

Half an hour later she reached the Music Building. The snow came pouring down, and the cold wetness dripped from her hair onto her face as she climbed the steps to the faculty office complex. The outside door was open; hurdle number one negotiated. She found the master key, made her way down the corridor to Gravesend's office, and let herself in.

She went straight toward the sideboard where the CD shelf system was and found what she was looking for, what had caught her eye that day she was in Gravesend's office. The cassette tape case was marked *bio #6*, and it sat on top of an envelope. She opened the flap and took out the letter. The note, printed on stationary from the Department of Music, Louisiana State University, was dated November 19, 1999.

Dear Quinn:

I wish I could have delivered this in person, but I hope this letter finds you well. Enclosed is the latest recording made on the seventh of this month. I have made my notes from it and am returning it to you for safekeeping, as per our agreement. Once again, I wish not to seem anxious, but I urge you not to erase the tape until I have written and finalized this section of your biography. I am not used to having my research materials out of my hands, and I do not have much faith in my ability to pre-select the information I may need via my notes.

I wish you good health and happiness, and once more I extend the invitation for you to join me for Christmastime at my home in Jamaica. We should have time enough to celebrate the season and complete the final tapes for the project. I hope you will agree to come.

Yours in music,

Papaté

Autumn double-checked the door lock and loaded the tape in the cassette player. Seating herself in the chair behind Gravesend's desk, she pressed the play button on the remote control and concentrated on every word:

.   **Papaté:** Why have you stopped composing?

Gravesend: That question implies a conscious choice.

Papaté: The action wasn't conscious?

Gravesend: Absolutely not. One doesn't say, "Well that's that, I'm not going to compose anymore." That choice is different than choosing a direction at a crossroads. I can't say for certain that I'm finished. I just feel that I am.

Papaté: Throughout our interviews, you've mentioned many times these feelings that seem to guide all you do. Can you explain what it is you feel?

(Long pause)

Gravesend: For as long as I can remember, from the time I was very young, I was aware of rhythms that went beyond music. There is a rhythmic quality to all living things, and be it a gift or just a different level of awareness, I was tuned into those rhythms. I learned quickly enough that when I acted in accordance with those rhythms, I was happy. And when I went against the rhythms, I had trouble. As I grew older, I began to interpret the rhythms into music and started to compose. It seemed the natural thing to do. The results were my early symphonies.

Papaté: Including *The Julia Suite*?

Gravesend: Yes, although that composition was born out of the rhythm of what I was feeling for Julia, who at that time was my fiancée. I explored more general life rhythms in *1964* and *1967*.

Papaté: And these rhythms form the elusive critical link between all your symphonies?

Gravesend: Yes. But I didn't intend for them to be elusive because to me they were natural; I assumed every musician worked on that level of consciousness, so there was no more need to bring them up as there would be in discussing how one breathes. It wasn't until I reached the next level that I had any inkling that I might be experiencing something that not everyone experienced. I wasn't certain of that, however, until reading your paper in which you suggested a link between my final three symphonies. Then it became obvious.

Papaté: What brought you to this "next level?"

Gravesend: A book. *The Golden Bough.* A colleague on the English faculty when I was teaching in Ottawa mentioned it to me during a discussion about myth. I admit to reading only the abridged single volume, not the thirteen volume set, but that was enough to give fuel to some of the theories that had been simmering in my head. The book speaks about the fertility rites and mythic ideals of ancient peoples. For me, it became a profound discovery, one of those seminal books that stay with a person for a lifetime. Passages would pop into my head, which I believed at the time to be random. References from the book began to appear in my lectures, and the more I thought, the more I saw connections between what Frazer reported about mythic concepts of ancient peoples and what I thought about music and the rhythms of life. Well, all of this culminated in the idea that what humans know as ritual could be the method we use to attune ourselves to the rhythms around us. That thought was such a revelation that I began to study myth and human behavior looking for the central rituals in our existence which I then could set to music.

Papaté: Central rituals in the area of modern religion?

Gravesend: I started there, but that avenue died out quickly. Modern religion tends to dilute ritual or turn it into habit. So I began to simply study routines, and I discovered that the key rituals were much more basic than spirituality, more mundane everyday things. Sharing experiences, such as attending a hockey game for example, or the sense of well-being one finds in a familiar object or routine. Even basic expressions such as laughter and crying as an expected response to stimuli could be interpreted as an automatic ritual, in a sense. Then I began to compose around what were, in my view, the most key rituals. Those compositions turned out to be my final three symphonies.

Papaté: Did you see them as a trilogy while composing them?

Gravesend: I thought of them as linked because they all sprang from the same well, but I was not aware that my background ideas created links between the music. Once I read your papers on the subject, I remember clearly saying to myself, "Yes, he's right!" That is an irony of the artistic process, that others see what we cannot, even though we are the creators—

The sound of a key turning in the lock froze Autumn. The door swung slowly open, then a doughy looking man with thinning hair and a limp entered the room. Mechanically he started for the trash can before the sounds and lights registered in his brain. He looked up with the same fear in his eyes that Autumn imagined were in hers.

"I'm a student," Autumn said, drawing his gaze, which had been contemplating the voices coming from the stereo. "Mr. Gravesend's student. I'm doing some research work for him."

"Who are you?" he demanded in a tone he might have used if he just caught her sneaking out the door.

"I'm a student doing research for Mr. Gravesend," she said in a louder voice and pressing the stop button on the remote. The voices went silent. "I thought I would come in now, when it was quiet. Mr. Gravesend gave me a key and told me to use his office."

"Oh," said the man, clearly relieved but still ruffled by the unexpected break in his schedule. He gave the stereo a suspicious look, shrugged, and picked up the trash can. After he emptied the contents in his janitor's cart just outside the door, he replaced the can and said, "I ain't responsible for lights being left on in here." He slammed the door shut behind him.

Autumn drew a deep breath, pressed the rewind button, and continued the playback.

Gravesend: Of course, I discussed all of these theories with Julia. And that led me to a third level. Working with all the rituals made me keenly aware of my own personal rhythms and Julia's and how tightly they were intertwined. I remember a notation in one of my journals that said something to the effect that a marriage of the soul is the best way to achieve a true harmony with the rhythms of life. That was to be my next compositional challenge, to interpret and translate that harmony between two people who have joined body and soul.

Papaté: But Julia died soon afterward?

Gravesend: Not just Julia but truly my other half. We were married for fourteen years and not until her death was I aware of the large role she played in my own rhythm. It is not a cliché to say that a good portion of my rhythm died with her. The irony of all my studies is that they led me to the ultimate musical rhythm — that of two people together — but by the time I learned that lesson, Julia was dead. Everything, every note, I composed was literally written *with her*, if you will. In an instant, all of that was gone. I can teach music, write about it, critique it, and, if I must, conduct a piece. But Julia provided the harmony, the intangible element that enabled me to compose at that high level. I spent the next two years after her death feverishly trying to regain the sound of our rhythm through music, working from memory, but I never succeeded. It just faded. And that's when I realized I probably would not compose again. I'm sure I could write some good pieces, and maybe my reasoning is selfish, but if I can't work at the level where I was, exploring rhythms that were leading to the sounds of life itself, I cannot go back to the mundane. Julia died, those rhythms died, so composition died. No reprise, no coda. Piece over. Gravesend at rest.

Autumn rewound that part and listened again. Then, she turned off the tape player and put everything back as it was before she came. But she didn't leave. She turned out the lights and retook her seat in the desk chair, turning to face the window and think about what she had just heard. The snow continued to fall, and she watched it, aware that it somehow fit in with her thoughts, as if both the snow and Gravesend's words were falling all around her.

December

❧ 1 ❦

Paradox, to Gravesend, was a minor idea, and one that he never thought to include in his musical explorations of the rhythms of life. He never gave it much thought at all. And like all aspects of life that are neglected when they shouldn't be, Paradox was now rearing up and devouring him.

He was on his way to teach the class he least enjoyed out of the entire term. "Least enjoyed" was a bit tame. He loathed it. This morning would be the open session on the topic of his own works in the Philosophy of Composition class. As he drove, his mind wandered to the subject of youth, those people waiting to learn from him. How assured they were of their futures, the successes that awaited them, the triumphs. Forget that they didn't know what success and triumph meant or what cost success and triumph demanded in exchange for coming into one's life. At this moment, they viewed success like fruit on the bough, merely to be picked, and Gravesend would only be one of many to direct them to the proper tree.

There could be no more distinctive quality of youth than this cockiness of victory assured in everything. He didn't doubt that for some of his students success *was* only a matter of time. Indeed, there had been such a time in his life, a time that extended a good many years beyond his youth, when he knew he had the Midas touch; success and triumph were his minions from his first composition until ...

Well, he thought, that was the problem with memory and age, wasn't it? One always reached an until, a wall, a spot in time where the champion finds himself fading from the winner's circle. Perspectives change then. When viewed from the vantage point of youth, a retreat is merely a setback that delays the eventual victory. But when one matures and views life from the other side, one realizes that each victory really only delays the inevitable loss.

Gravesend frowned at his own thought. What internal jackass or devil made him think such fatalistic trash as that? Was it a Romantic rule that if one lives long enough, one's self-opinion must sour to the point that one must feel sorry for continuing to exist? The building looming before him was filled with people who thought him one of this fading century's pillars of music. What happened to the voice inside him who believed he was a champion as well? Most importantly, how did one find that voice again? He didn't know; he didn't even know where to begin to look for it, ergo, Paradox.

His thoughts stopped with the car. After a brief moment in his office, he went on to the classroom and made a quick survey of the students while arranging his support materials on the lectern. Everyone present, plus one. Autumn sat with a casual posture, notebook open and a face ready for anything. She was dead ahead of him, third row center, and three seats in front of Lyle Glasser, an arrangement Gravesend found to be strange.

"Good morning. As I hope to make this more of a discussion than a lecture, my opening remarks will be brief. The guiding metaphor in this class has been the hunt for the mythical beast. We have dug into and around, through and back through that metaphor in a variety of ways to understand what is involved in the creative process of composition. We've centered on music, obviously, but the analogy holds for whatever art you might choose to pursue. I believe examining works in this way helps students to get past the physical nature of the work-in-progress and delve into the soul of that work. So the exercise I hope to lead you through today will follow that thematic line. We will be examining several of my symphonies, looking for the mythical beast, the underlying reality of each. Now, you might think that I have an unfair advantage. 'After all, Gravesend,' you could say, 'you did write the bloody things.' But it is the listener or the reader or the viewer who interprets the work, too, and the sum of all opinions about the work, I believe, make up collectively what we term the 'meaning' of that work. So let's get to it. Do we have any opening comments?"

Ms. Green's hand was the first in the air, as always, and usually her comment was something complimentary toward him. The younger Gravesend would have appreciated the attention. The older Gravesend thought that it was a miracle his cholesterol level hadn't spiked due to her buttering him up.

"Yes, Ms. Green."

"I want to say that *The Julia Suite* is one of the most beautiful pieces I've ever heard. It's warm, loving, romantic…"

"Romantic," repeated Gravesend, cutting off her praise before it had the chance to flower. "Do you mean Romantic in the sense of its compositional structure or romantic in the way of a love ballad?"

"Both, I guess."

He pointed to another student. "Ms. Rochefort?"

"I don't think the piece is quite as fluffy as that."

Gravesend enjoyed the look of annoyance on Ms. Green's face. "Explain, please."

"I found it to be very erotic."

Autumn's hand went into the air.

"Our guest today, Ms. Gilhain."

"I can see where someone might think that, especially if you study the idea behind *The Julia Suite*; I mean it was written for your wife at the time of your engagement. That would make it seem erotic. And the music does follow a sexual pattern: toward the end it rises higher, each instrument heightening the pitch one at a time to a crescendo, then falling away in the same manner, until only a piano is left to tap out the final sequence of notes. But if we're going to talk erotic, *Symphony Number 1964* was erotic, almost pornographic in some places. I wasn't expecting it. It was arousing. Music to make love to."

Several students clapped in agreement. Ms. Rochefort frowned, and Ms. Green looked embarrassed.

Another student raised her hand and asked, "What's the mythical beast analogy have to do with the erotic nature, or any nature, of a finished piece?"

"A good question," said Gravesend. "This would be the perfect juncture to demonstrate the metaphor as a critical tool. What we've heard so far were several points dealing with the superficial nature of both *The Julia Suite* and *1964*: romantic, erotic, etc. But in order to find the meaning of those pieces, we must look deeper than the sensual flesh of the works. What beasts were the pieces chasing? Mr. Willis, it's good to hear a gentleman's opinion. Go ahead."

"I think the beast you're chasing in both pieces is love. Trying to define the music of love or to translate it into music. The two symphonies do it in different ways. The first is kind of the anticipation, you know? The waiting-for-it-to-happen kind of love. And the second one is the ... the ..."

"The happening of love," said a fellow in the back, which drew a laugh from most of the class.

"Yeah, right. The actual act."

"I agree," Autumn said. "*The Julia Suite* is more heartfelt, more in love at the beginning, when love is fresh and ... I don't know ... promising I guess. I'd say that the beast for it was the promise of love. *1964* is, as he said, more of the physical side of love coming on. Its beast then would be desire and passion. The beast in *The Julia Suite* is a young, timid thing; *1964*'s beast is a roaring, powerful one."

"Good. Mr. Glasser, you usually have a way of cutting to the heart of a matter; can you add anything to what has already been said?"

Lyle returned the question with a shrug. They locked eyes, and Gravesend directed his best "you-can-do-better" look toward him. But, nothing came back in return. Gravesend's first instinct was to force Lyle into some comment, any comment, but with Autumn present, he checked the urge.

"All right, shall we move on to the next topic, *Symphony Number 1967*?"

The debate raged over the schizophrenic nature of the piece, both driving and intense and relaxed and floating. Autumn didn't offer an opinion in that discussion, nor for symphonies *1970* and *1973*. But when Gravesend introduced the final symphony, *1976*, her hand shot into the air.

"I listened to those last three symphonies with a friend, and we both agreed that rather than being able to look at them as three individual works, they had to be seen as one work in three large movements."

"Would you explain that comment in more detail please, Ms. Gilhain?"

"Well ... all your works are emotionally crowded. By that I mean the sensitive listener can feel every note like a punch coming out of the speakers. But in these three, the emotion was thinner. That was confusing until we listened to all three in a row and discovered that the emotion built up through all of them. By the end of *1976*, you're left with this profound sadness because of the realization that this was truly *the* end."

Several others nodded in agreement. The two jotters, whom Gravesend, much to his dismay, had not broken from their habit, crowned her comment with a note.

"The sadness," she continued, "wasn't something lost and hopeless, but a beautiful sadness, like the way ... I don't know ... a rose is sad because it'll wilt and dry out, or the sound of a flock of geese is sad because it fades away. *1976* just fades away. It was like, subconsciously, you knew it would be the last piece you composed. That gave the symphony an overwhelming power."

"The suggestion that there is a link between those three symphonies is not new."

"No, but is the theory that there's a link between *all* your symphonies new? I found a link defined by one sound, one feature that I couldn't isolate until I went back and listened to them all in one sitting. It's the way you use the piano to underscore the other instruments, like you're hiding it in the background for some reason, and then somewhere near the end it bursts out and becomes the key instrument, tying all the others together. In *The Julia Suite* it came at the very end, and each note hit the center of all the earlier melody lines. In *1967*, the piano tinkered in the back like it was just along for the ride until the end of the third movement. Then you jump it to the front of the piece, playing a march-like bridge into the fourth movement where it sails along as one of the featured instruments. By the end, the piano is summing up the entire work while leading the symphony to a close. Why do you hide it and then bring it out in that way?"

"Because it is the only instrument that is capable of doing all that you describe. The piano becomes the favored sound. It is used when the composer wants the listener to feel a certain way, but if you overuse the sound, be it a chord or a note, that sound loses its impact or it damages the surrounding sounds. Likewise, if I use the piano too much, all the other instruments seem weaker."

"And yet you've never written anything just for piano. You introduce all these strange instruments like bagpipes and whistle and bells."

"For the same reason. The piano's superiority can raise the other instruments to a higher level. So, I let it shepherd the other instruments along through any given symphony; near the end, I single the piano out to 'sum up the piece,' as you say."

"So, my analysis of a link is correct."

"I'd characterize it as observant."

"Good enough for a paper in my music class with Dr. Spire?"

The class laughed again, and even Gravesend smiled.

"It's a starting point, Ms. Gilhain. Read the critical papers written by Argonne Papaté on my symphonies. He was the first to advance the theory you just described."

"Never heard of him."

"You'll need more study before writing any paper then. He is one of the foremost scholars on American Gospel music and has published some brilliant articles relating Gospel to earlier chants and other forms used in pre-Christian rites. Before that, however, he came to NAUFA on a fellowship in the mid-seventies and took an interest in my work. He published several papers on my symphonies and has kept up with my work as a side interest. He was the first to identify the musical link between my last three symphonies, as well as the first to propose a thematic link between all of my symphonies in some way. What you proposed, Ms. Gilhain, is a technical link. Observant, but not quite all-encompassing."

"Is there a thematic link?" asked Rochefort.

"One never knows. As an artist, I dare not infringe upon the genius of my critics, even when they have been dissecting my works for the past two decades in an attempt to find such a link. Nonetheless, Dr. Papaté is a brilliant fellow. If there is a link, I'm sure he'll find it."

"But you have to have something to say about it," said Willis. "You're a critic, too."

"I have several comments to make, and I have made them: in my notes and papers, which are locked away in a vault. Upon my death, they are willed to Dr. Papaté, who has agreed to produce them in the appropriate form. In short, I'll answer your question when I am dead. And speaking of dead, our time is nearly gone; so, are there any other comments?"

The only response was the shifting rasps of book bags being loaded up for departure. Gravesend nodded, wished them a good day, and went to his office. He settled into his chair while turning toward the window. He didn't feel like moving quickly to leave. He felt tired, more tired than he could ever remember feeling following a class. Age had crept in. Autumn mentioned things fading into oblivion, and at that moment, he felt like one of those things: fading into a shadow, fading like the daylight at dusk.

As if on cue, he heard a knock at the door and swiveled around to find Autumn halfway between the door and his desk.

"When're you leaving?" she asked.

"In about fifteen minutes. I needed some time to collect my thoughts. Why do you ask?"

"Look," she began with a tone of sincerity and modesty he never imagined she could reach. She was looking away from him, as if embarrassed to meet his eyes. "I haven't been very serious around you, and I know I can be bold and bitchy and tricky, which means people don't often take me seriously when I am being sincere. But I'm being sincere now, and I want you to understand that what I'm about to ask I am serious about. Okay?"

"If you say so."

She squared herself to him, now, clear-eyed and intent, so intent that Gravesend's became alert. He could see her griffin's wings spreading in silhouette behind her.

"There is something I want to tell you ... about today. Something I couldn't say in class, and I can't say it here, either. I don't know why I have this need, and if you absolutely refuse, then I'll just have to say what I want to tell you right here and never bug you about it again. But ... I need ... I would really consider it a great favor if you would let me say what I have to say at your house."

"Ms. Gilhain…"

"I know, I know. This is an intrusion and it's really out of line, but I'm just saying what I feel. I don't have any good reason to ask, but could I anyway? Please?"

Gravesend studied her face. What a strange thing it is to see a person one thinks one knows with a wholly new expression. How that person appears to be completely different but also more familiar. Autumn, who could be so cagey and who used misdirection like a magician, was standing in front of him with an earnestness so genuine that she looked vulnerable. To her, this was a deal-breaker, and Gravesend could recognize a crossroad when he came to one. He could say "no" and send her on her way and be reasonably sure he would never see her again. But if honesty were going to rule the moment, he had to admit that he wasn't ready for that to happen. He said he wanted his privacy, and he meant it. However, if he followed that desire down to its root, he understood that his privacy was the weather stripping he used to seal himself off from reminders and emotions connected with his life before Julia died, a life when Gravesend and his house were open and well-trafficked. For whatever reason, this young woman had become a persistent wind. She annoyed him. She aggravated him. She threw him off balance. But the truth of the matter was that it had been a long, long time since he felt that pride when a newcomer got bowled over by the house and the life that he and Julia had built. It was that pride and desire he detected in his voice when he heard himself say, "Come along, then."

"Really? Great!" She backed toward the door. There was no sign of victory on her face, only relief. "I have Gaston's car so I'll meet you at your place in twenty minutes."

That pride turned queasy as Gravesend was getting into his car. Some invisible line had just been crossed, and, like all lines, he knew that once it was crossed it could never be redrawn again. He could excuse putting a toe over the line from time to time when it came to school decisions, but he had just invited to his home a person who was, for all intents and purposes, a dangerous stranger. It had taken him a week to rid his mind of the psychic paw marks left by the Home Society's soirée in September. For nearly a quarter of a century, he had made a habit of politely steering away interviewers who hinted that his home would be a much more relaxing setting for their work than his office at the University. He avoided checkout lines in stores where one of his students was stationed simply because he didn't want students to see what he bought for his personal use or consumption. Home was home, school was school, music was music, and life worked better if the three roads never converged. But along with the queasiness, a sense of relief, albeit with trepidation, was palpable.

The queasiness, relief, and trepidation continued to mix together in an uneasy stew as he watched Autumn walk up to his front door. He swallowed all three with a smile as he held the door for her. She walked in past him, hanging her coat and purse on a branch of the coat tree, and viewed the hallway in a slow whirl, clasping her hands in front of her and leaning in toward Gravesend.

"I'm ready for the guided tour."

They started with a quick look at the kitchen, and then Gravesend gestured for Autumn to turn right and enter the dining room. Each room had a special, elegant item, and Gravesend noted that none of them escaped Autumn's eye. In the dining room, she paused first at the painting that had thrilled Mrs. D'Abonne, then at the carved oval table and high-backed chairs, commenting that they looked like thrones from medieval times. In the formal living room, she sank into the eighteenth-century Queen Anne's chair and tossed Gravesend a coquettish smile. And in the sitting room, she ran a finger along curliqued hair and beards of the godheads stationed at each corner of the castle-like coffee table and pointed at the reproduction of the same faces carved into the joints where the floor-to-wall bookcases came together.

"This is really cool," she said. "Who decided on the theme of this room?"

"Julia. She designed all of the rooms, except for the Great Room."

"The Great Room? Is that where your piano is?"

"Patience. You'll see that in time."

They exited the sitting room, and Autumn pointed to the staircase in the middle of the central hallway. "Up we go?"

She ran her hand up the carved banister all the way to the top. After gaining the landing on the second floor, she stepped into the first bedroom on the left and crossed the room to the bank of windows forming the far wall.

"What a view of the city! Your bedroom?"

"No. We planned this to be the guest room, although Julia would sleep in here if I were composing late at night."

Autumn plopped herself down on the canopied bed. Kicking off her shoes, she curled up on the thick coverlet. "Does the fireplace work?"

"Of course. Each room on the second floor has one. But other than a few of them, they haven't been lit in many years, I'm afraid."

"This'll be my room if I ever get too drunk to leave sometime."

She rolled over onto her back and stretched, arching her chest and her stomach. Then she closed her eyes and put her arms behind her head, stretching again, this time to extend herself down the middle of the bed from pillow to foot rail. Gravesend retreated into the hall and quietly pulled his bedroom door closed, then came back to the doorway to the guest room, but didn't enter. Climbing off the bed, Autumn brushed past him with a smile. She glanced into the library and the two bathrooms before turning her attention to the two rooms facing the front of the house. One had a standard size doorframe, but the room next to it featured a wider entrance with double doors.

Autumn pointed to the room fronted by the standard door. "This your bedroom?"

"Yes."

"And you're not going to open it, I take it."

"No."

She nodded before stepping over to the closed double doors, and finding them locked, she knocked on the oak with her knuckles. "What's in here?"

"An extra room. I don't use it anymore."

"Is there an attic?"

"Just a crawl space, not high enough for you to stand straight, let alone me."

"What about this Great Room you mentioned?"

"Ah! Follow me."

Gravesend led her back down the back staircase which deposited them in the kitchen. He pointed to the round, hewn door in a recess opposite the entrance to the dining room. Instead of a doorknob, a thick leather thong hung from the three o'clock position.

"Pull that and step inside, but be careful; there's a step down into the room."

The door creaked open and Autumn dropped her foot down onto the flagstone before the door. Light streamed in through the clerestory windows high up on both side walls, making the arching ceiling seem higher than it was. Two rows of stone pillars conspired with the stone floor to form a wide path down the center of the room, leading to a group of chairs before a cavernous hearth that reached nearly halfway up the far wall. Candle holders extended from every pillar, each holding a thick electric candle. To the immediate left stood a concert grand piano, which would have dominated any normal room but had the appearance of a dollhouse piece in this one.

"Wowzer! Is this place cool!"

"This used to be where we entertained, and I dare say the room got a lot of use. It's quite romantic at night, with the fire lit and the electric candles guttering. We would set up a table in the back with the food on it and some discreet floor lamps to round out the lighting. But that was in another age. Thus, we conclude our tour of Gravesend Manor."

He stood at the open doorway, indicating that they should leave, but Autumn remained, doing a slow spin and taking one final, appraising look at the room.

"The perfect setting for a Society meeting."

"Please, don't connect my home with any visit by any society in this city. I've already performed my charity in that line by allowing the Home Society to prowl through my house, and I'm not anxious for an encore."

"It's not that type of society. I'm talking about an old-fashioned arts society made up of musicians, an artist and a would-be-writer: *Société de l'Esprit Artistique*."

"Ah, yes. I saw that name on the exhibit in the Art Gallery last month. It was a rather good show."

"That was our artist, Chet Kunzler. Gaston, Lyle, we're all in it. Everyone would love this room! It feels like a place to touch the creative, especially in winter. What about a Christmas party? We could get some food and drinks, and play music, write and paint or draw, depending on Chet's mood."

"So, you are part of that group? Several of the faculty members were talking about the Society, wondering who the members are. How dim-witted of me not to have guessed that Mr. Gunn and you are involved."

Autumn's face went dark. "Look, no one's supposed to know about that, about who is in the group. It was stupid of me to, you know…"

"Your secret is safe with me, as long as the secret of my house is safe with you."

"It is, at least until we have the Society gathering here. Then, you'll be an accomplice.

"But then everyone will see the house. As delightful as that sounds, I'm afraid a Christmas party cannot happen. I have plans for the holidays. Besides, aren't all of you going home over Christmas break?"

"Patrick's going back to England. I might go to Pittsburgh or stay here with everyone else. I don't know. But, we could do it before Patrick leaves. A Winter Solstice party. I could arrange everything."

"I must decline; I'm sorry."

"What, you don't want amateurs working in the room where you wrote all your great compositions? Wait, you didn't compose in here. You used your studio for that."

"My studio?"

"The room behind the locked double doors. Your 'extra room.' Do I look *that* stupid? You said your wife used to sleep in the guest bedroom when you composed late, and in a house this size, I'm sure the piano in this room wouldn't have bothered her. I bet you have a whole studio set-up in that locked room, a room you've kept shut tight since the day you stopped composing."

She threw back her hair and gave him a knowing smile. The griffin's smile. His queasiness kicked into overdrive again.

"So, will you think about hosting the party?"

"If you truly are trying to convince me to have your friends over to my house, you must stop using words like 'society' and 'host.' Neither go very far in persuading me to lend my house out for an evening. Now, I have given you the tour you so eagerly wanted. I believe you said something about having a comment to make, one that couldn't be said at the college?"

"Right. I want you to compose again."

Gravesend laughed. "Just like that, eh?"

"Yeah, just like that."

"I'm not sure that composing is possible."

"That's what Gaston said you'd say. Why? Why is it so damn impossible? I don't understand."

"No, I'm quite sure you don't. And frankly, I don't think I could explain it to you so that you could understand. All I can tell you is what I have been telling people for more than twenty years. I never said I wouldn't compose again. Up until now, I have not. But I cannot say with any conviction that I will or will not compose again in the future."

"Not even during a Winter Solstice party for the greatest artistic society of the modern era?"

"Not even for the greatest artistic society of the modern era. Neither having a party here nor composing again is feasible."

"That's bullshit."

She brushed past him and out of the Great Room. Gravesend followed, closing the door, and found her standing in the doorway between the hall and the dining room, watching the light rain mist the panes of glass.

"Autumn…"

She put up her hand. "Before you say it, I know, you don't want people in your house; this is your private place, and I'm sure I don't fully realize the privilege granted unto me for having been allowed to view it once. But maybe you should think of it this way: if I hadn't come here today, I never would have opened your locked room."

"Pardon me?"

"I'm not talking about the room upstairs. I'm talking about in here." She came to him and lightly tapped the breast pocket of his dress shirt. "You've been locked away for far too long, Quinn Gravesend. That's truly your locked room. But you opened it, briefly, at the lecture today, and the key you used was your art, your music. You should've seen and heard yourself. Your voice swelled, and you looked happier than I've ever seen you. That's what art does for you and for us; it brings out the spirit in us, which is the only goal of our Society. We don't care about grand parties or house tours. We arrive, light the fire, and let the night and creativity take us wherever. You don't have to take any larger part in creating anything other than providing the place for it to happen. That Great Room is aching to be used. Won't you just think about it? Please? Isn't there any kind of a deal we can strike, something you need that I can help you with?"

Gravesend thought for a moment, facing the painting in the dining room, deliberately looking over Autumn's head. "You want to negotiate, do you? Fine. Perhaps we can make a deal. I'll think about permitting a gathering for this Society of yours and Mr. Gunn, if you will work on getting a member of your group motivated in my class once again."

"Lyle?"

"He's sliding rather sharply, and if he's not careful, he'll slide straight out of the course with an "F." Earlier in the semester, I counted him the brightest, most promising student in the class, one of the brightest I have ever had. But in the past three weeks, he has dropped off the end of the earth, and although he comes to every class, he rarely seems to be present. Like today."

Autumn scowled and didn't reply.

"Autumn? Is there a problem?"

"Yes. I mean, no. Lyle's quiet by nature, but over the past several weeks, he's been more than quiet, even at the Society's get-togethers. It's exactly like you said: present but not present." She stopped, opened her mouth to say something, and then closed it again. The scowl deepened.

"You think he's in some sort of trouble?"

She shrugged, the scowl remaining. "I don't know. I see him all the time. But if someone who doesn't see him as much is picking up on something … I don't know."

"So, we have a deal?"

She nodded. "Deal. I'll kick him in the ass about your class, about all his classes."

"And I'll consider having your people here."

She put on her coat and stepped to the door, but instead of opening it, she laid a hand on the flat surface and then turned back around to Gravesend. An embarrassed half-smile made its way across her face as she put her arms around him in a gentle embrace. She had enough height to lay her head against his shoulder bone, and Gravesend found himself pressing his cheek against the back of her head.

"A hug's not much," she said breaking the embrace and smoothing the buttons of his shirt with her hand, "but that's the only way I can express how your music makes me feel. That's what I really wanted to tell you here that I couldn't tell you in class." She pulled open the door, and Gravesend watched her saunter out toward her car. As she opened the car door, he closed the door to his house and stood, thinking.

Paradox. Yes, he had been negligent in studying it.

$\approx 2 \approx$

Patrick handed Autumn her beer and took the seat across the table from her.

"Did Gaston tell you about the party?" Autumn asked.

"Now, be a bit more specific with that question; Gaston's told me of a hundred parties since August."

"Did Gaston tell you about the Society meeting at Quinn Gravesend's house on the 20th of December? And more importantly, will you be able to come?"

Patrick took a deep draw on his cigarette and blew a stream of smoke out of the corner of his mouth, away from Autumn. "No and yes. He didn't say a word about it, but my plane leaves on the 22nd."

"Good. When will you be coming back?"

"After the New Year, sometime around the fifth. My mum wants me to go and see the entire family and all that. Ever read James Joyce's short story 'The Dead?'"

"I saw the movie."

"Righto. Anyway, remove the maid from the story, and you'll have an accurate view of the Mallard family Christmas dinner. So, we're going to the Master's house, are we?"

"The Master?"

"That's the name some of the seniors in the music program call him. Because he's so far above the other professors, I suppose. A legend. The sort of fellow you can't approach without feeling just a bit of awe. Who got him to agree to this party?"

"Actually, it was me. He gave me a tour of his house, and you can't believe this one room. It looks like a hall in an old castle. It's a perfect place for a Society meeting."

"Sounds interesting. Mind if I ask a personal question?"

"Nope."

"Is there any romance between the two of you?"

"What?"

"You seem to be quite thick with him, and there's been some talk within the group. Nothing sordid or serious, only curiosity. So, I'm asking is there any romance going on between the two of you?"

"Our relationship is friendly. That's it."

"A relationship is it?"

"You know, other than the accent you're as gutter-bound as American men."

"The question isn't such nonsense, you know."

"Yes, it is nonsense. The guy fascinates me, okay? He has some brilliant musical theories that say a lot about life, and you said yourself that his symphonies are legendary. I mean, imagine if your professor was Mozart or Gershwin? That's pretty attractive. But that doesn't mean we're screwing around. Yes, I feel drawn to him, but it's not sexual."

"What sort of draw is it then?"

"I don't know, just a draw. We connected. There's something about him that, well ... draws me. I mean, can anyone truly know what attracts them to someone else? Can you explain why you're attracted to Mary?"

"Sure. My dad."

"Your dad?"

"My dad has always been extraordinarily attracted to Asian women. Obsessed you might say. A lot of Englishmen are."

"Why?"

Patrick held out his hands, palm upward, and pretended to weigh something in each. "Princess Di or the Queen Mum. English women lean toward being slender with little figure or matronly. Now, there are some beautiful English women, but they are mostly of those two body types. Even with immigration rising in England, when you step outside the cities, you see fair complexions, long faces, slender or matronly body types."

Autumn pointed to her own cheek. "What's wrong with a fair complexion?"

"Nothing, in amongst many other complexions. America's a smorgasbord of looks and body types. But we live in Salisbury, not London, and when ninety percent of the women have the same look, and the majority conform to two body types, there isn't much variety. Now, pop in an Asian woman, Chinese, Japanese, Thai, it doesn't matter; she's going to look exotic."

"Wait a minute. Mary's American."

"She's *Asian*-American, born to Chinese parents, both of whom came here when they were in their twenties. In fact, her parents met on the trip to America. That's what I mean about the smorgasbord American population. Mary's an American, but she looks Chinese."

Autumn shook her head. "You're kidding, right? I mean about your dad?"

Patrick grinned. "It gets worse. My dad'll see an Asian woman, and he'll tug at my mum's arm. She's almost as fascinated by Asians as he is, and then, they'll discuss it. Strange. I have peasant parents, and they have global children, another reason why Christmas dinner can be contentious. But you asked about my attraction to Mary, and there it is. I have bred within me the Englishman's obsession with Asian females, which is why, when I look at Mary, she appears to be the most lovely, exotic creature I've ever laid eyes on."

"That explains some of it anyway. But you and Mary are totally mismatched."

Patrick lit another cigarette and flicked the match into an ashtray. "You say that because you don't like her; you don't think she's mad about her art the way the rest of us are. Well, let me tell you something, Autumn Gilhain. You're bloody well right."

"Right?"

"Yes. On that one point only. She doesn't have an all-consuming passion for her art. But thinking she has no talent is dead wrong. Simply put, she's a lovely writer, a sensitive soul, a word conjuror. You don't really know her as I do. You see 'Expected Mary.'"

"'Expected Mary'? What the hell's that mean?"

"Mary has this ability to conform to whatever she's doing at the moment. She's in with us now, an artistic lot, so she puts on the artistic face. Only, that's not truly who she is. Mary's no bohemian, but she can play that role. The trick is she has the talent. Her ability is real, but her actions are a facade. She is 'Expected Mary,' playing the part she's expected to play. When I told her once that she was beautiful, she said, 'Yes, I am, but female poets are ugly, right?

Beautiful people inspire poetry, they don't write it.' Nonsense that, but she believes it."

"I believe it, too."

"What's this now?"

"I tell myself that I don't like her because she's shallow and untalented. But underneath maybe I'm shallow and untalented, and I turn that on Mary, then hate her for it."

Patrick stubbed out the remains of the cigarette. "Rubbish. My God, I hold you up to her as an example. 'Look at Autumn,' I said once. 'She's talented and beautiful and dedicated to her art. You can be the same.'"

"Oh, good move! I'm sure that's just what she wanted to hear. If I were her, I would've ripped your tongue out through your nose."

"She didn't talk to me for three days."

"You deserved it. So, who is the real Mary Han?"

"The real Mary Han is an American suburbanite. She'll take her degree and wind up employed as an advertisement writer or something in that line. She'll be splendid, of course: make a lot of money, raise a family and live out her life. And there's nothing wrong with that. It's just not the life I want."

"What do you want?"

"That's the key question now, isn't it? I'm a thoughtful wanderer. I like to keep my eyes open for the opportunity and then seize it. I don't know what that opportunity is, but I have some parameters. I would like it to involve music. It must be something that grips me in its claws and won't let go. Then I'm after it, and let it take me wherever it may. I'll go. Like coming to this school. I read about NAUFA, researched it, and the more I learned, the deeper its fingers dug into me. I had to come. I'll probably leave the same way. Not on a whim, mind you, but in the throes, as the poets say."

"I think I understand what you mean."

"And I understand that Autumn Gilhain is a witch."

"What?"

"I started a conversation meaning to learn the secrets of the Master and you, and I end up going on with these personal tales about me."

"Getting people to talk about themselves is one of my many great talents."

"Along with humility."

"Forget humility. It's a false virtue. Gilhain is Irish. I'm proud, strong, able to drink most people under the table, temperamental" — she put on a teasing smile — "beautiful."

"That stereotype fits you better than it fits the true Irish. Add to that you are cocky, vulgar, self-centered and brash, and the Irish tag won't stick. The Irish are more refined in all things, except joy and conversation. They're mad with celebration and talk. So, don't be so bloody quick to hang the Irish tag on yourself. No, Autumn Gilhain is a Celtic woman, not an Irish one, I say. Hold on." He went to the bar and returned in a minute with two more beers.

"Celtic?" Autumn asked, taking her mug from him. "Doesn't that mean primitive and crude?"

"After a fashion, yes."

"You're one hell of a sweet-talker."

"I can talk like a nightingale sings, love. Unlike you who spits out words like a volcano. No, don't protest that. What was it you said a minute ago? You'd rip my tongue out through my nose for saying what I did to Mary? Proves my point, doesn't it? That's a Celtic response, which isn't meant as an insult. The Celtic women of old were tall and beautiful, but quick to anger and terribly nasty when angry. They were fierce enemies but passionate and seductive lovers. Now, deny that description doesn't fit Autumn Gilhain."

"Maybe. And maybe not. Maybe I'm more like Mary than you're aware of. We do have something in common, you know."

"That being?"

"I'm not sure I should say now. It's something illegal."

"Then you have no link to Mary Han. She never committed an illegal act in her life."

"Well I *have* committed them, and I've had them committed against me. But what I'm talking about is illegal in a social sense, a crime against art and friendship, although artistic enough to my nature."

"I don't follow you."

"There's a notebook."

"A notebook?"

"Nearly two notebooks. About the Society. Our Society. I'm writing them, recording what it is we do."

She scrutinized his face, waiting for the barometric expression to fall, but she saw no reaction. He seemed to be waiting for the punch line.

"It's something I started at the very beginning, in the planning stages for the Society. To tell you the truth, I don't know why I did it. Maybe I wanted a record of what we did just so I would have something to look at and remember this group by years later after we go our separate ways. I've never been a part of anything like this Society. An old separation fear of mine, I guess. Whatever. But the notes and observations and commentary are leading me down paths I never knew existed, down to what's inside me. Now when I sit in at Society meetings, I play my music, but I'm really listening, watching, absorbing it all. When I go to the bathroom or the bedroom, I frantically note down all I've absorbed since the last trip. And when I read it later, I don't believe it. Patrick, what's in those notebooks is really excellent. I'm not just being cocky. It really is good stuff."

"And what are your plans for these notebooks?"

"I don't know. Being around you and Gaston and Lyle and even Chet has brought me down as a musician. You're all geniuses who come out with this incredible stuff, and I'm not capable of playing and composing at that level. Maybe that's why I'm so fascinated with Quinn. He doesn't make me feel like I'm competing and losing. Anyway, one of the things I've discovered by writing in the notebooks is that I love writing, and I think I'm good at it. Maybe this will become a novel or non-fiction book. Or maybe I can blend the two arts into a recording of songs or an opera. I don't know. I don't have a plan; I'm just pursuing it. After hearing what you said about going after what you want with a passion, I thought you would be the one who would understand."

"I wouldn't claim understanding of the female mind in general, yours in particular, but thank you. Does Gaston know of these notebooks?"

"No! Jesus, no one does."

"What's this something that caused – what did you call it – separation fear?"

"That doesn't matter."

"The Master affects that too, in some way, doesn't he? Which is why you're drawn to him?"

"Maybe he does."

"I'm only looking after him, you know. He's a bloody good teacher by all accounts, and a musical genius in any age, which means more in my part of the world than yours. I don't think you should let him drift into your Celtic heart — and anywhere else he may drift — ill-prepared."

"I told you…"

Patrick held up his hands in surrender. "I'm saying what I think only because I must dash. Mary's class will be finishing soon, and I promised to meet her afterward. We may be coming back. Will you be here?"

"I don't know. My Celtic stomach is kind of hungry. Maybe I'll be out trying to catch some unsuspecting animal and then eat it raw."

"And after you leave the Master's house?"

"Go to hell!"

Patrick stood, drained his mug and gave Autumn a wink. "Until later, you Celt."

∾ 3 ∾

A sweet ache overcame Gravesend as he stood on the threshold of the Great Room. This room, his most favored in the house, always looked its best when arrayed for a party, and the half-lit shadows in the mellow light of the hearth fire lent the final ingredient to the character and the magic of the room. On this night, Autumn and her friends, as well as students from his Philosophy of Composition class, made up the guest list. There was Gaston Gunn atop the back of the couch, feet extended along the arm, his back against the last stone pillar. He wore the guitar but no sunglasses. There was the hearty fellow Autumn introduced as Chet Kunzler enstooled before his easel near the food table, being observed by three of Gravesend's students. And Lyle Glasser? Gravesend expected him to be at the piano, but Patrick Mallard and one of the Philosophy of Composition students occupied that seat.

From his vantage point, Gravesend counted thirteen heads. He peered into the darker areas and spied Glasser sitting against the wall, barely visible inside one of the shadow pockets. That made fourteen. He was the fifteenth and Autumn was the sixteenth, the number who had come through the door so far. But Autumn was not in sight.

He ducked back into the kitchen and searched the first floor, then the upstairs. He found her in the master bedroom, standing in front of his desk. In her gray-green knit sweater and gray knit cap, she looked every bit like fall moving into winter, the color of light on a winter's day beneath rolling gray skies.

The creak his foot on a loose floorboard made her spin so hard she nearly lost her balance. She held a pen and a steno pad in her hands.

"What're you doing here?" she asked.

"I might ask you the same question."

"I needed something to write with." She looked down at the things in her hands and coolly tossed the pen back onto the desk while stuffing the steno pad inside her purse. "And, I needed some privacy."

"There are pens in every downstairs room and plenty of private spaces in a house this size. What are you writing that demanded so much privacy for yourself that you had to infringe on mine?" Gravesend came into the room and surveyed the top of the desk. A few bills and two letters, one from a colleague in Germany and another from his sister-in-law, were the only items in sight.

"Boring stuff, but important to me. I'm sorry. Come on." She took his hand in hers. "I was just coming down to rejoin the party. Unless you came up here to get me alone?"

"You say such things to throw the person you've angered off balance, but if I catch you in here again, the only thing I'm going to throw is you out of this house. Do you understand?"

She nodded, but her smile remained undiminished. Gravesend shook his head and let her lead him back downstairs to the Great Room. Most of the guests had migrated to the chairs that Gravesend had placed around the piano, except for Kunzler, who remained at his easel, Gunn on the couch, and Glasser in the shadows. The talk had turned to obscure love songs. A student named Jamais Shears took a pair of bongos out from under the piano and sat cross-legged in front of a chair, tapping out a rolling rhythm. He sang a song weaving in and out of English, French, and Swahili. When he finished, the listeners broke into applause.

"Grandmother's song," he said, holding up one hand. "I don't know what it means, but I could sing it from the time I was a child."

A student at the piano tinkered out a version of Randy Vanwarmer's *Your Light*, and as he was hitting the last few notes, Gunn strummed a segue into a slower, more raw version of Dylan's *Tangled up in Blue*.

"That's no love song, Gunn!" Kunzler called out.

But Gunn continued. When it came time for the vocal, he lifted his head and sang, and in that singing, the feel of the room changed from a cavernous, firelit hall to a place open to the air with dusty sunlight slanting down through the trees. The sound of the words, not the words themselves, floated around Gravesend, around the room. The chattering that had been going on during the first two songs quieted. Autumn, standing between Gravesend and a pillar, leaned toward him until her shoulder and head fell against his arm, but her eyes remained on Gunn. Gravesend looked at her, at her hair spilling out from under her cap and onto both his sweater and hers. His gaze followed those curls and waves down past her shoulders to her breasts, and he found himself wondering about the shape of those breasts without clothing to fetter them.

The thought froze him for an instant, and then he snapped his head up and away from her body, expecting to see people staring at him as if his thought had been broadcast through the room. No one else had moved, but the spell in Gunn's voice lost its grip on him. He searched for a neutral place to focus, anywhere away from Autumn. He looked beyond Gunn's outstretched feet and over the top of the piano, and that's when he met Glasser's eyes staring back at him from the shadows. At first he thought, somehow, that Mr. Glasser had intuited what he had just been thinking, but even as he felt his face begin to burn with embarrassment, he saw that wasn't the case. Glasser was staring right through him, and, for all he knew, through the wall behind him. Gravesend watched the young man's body tense. Gunn's song acted like a winch drawing a pail full of pain from a shallow well inside Glasser. Gravesend tracked it until that pain splashed all over Glasser's face. Gunn's melody turned mournful in Gravesend's ears. Tangled up in Blue. Tangled up in sorrow. Tangled up in a web unbreakable. That's what Glasser's expression was saying to him, and in that instant he recognized not only his student's predicament but his own. Gravesend couldn't tell what web had ensnared Mr. Glasser, but what had caught Gravesend had become very clear: a sexual attraction to Autumn.

The thought triggered his flight reflex, but he couldn't move. The gravity of emotion spilling out of Mr. Glasser's gaze was both too painful to watch and too fascinating to leave. Gunn swept the song aside in three final downward strums, and the room erupted with applause. An enthusiastic student jumped up directly in front of Gravesend and broke the visual link with Glasser, so Gravesend wasn't sure what happened next. He heard what sounded like a squeal, then the short, quick pounding of hard-soled shoes on the stone floor, and he felt the group take a collective step back. The student standing in front of him moved away in time for Gravesend to see Glasser literally push Mr. Willis off the piano bench and onto the floor where he sat with a look both dazed and confused.

"You want emotion?" Glasser yelled. "I'll give you emotion!"

Glasser played the opening chords of a rock song Gravesend didn't know. The young man's hands worked the piano like a professional, but his body shook, tears ran down from his eyes, and the anger and emotion rushed through his throat like a prairie wind forced into a tunnel.

> Go all the way back to the moment you first came
> All the times we had together, times of sun and games.
> You in a shirt and tie, me in something blue
> What I wanted most of all was to be a man like you.

A man, a man – what's that phrase really mean?
It's to keep a dream together, to know the in-between.
So I walked a road away from you, out another door.
I sat in all the shadows, and I sweated every score.

And there's more, and there's more, and there's more
Always, always more.
The sinking of the sun, then the waves, then what's
Closest to the shore.

The emotion Glasser was expelling reached such a level of violence that the sensory vibrations Gravesend picked up made him hurt. And the sounds were still cresting, not falling back. Gravesend tried to deflect some of the sensory waves by looking around the room, but doing so became as surreal as the song. Everyone else had turned to stone. Willis remained on the floor looking up at Glasser. Gunn's guitar dangled from his neck unrestrained. Kunzler sat half-turned on his stool, indistinguishable from the paint on the canvas; only the drop of brown on his brush was in motion, falling to its end on his leg and pooling in a line following a crease in his jeans. And Autumn? She had disengaged herself from his shoulder and leaned forward, taking in every word Glasser was singing as if the song were explaining all the secrets she ever wanted to know.

There's a greater purpose sitting inside every lie
I bore every contradiction and I wore the suit and tie.
Sons are sons forever, and loyalty's the aim
To the lonely point when it's no longer just a game.

But alone in the sea with the sharks on every side?
Shall I let them bite my heart so you'll run away and hide?
What's red isn't red enough: Let it wash away the strand?
Shall every single in-between become another also-ran?

The song segued back into the chorus "And there's more, and there's more, and there's more" but instead of moving through that verse, Glasser moved into a crescendo, pounding the keys and repeating "and there's more" in a voice so primal and filled with anguish that the sound stuffed the chamber beyond even its ability to echo. Then the music went out of tune as Glasser, still repeating "And there's more," began to pound the keyboard with the sides of his fists. Gravesend heard the cracking of wood at the same time Shears and Mallard came out from the shadows to restrain Mr. Glasser. It took both of them to do it. At this point, Gunn and Kunzler were scrambling toward the piano, with Autumn following. Gravesend felt the urge to flee overcome all other sensations, so he grabbed his jacket and left.

The temperature had dropped into the teens; nevertheless, Gravesend plowed through the empty streets, cutting through the cold rather than the other way around. He avoided pools of light from the streetlamps as if they were pools of water. He ducked behind parked cars or poles at the approach of headlights. He kept his eyes focused straight ahead, away from the frosty windows of houses. Every sense and nerve felt exposed to the point that the clouds became resonant, ashen in feeling, hanging like the underbelly of some great dragon about to crash down on his head. His flight finally came to rest against a pole attached to a dysfunctional streetlamp near the center of town, and he stood against that pole puffing out breaths in short bursts.

"What happened back in that room?" he said to the pole, still trying to get his breath. From the moment Autumn put her head on his shoulder everything had gone haywire, like an orchestra coming unhinged, each instrument splitting off to play its own melody, tempo, and style. He tried to plumb the actions of Lyle Glasser, but what poked through all the roiling emotions at the moment was his thought about Autumn. What could he possibly have been thinking about a student? And one who was forty years his junior? Where was the professionalism to have a thought like that in a room full of students? What did it mean to have that thought in a room where Julia and he had shared some of the most defining moments of both their lives? To be standing in the same room wondering about the shape of a woman's breasts?

Gravesend kept repeating those thoughts, trying to whip up a froth of indignation and self-recrimination, tamping the snowy grass with his feet, but thinking of the touch of Autumn against his shoulder was no less exciting in memory than in the happening. He closed his eyes, leaning back against the pole, seeing Autumn beside him, and forcing himself to think of something else: that horrid, frightful ride that Lyle Glasser conducted. Gunn's mesmerizing song. All of it blended together and drained away, leaving only himself and his emotions for Autumn Gilhain. How could this happen? How could he who had been so careful to hold school, art, and life apart for so many years ever allow it all to come undone so quickly? How did he not notice any of the danger signs? At least he knew how to answer that question. He did notice them. Every single one of them. He just ignored each signal, driving straight through every red light going off in his head.

He heard a car approaching, but the sound of it braking to a stop didn't register until he heard a voice call, "Professor Gravesend? Professor?"

Gravesend opened his eyes. Five pairs of student eyes, at least three pairs belonging to students from his graduate level Conducting Seminar, peered at him from the inside of the car that had pulled up to the curb.

"Is something wrong, Professor?" Grace Amin said from the front passenger seat. "Do you need a ride to somewhere?"

"No. No, thank you. I'm out for a stroll and ... ah ... only stopped for a moment before starting back."

"You're sure?"

"Quite sure. Thank you again."

"Okay. Merry Christmas!"

"And to all of you."

Amin rolled up the window and the car went on. After a minute, Gravesend turned around and started trudging his way back toward home, his heart as heavy as his legs. If given the choice, he would prefer finding the door to his house swinging wide and the whole place ransacked to Autumn waiting in the Great Room for him alone.

He found the front door firmly closed. One unknown vehicle remained in the driveway, but because he had not seen which vehicle each person brought, he had no way of knowing who was inside. Well, he couldn't stay outside all night, although freezing to death felt like a viable option. He entered the house and fell back against the door, listening.

Autumn's voice came through the open doorway to the Great Room.

"Quinn? Is that you?"

"Yes."

"We're in here."

"*We're*," he thought. "Plural. Thank God!" Gravesend took off his jacket and headed for the round door.

Autumn sat on the couch, shaded in the light of the dying fire. Glasser lay in a fetal position perpendicular to her, his head in her lap, uttering soft, low moans and bleats at random intervals. Otherwise, he appeared ready for burial.

"What happened?" Gravesend asked. "I was expecting—"

Autumn stopped him by putting a finger to her lips and motioned for him to sit in the tight space between her and the arm of the couch. Gravesend sat with as much grace as he could, aware of her thigh, hip, and arm pressed against him, of the mixed scent of burning wood and jasmine.

"You look like death," she hissed. "Where the hell have you been?"

"I had to ... I needed some air, so I went for a walk."

"Well I wish you'd have taken me with you!" She jerked her head toward Glasser. "What a mess."

She lay the side of her head and cheek against the point of his shoulder. Somewhere in the chaos her knit cap had gone missing. Her hair tickling his neck sent chills through him.

"Lyle snapped," she whispered. "Did you hear the song he played after Gaston finished?"

Oh, the wave of relief in that question. If she had to ask, Gravesend figured, then she hadn't intuited any of his thoughts, which was his greatest fear. It wasn't like Autumn to miss even a trace of a sexual scent, but the night hadn't been a normal one. If Autumn had been distracted enough not to sense his feelings, then she couldn't have been paying enough attention to track his movements. In other words, she realized he was gone but not that he had fled. For the first time in the last couple of hours, Gravesend felt his senses begin to uncoil. "I was here for the song. The intensity drove me out of the house and into my walk."

"Well, when he was done, he began pounding the keyboard with his fists. Sorry, but he did some damage. Patrick and the guy with the bongos had to pull him away from it. Lyle kept screaming and flailing, but they finally managed to wrestle him to the floor and hold him. Then he really started freaking out—"

Gravesend held up his hand and pointed. Glasser had rolled his head and said something unintelligible. He still looked like he was in another world, but Gravesend didn't want to risk a repeat performance if he should overhear Autumn detailing how and why he burst his seams. Gravesend got up and found a blanket and a cushion. He smoothly swapped out Autumn's lap for the pillow and covered Glasser with the blanket. Motioning for Autumn to follow, he led her out of the room and into the kitchen, closing the door softly behind them.

"Would you like some tea?" Gravesend asked.

"Yeah, with a good shot of whiskey and some honey. So, Lyle's on the floor calling out how the world is full of liars and pigs and, well, ranting. Gaston took over for the bongo guy and tried to talk Lyle through it. Gaston is one of the two people Lyle looks up to in his life. In fact, Lyle's the reason Gaston and I are here, but even Gaston couldn't get through. Lyle kept trying to roll free and he kept yelling and swearing, which if you know Lyle, that isn't him. No one had any idea what to do; I mean, how do you react to something like that? So Patrick and Gaston just held on and we were all milling around, trying to be cool."

The kettle boiled, and Gravesend set it aside to steep. He took out two mugs and added some Crown Royal Reserve and honey to Autumn's.

"Finally, Lyle calmed down and stayed on the floor sniveling. That's when the party broke up, and your students began to drift out until only Lyle, Chet, Gaston and I were left. We sent Patrick with the others; he has a plane to catch. Gaston was really shaken; I've never seen him like that before. Chet kept trying to get Gaston out of here, but before he would leave, I had to promise that I would sit with Lyle and wait for you and that I would take care of him when you got back. Once Chet and Gaston left, I got down on the floor and tried to talk to Lyle. It took me about half an hour before I could get him off the floor and onto the couch. That's when it all came out."

"What came out?" Gravesend said, pouring the tea and bringing the cups over to the table.

"What's been going on with him. Why he's been so out of it lately." She took a sip of the spiked tea and her face relaxed. "Thanks for this."

"So, what's behind Lyle's behavior?"

"I told you Gaston was one of the two people in Lyle's life that he looked up to. The other is his step-father. Lyle's real father ditched his mother before Lyle was even born. His mother remarried when Lyle was about six to a guy named Kroft, who at that time was just beginning his first term in the Pennsylvania House. He was a good father, despite the fact that he was gone so much. The guy went from the PA House to the U.S. Senate and got really powerful there. And of course you know about what he's doing now."

"No," Gravesend said. "I don't. I follow Canadian politics more than the American version."

"God, I don't follow any of it, and even I know Senator Mitchell Kroft."

Gravesend thought for a moment. "Wait. Yes, I do recognize the name. Are you telling me that Lyle's step-father is one of the fellows running for President?"

"Yep. The primary elections begin in January or February, and Lyle's told me that people think Kroft has a good shot because he's a moderate Republican who a lot of Republicans and Democrats like. The problem is that the more conservative Republicans don't like him. They want their guy in. Then there's the second thing."

"Which is?"

"Lyle's gay."

Gravesend made a face. "That won't be a good vote-getter, not the way homosexuals are thought of in the U.S."

"Right. Lyle came out to his parents when he was sixteen, shortly after I met him. His father's cool with it, but Lyle's always been super careful not to let anyone outside of his family know, except Gaston. I didn't know until we came here. One of the reasons Lyle chose NAUFA was because it was close to Canada, and he thought being so close to Canada, eventually, he might be able to pursue a relationship there where the scrutiny would be less. Of course, his dad hadn't decided to run for the presidency at that time. Even now, he's only one of what, four or five Republican candidates? The press has left Lyle somewhat alone right now, but he knows that if Kroft starts to win, that'll all change. He wasn't even looking for a relationship, not until the election gets sorted out. But then, he met a guy named Jacques-Yves, and even though it's probably the worst thing in the world right now, Lyle fell for the guy — hard."

Thoughts of Autumn earlier in the Great Room started to rise up in Gravesend's mind, but he pushed them down. "I know a bit about having ill-timed romantic feelings. What did you mean by the press has left Mr. Glasser 'somewhat alone?'"

"A couple of times in October, Lyle felt like he was being followed. Also, he thought someone had gotten into his apartment and looked around; he doesn't always think to lock it. But nothing was taken, so he just said probably some reporters were snooping. I was pissed, and wanted to call the cops, but he wouldn't. He didn't want to do anything to draw attention to himself and, through him, to his dad. Then came the trip to Montreal in November."

"I assume that's where the problems started," Gravesend said.

"Yeah, big-time. Jacques-Yves met Lyle in the park and told him that their relationship was a set-up. He was paid $50,000 to get it on with Lyle and provide evidence that Lyle was gay. He said that he never loved Lyle and that the whole thing was about politics and money."

"No wonder he went off his head!"

"It's been building for a long time, and worse than any of us knew. Not only did he fall in love and get dumped, but now he's worried that he just blew his dad's presidential chances. What's really bad, though, is that he told me he's starting to think he'll never be able to find someone to love, at least not while his father's in politics. He's afraid people will be watching now, and he'll doubt the motives of any potential lovers. The way he was bawling and saying unintelligible things between what was coherent had me worried he would start going crazy again, and I couldn't stop him on my own. I didn't think you were ever coming back."

Gravesend finished his tea. "We better look in on him and decide what to do."

They went back into the room where Glasser was still moaning incoherently. What was to be done with him? And with Autumn? He could offer to drive them somewhere and help Autumn get Glasser where he needed to be. Looking down at the young man, Gravesend also wondered if he shouldn't call an ambulance, although that seemed extreme and would call unwanted attention to Glasser. The one solution Gravesend didn't want to think about was having them both stay here, but what if Autumn suggested it? Didn't she say something to that effect when she was touring the house? "This'll be my bedroom if I'm ever too drunk to leave?" Gravesend didn't even want to think of that, of him and her in this house on this night with Lyle Glasser lying in state in some other room. Gravesend went over to Glasser and brought his hand down firmly on Glasser's shoulder, giving him a rough shake. "Mr. Glasser! Wake up! Mr. Glasser, Lyle, it's Professor Gravesend. Listen to me!"

The moaning and sniveling subsided, and Lyle raised his head a few inches off the cushion, but his eyes remained closed. A thin strand of slobber spun down from his lip like a spider's thread, coming to rest in a gooey spot on the pillow's fabric. He put his head back down.

"My God," said Gravesend, "he's catatonic. Maybe I'd should call an ambulance."

"And what? Have it reported that Mitchell Kroft's son was hospitalized after a huge party at the home of the legendary composer Quinn Gravesend? If you don't want me invading your privacy, you'll certainly love having reporters storming this place. No, we're not doing that to Lyle. Look for his car keys. They should be near his coat, maybe in the hallway."

Gravesend left the room and returned with a leather jacket in his hand. "Keys are in the pocket."

"Great. Help me get him up and out to his car. I'll drive him home."

"And you? How will you get home?"

"I'll crash at his place. I don't think he should be alone tonight, and if he gets worse, I can call an ambulance from there like he just got sick." She pushed Lyle into a sitting position, and his head lolled. Gravesend took a napkin from the food table and wiped the drool and sweat from Glasser's face. While Autumn went out to start the car, Gravesend managed to wrap the jacket around the young man's shoulders and pull him to his feet. Then he half-dragged, half-led Glasser out of the house and deposited him in the front passenger seat.

"Do you want me to follow and help you get him into his apartment?" Gravesend asked.

"No. Thanks. I can handle him as long as he's not fighting me. And I wouldn't put it past Gaston to be camped out at Lyle's place anyway."

Gravesend watched the car disappear down the drive before re-entering the Great Room and taking a seat in one of the leather chairs before the fireplace. His relief was palpable. Most of the wood behind the grate had burned and the embers glowed as the light faded. Instead of stoking the blaze, he sat, watching it burn lower and darker. In two days, he was expected in Jamaica to spend Christmas with Papaté. He tried to focus on that, on how different Christmas would be in a tropical climate. He really didn't care. His mind replayed party scenes until the fire finally dimmed from his view.

He started awake with a sharp pain shooting through his back and neck when he moved in the chair. The fire was cold. He eased himself up out of the chair and stumbled back toward the kitchen. The hands of the grandfather clock stood at 4:14 a.m. He was going to be a mess when he got up later in the morning, and he still had packing to do and errands to run. He moved through the kitchen wondering what woke him. He had been dreaming about some foreign place where the people all rang bells, but the bells reminded him of his own doorbell. He stopped just as he was about to start up the stairs. Turning around, he hobbled back out to the entrance way and opened the door. No one was there, but a compact disc clattered as it fell at his feet. He picked it up and read the label: *The Book of Secrets* by Loreena McKennitt. Gravesend opened the attached card:

Dear Quinn,

Here's something that is _you_. I know that you aren't a big fan of popular music, but this is different, complex, and just a little mysterious. My copy reminds me that there is a person who can surprise me and who I can surprise. That's you. Merry Christmas.

Love,

Autumn

January

≈ 1 ≈

"New Year's Eve," Gaston said looking up from his dinner, "is the only night of the year where it seems like the night is spending you instead of you spending the night."

Autumn stared at him. "What the hell made you say that?"

"I don't know. The thought just came to me." He shrugged and returned to his plate and usual mealtime silence.

"This'll be the first time we're all together since the Solstice party. Is Patrick back from England?"

Gaston nodded.

"And Lyle's still lost in space. Did he go with you to Montreal over Christmas?"

"Nope."

"Has he talked with his dad?"

"I don't know."

"Gaston, I was in Pittsburgh over Christmas; you were here. What went on?"

"He played the piano, mostly. Working things out."

"What things?"

"Things. You know, the same way I work things out with the guitar."

"What the hell does that mean? You didn't spend two years acing music classes and then bomb the entire first semester of your junior year. You didn't flip out at a party in front of a crowd of people, and then go practically comatose. You didn't make an admission to something that mortifies you and then withdraw from everyone and everything. And, oh, by the way, you didn't almost ruin your father's presidential campaign. He's your best friend, goddamn it, so could you cut the cool-man crap for one minute and talk to me?"

"What're you getting so excited about? He's got things to work out: his parents, his music, his life. He didn't go to Montreal or see people or call home. He stayed in his apartment and played the piano. He's working through his problems the best way he knows how. It's a way I understand, so I stopped by occasionally. The rest of the time, I let him be. We'll all be at his place tonight. See what happens then."

"What'll happen is the night will spend us instead of us spending the night."

Gaston shrugged.

The phrase remained inside Autumn as she dressed for the Society meeting. She replayed it in her brain, and with every replay it wormed deeper into her chest. She tried thinking of the party to clear her mind but found herself dreading the night. That dread combined with Gaston's words weighed her down even more. Why? Because of Lyle? Or was Gravesend, off somewhere in Jamaica, the cause?

She went to the kitchen and opened a bottle of wine.

"Starting early?" Gaston asked.

"Yeah. I thought I'd get in the mood." She had a deep drink from the bottle and watched Gaston restring his guitar. "Do you think anything'll be different at the meeting, you know, because of what happened at the Solstice party?"

"No. Why?"

"I don't know. I feel like something's not right, and I don't know or don't remember how 'right' is supposed to feel. Maybe it's all this Y2K crap."

He made no reply, and she returned to her bedroom, leaning against the pillows thinking and drinking. But when she put the empty bottle down beside her bed, the feeling had grown, not diminished.

"Time to go," Gaston called, rapping on her door twice. She got off her bed and followed him out of the apartment, hesitating at the car door.

"What's wrong?"

"Nothing. I don't know." She brushed her fingers along the snow encrusted rubber lining of the passenger-side window. "I think I'll walk over to Lyle's. I have someplace I need to go first."

"Where?"

Instead of answering, Autumn took another bottle from the box they were bringing and headed away from the car over the icy and uneven sidewalks. She had no idea where she was going, and after she heard Gaston's car pull away, she didn't care. She walked aimlessly, bumping into people who knew their destination, where they belonged. She felt hungry, probably from not eating enough dinner. Two more blocks and a popular diner materialized. She went up the steps and inside the door, but the hostess, seeing her take a long swig from the wine bottle, told her firmly that she had to leave. Shrugging, Autumn turned around, tipping the bottle and spilling wine onto the sweater of a man coming in behind her. She said something about not watching. He said he needed to go home to change. She thought she smiled, or maybe he smiled. No matter.

The arrival of the Millennium dimly registered on her brain while she and the man were making love on an unswept carpet in the middle of his living room. His name was Mick, or something like that. What's in a name or sex with a stranger or a nagging sensation? They finished, he changed, and she took what remained of the bottle of wine and left to wander some more.

Snow came, light and frosty. It laid a paper thin covering ahead of her like a bridal carpet leading down an aisle that was really a driveway. She walked toward a bench beneath an oak tree. The bottle was empty, and she was sick of it, so she tossed it onto the slick, snowy grass and watched it slide out beyond the light. She thought she had been on her way to Lyle's apartment, but this place would do. She fell down onto the bench, amazed to have landed in a sitting position. Too much wine. Somewhere she thought she heard a phone ring. Quinn? But he was in Jamaica with that Papaté guy. She remembered his biography and some secret she wanted to know. Was he on the phone? Did he call? Would he even think of calling?

Maybe he was like her father, whose voice called to her now, from behind her as she walked out the door because he didn't have the guts to face her, to stop her.

"You had help! Someone brung you here! Couldn't make it on your own, you bitch of a girl! If you was a boy, you would've done it. A boy would've, you…" and she slammed the door: Just like that her father was gone from her life. Good riddance.

Autumn shook her head, letting it fall back, letting the snow lay on her face and neck like a veil. For a moment she knew exactly where she was, aware of the cutting wind, feeling the snow, seeing the branches of the tree above her sway. They clicked together in an odd way, and remains of leaves brushed and hissed like spray in a fountain: like the water that perpetually hissed in the fountain at the Point in downtown Pittsburgh. The fountain was bordered by a thick concrete surface — just beyond the range of the pluming water. Gerry appeared beside the concrete border, then came and sat down on the bench beside her.

"I haven't seen you since we were in high school," Autumn said. She couldn't feel her lips, and the words seemed to slide off them, tumbling out into the air.

"I been around. And I seen you. You and him. Seen it coming; a lot of people did."

"You have anything to drink? I could use something."

"Don't you ever listen, for chrissake? Shut up and listen for once, okay. You gotta listen to him, you know?"

"Know? I don't *know* anything!"

"Don't think that way, or you'll miss out. I'll help. I always helped you and then Gaston and that Lyle kid. Lyle won't need me much anymore, but the rest of you do, no matter how great you all think you are."

"Then tell me something, Mr. Genius: if you have all the answers, what about you, huh? You couldn't stick it out, could you?"

"I'm not important. He is. You and him. Go there."

Gerry stood up and walked over to the fountain. He loitered there, his hands in his pocket, the mist spraying around him. He wasn't smoking. Autumn thought hard, but she couldn't remember ever seeing him without a cigarette in his mouth or hand.

"You quit smoking?"

He made no reply. The wind picked up, and the spray screened him even more. She thought she saw him take a step back.

"Gerry? Where are you going?"

He shook his head and the wind blew harder still, spraying more mist between them, obscuring him.

"Gerry wait!" called Autumn, but the wind carried her words away as soon as they left her mouth. It blew so hard that it began to slap at her face with what felt like a bony hand. She felt the slap but not the sting of it. Again and again, and then another voice came from the wind, a voice calling somebody named Missie. Autumn closed her eyes and moved her head to avoid the slapping wind. When she tried to open her eyes, they were stuck shut. Finally, she pushed her lids up enough to form a crack of sight.

The voice came again, louder, more coherent. "Wake up, Missie. You sick? Or you just drunk? Wake now, I say!"

The slaps became harder, or maybe they just felt harder. Her vision began to clear, and she saw the snow and the driveway and the face of an older man bending over her with deep worried eyes. He brought his hand down across her face again.

"OW!"

"It hurt? Good. That's good." He stepped back and watched her closely.

She looked around, following the driveway down to where it ended next to Gravesend's house. She tried to stand but couldn't. She couldn't feel her body, but she shivered. The old man took off his coat; Autumn waved at him to stop, but she didn't have the strength to prevent him from wrapping the garment around her.

"You not sick now?"

She tried to make her mouth work. "Fell asleep."

"Fell asleep, you say? You drink too much and that can happen. You shouldn't drink and be caught outdoors on a night like tonight."

Autumn nodded.

"I came to check on the place. My wife is the housekeeper. I help out with the grounds here and watch over the place while Mr. Gravesend goes away. I was coming over to see that the pipes don't freeze. You a long way from where you're supposed to be?"

She nodded again. "I'm a friend ... Mr. Gravesend's. Forgot he was gone."

"Being drunk kinda puts the memory to sleep. Wonder you didn't fall in a street and be ran over."

She shook her head. "Didn't drink much."

"You still were in a drunk snooze. I know. When you get to seventy-five, and you live along the way, you learn a thing or two. Now you come in and warm up before you start back. I'd offer to ride you to wherever, but I don't have a car. Never needed one. You know someone you can call to come get you?"

"I'll be fine. Just get warm."

"Need some sobering too, maybe. Wonder you didn't fall in the street."

The man put a firm arm around her and helped her to her feet, but they felt like round globs at the end of her legs. So he dragged and guided her into the house, depositing her in one of the kitchen chairs. He disappeared into the living room and returned with two thick afghans. He wrapped one of them around her shoulders, the other around her feet.

"Make yourself a seat while I go to the basement and check on those pipes. See if you can't get your legs feeling again."

The feeling returned slowly and in the form of a thousand needles pricking her entire body. She stood and the pain grew worse, but she kicked away the lower afghan and stumbled around the table, holding onto the chairs as she went. Soon the pain abated enough that she could walk unaided. She wanted to go into the Great Room and start a fire, but she didn't want to be alone inside that large hall. She didn't even want to be alone in this room. Although most of what went on during her time in the snow was hazy, she remembered the voice and face of Gerry Powalski with perfect clarity, and that spooked her. Gerry died in a car crash during their senior year in high school. Didn't people talk to a dead person only when they were close to death themselves? She remembered Gerry saying something about listening to *him*? Who was him? Quinn? The thing left her feeling eerie. She was glad to hear the sound of her rescuer's heavy tread on the cellar stairs.

"You warming, Missie? Good. It don't take long. A tall girl like you oughta warm up quick as a hurricane. Them pipes are fine so I'm about done here. I'd offer you to stay, but I don't know you well enough. Not that I doubt you're Mr. Gravesend's friend, but these days, well, I couldn't take that responsibility. You're welcome to come over to my place though. Mrs. Carter can fix you a toddy that'll be warming you next New Year's."

"Thank you, but I'd better go before it gets worse outside."

"You sure everything's all right?"

"I'm fine, really."

The man gave her the once over, then nodded. Outside, he wished her a happy New Year and goodnight. Despite her weak legs and the thick winds, she started for home rather than Lyle's apartment, which was closer. She crammed her gloved hands as deep as they would go inside her jeans pockets, and the fingers of her left hand felt a wadded piece of paper crumple. Pulling it out, she stopped beneath a streetlight. She straightened the paper, recognizing it as a page torn from her steno pad. She tilted it toward the light to read the address she copied off the letter that had been lying on

Gravesend's desk the night of the party, the one signed by a Mary Gravesend. She hurried home.

⁂ 2 ⁀

The hunt for the mythical beast led down an alleyway, black and narrow, smelling of saltwater, heated brick, and fear. The darkness went beyond the night and beyond the shut windows, all with tightly drawn shades. The stillness was akin to a vacuum, and the pitch black was pregnant with the fear of the monkey figurine whose hands covered its eyes: see no evil, even when evil came creeping along the surface of the skin.

In the end, thought Gravesend, the metaphor — the composition of music as a hunt for the mythical beast — was stronger than any evil. The origin of the metaphor had long ago dropped along the paths of time and been trod into dust. The idea had become just another pedagogical device, a hollow symbol he hauled out before his students year after year as a staple of his teaching repertoire. So, how then could he explain, even to himself, the sudden random nature of walking along in one's own world, turning a corner, and running flat into that mythical beast, alive and well enough to fill an alleyway with its claws? This was the last thing he expected: to find himself adrift inside Daedalus's maze chasing a Minotaur. And yet, that's what this dusty back alley in a little town on the coast of Jamaica felt like. And he reveled in it, such a revelry that he had not felt at any time since Julia's death.

Each moment, each step deeper down that dark alley, was precious. He could die happy right here. Paradox once again.

He stopped at the end of the alley. His memory of the correct route was sketchy. He turned left and started down another street before turning about and going in the opposite direction. At the next T in the road, he heard the sound he had been waiting to hear: the faint thump of drums. He crept toward the sound, staying in the shadows of the houses until the buildings came to an end. He had walked toward the sea, and in the dimness of moonlight, he saw the tall grass blowing in the offshore breeze and heard the waves rolling onto the beach. Beyond, stood the dark mass he knew to be the grove of trees growing in a circle, skirted by ancient graves.

Gravesend moved forward to the edge of the grass and the outer rim of the graves, paused, and went closer still. That afternoon, he had counted seven rows of graves. Now he let his hand brush the top of each as he counted his way forward. He stopped at row four, ten yards from the grove, and crouched behind a stone marker.

He had no interest in seeing the ... worshippers? congregants? What was the proper term for those performing a Voodoo ritual? And he certainly didn't want to be seen. It was the music that called him, the rhythms and the feelings behind those rhythms. What feelings! Primeval, like breathing, as resonant and rich as notes formed in the absolute center of the soul. This was music played on the keenest of edges, that point where life and death meet.

"Pay attention, Gravesend," he told himself in a tone reserved for students. He couldn't afford to get caught up in the emotion of the sounds. He concentrated on how the sounds were put together, how the music was made. The chord progression was elementary. He could play it on any instrument; yet, twenty artists of his caliber would have trouble capturing the feeling of it. No matter. He was like a chef in search of an herb: he needed only a pinch, not a pound. His own emotions had formed the basis of music he wanted to compose. The sound coming out from behind the trees would give that music a distinct flavor, one few people have heard.

He stayed only until he was sure he had the sounds he wanted before scurrying away from the grove. All the way back to Papaté's villa, he married the sounds of the ritual to the notes he had composed in his head. It was long after midnight when he arrived, but Papaté was still awake. He eyed Gravesend with suspicion, and that suspicion dissolved into fear and anger when Gravesend recounted his tale.

"You have to be crazy, man! You say the houses were dark along the way to this place? You know why? Papa'll tell you why. The people who live in those houses are no fools. They know to kill the lights when the voodoo men pass on their way to a grave for the death chant. Even the houses don't breath. No, don't you smile like that, because I'll tell you this, man: there's more sense in any one brick in those houses than in your whole Canadian head!"

"But the sounds that those people played, Papa. You can't know what ..."

"Oh, I know what. I've heard that sound, man. Make no mistake. Papa knows the sound you have going inside your head. You think you heard just the death chant? Not on this night. No way. You know the date? The date of this day?"

"It's January sixth."

"January sixth. Epiphany. The day the three wise men come to the manger that holds the Christ Child and give him his first gifts. Do you forget that the Christ is a key figure in the real voodoo, and the actions of his life carry great significance in the rituals of their worship? A man who dies on Epiphany is a powerful man indeed. He becomes the gift carried to the Christ by the spiritual Magi. And so he is honored with special jukes put on his name and his grave. Those who take part in his burial receive a piece of his mortal power, which they believe is great indeed. So what you heard was not an ordinary death chant. No, that sound was the sound of the spirit-gift, a sound that all but fools fear."

"The sound was beautiful."

"Yes, but the price to hear it is heavy. Do you know what would have been done to you had you been seen? Oh man, they would have thought you were there to try and steal the dead man's power from them. They would have thought you were a black spirit trying to kill them and the dead man's afterlife. And they would have killed you and hacked you with machetes until you were small enough to burn so that your ashes could have been spread over the dead man's grave. Then Papa would have had to begin writing that biography sooner than he planned. So, say goodnight now, fool.

Go to your bed and pray to your God a prayer of powerful thanks that you're safe."

Gravesend went to bed, but he lay awake with the chants and music playing and replaying in his head. With each replay, the sounds changed, mingling with other notes and chords arising from his own creativity, forming a mold of coherent music. He let it play and change on its own, hardly daring to breathe, let alone think, so as not to interrupt the delicate process.

Sometime in the night, he rose and padded out into the hallway, then up the stairs to Papaté's studio. With the door shut and the room dark, he stumbled around until he found the light and a blank reel of tape. With trembling hands, he set the console controls and punched the square button at the side. A red light snapped on, and, for the first time in nearly a quarter of a century, Gravesend sat behind a piano miked into a recording console.

Near dawn, he returned to his room and lay down. The box of tape went beneath his pillow, and sleep finally came.

❧ 3 ❧

Mary Gravesend stood behind the screen door, prim and correct, with not so much as a pleat out of place. She had one of those faces that was not so much lined as it was folded, and between the folds the skin was as creamy and smooth as brie. If she wore any make-up, Autumn could not detect it. She was petite, but there was nothing small about the woman. When she spoke, her voice had the cant of someone schooled in speaking from a very early age, a music-box tone, and no trace of an accent.

"You are Jeanette Malloy?" asked Mary Gravesend.

"Yes, ma'am."

She nodded and opened the door. Autumn stepped into a cottage with its fresh, living smell, not the packed-away odor that lingered so often in houses where elderly people lived only in memories, nor the rime smell of most seaside homes. Mess in any variety was not welcome here. Even the crevices of the hall mirror's gilded frame shone with a polished luster. Autumn thought of the sand that lay everywhere outside the cottage and instinctively bent to remove her shoes.

"Oh, there's no need for that," said the woman in polite and contradictory protest. She led Autumn into the living room and motioned for her to be seated on the couch. She left the room and returned with a tea service, which she placed on a table beside her chair.

"If I understood you correctly on the phone, you are from Quinn's college. Cream and sugar?"

"Just sugar, please, thank you. Yes, I'm a student there."

"And you write for some paper or other?"

"*The Artisan*. It's the college paper. Once a month we run a feature story on a major figure at the college. This month the editors have chosen Mr. Gravesend."

"If you don't mind my asking, why not simply interview him? I'm sure he will grant you an interview if you characterize the article as you have for me."

"I've spoken with him already. But the editors like to get outside points of view. They don't want us to summarize a biography or retell stories that are well-known on campus. That's why I need an outside opinion, to get the things that students don't already know about Mr. Gravesend. And let me say up front that it's very good of you to meet with me like this. I appreciate it."

"It's my pleasure, dear, although I'm not sure how much I can help you. I must say, you're a dedicated soul to travel all the way to New Jersey when I could have simply told you what you needed to know over the phone."

"I was coming to the area anyway. Visiting friends. That's how I got the assignment. You're Mr. Gravesend's sister-in-law?"

"That's right. I married Quinn's elder brother, Peter. He passed away in 1993."

"I'm sorry to hear that. There's a girl in the family too, isn't there?"

"Ingrid. Ingrid Banes. She and her husband are archeologists. They live in Cambridge, England now, where they both teach."

"When was the last time you saw Mr. Gravesend?"

"Let me see ... I would have to say it was about two years ago. We met by accident in Toronto and spent a small amount of time together."

"If you had to name one source for his musical ability, what would it be?"

"His parents of course. They were both musical people, although not quite as talented as Quinn. His father was a mathematics teacher and quite a capable musician; the piano was his instrument. His mother could produce the loveliest sounds on the harp. She gave Quinn his rudimentary training. But he put both of their strong points together: his mother's flair and melodic bent and his father's more practical, technical skill. Music is very mathematical, you know. Quinn seemed to be able to blend the best of both parents."

"I've listened to all his works, and he is a great musician by all accounts — except his own. Has he always been so modest?"

"I don't know if he were ever modest. One can hardly be modest when the world attaches the tag of genius to one's name. More than likely, Quinn was being private. He is always careful with interviewers."

"Why is that?"

"I'm sure he is the only one who can answer that question sufficiently. I wouldn't presume to speak for him."

"He mentioned that his wife was a great influence on him. What was she like?"

"Julia was as dear and lovely a woman as you could ever imagine. Very proud and supportive of Quinn. And very much her own person. When critics first began to praise his music, Julia used to tease him, saying things such as, 'Don't think you're too famous to carry out the garbage, Quinn Gravesend!' But she was prouder of him than anyone. Whenever one of Quinn's symphonies was broadcast over the radio, even if just a movement or two were played, Julia would simply beam. And she was a splendid hostess. She loved to entertain. Then, of course, she contracted cancer, and when she died, well, everyone missed her terribly. I have a picture of her if you are interested in seeing it."

"Please."

Mary Gravesend left the room and returned with a silver frame. The photograph of Julia Gravesend stared out from behind the glass with life. That was the word that leaped into Autumn's mind — life. Everything about the face was alive. Her hazel-brown eyes had the roar and dance of firelight to them, stray strands of bobbed brown hair blew in a breeze, and her smile conveyed warmth and a puckish sense of humor. She placed the photograph on the coffee table.

"I realize you don't want to tell a lot of stories about Mr. Gravesend, but could you tell me what he was like when he was younger. Was he always so private, as you say?"

"I only want to say what is appropriate dear. Family business is just that, for families. But no, he wasn't always such a private man. He was of two minds. One was very moody. I would call it 'within himself.' The other was quite outgoing and bright. He could be mischievous as well. Gefr." A smile crept across her face.

"Gefr? I don't understand."

"Perhaps I shouldn't have mentioned that. It might prove embarrassing for Quinn."

In ten minutes of knowing Mary Gravesend, Autumn was sure of one thing: the woman wouldn't let something slip. Her smile seemed to invite prodding, as if she had spotted an opportunity to turn the screw in a long-standing, good-natured game of one-for-one. Autumn, suddenly liking this side of her hostess, chose her words with care. "If, as you say, Mr. Gravesend was mischievous when he was younger, isn't there some little prank he put over on you, or your husband, that you would like to pay back. An innocuous little story could do that, as long as it didn't betray any family business, as you said earlier."

Mary Gravesend tilted her head to one side. "If my husband were here, he, no doubt, would be telling you stories faster than you could write, my dear. At any rate, Quinn will certainly recognize the source of this tale, and maybe it will prompt him to call. Very well. Gefr was his secret name."

"His secret name?"

"The secret name is an ancient concept in many cultures, but especially in Scandinavia, and his mother was Danish, as you no doubt know. I suppose the notion has always been romantic to me, which is why I just now thought of it. Not used much today, I'm afraid. Modern childbirth practices and the wish to strip everything down to its physical nature have stopped the tradition, and that's a shame. The secret name is whispered into the child's ear by the mother just after birth, and the name is not revealed until the child reaches a certain age. The age of revelation varies with the culture; thereafter, the mother will sometimes call the child by his secret name when they are alone. The tradition is a wonderful expression of the continuing bond between the mother and the child. At any rate, Gefr is Quinn's secret name."

"What does Gefr mean?"

"Gefr was one of the names of the Teutonic moon-god. There is a story that tells how the moon-god lent a hand in bringing mead to the ancient peoples, which was seen as both a blessing and a curse. Like mead, Gefr was supposed to be a curse or blessing: a serious and secretive entity, as well as one who enjoyed creating illusions and a bit of mischief now and again. When Mother Gravesend got her first look at Quinn, the name came to her. Understand that this story comes to me through Julia, who was known to pull a leg now and again, so take that under advisement. Julia claimed to have heard the story from Mother Gravesend, who was very Old World. Anyway, whether because she gave Quinn that name or because she knew something about him from birth, he has lived up to his secret name."

"In what way?"

"Suffice to say, Quinn's music and talents are a blessing, but his attitude can sometimes be a curse." Autumn opened her mouth to ask a follow-up question, but Mary Gravesend raised her hand. "I think we should leave it at that."

Autumn nodded. "When did you first meet Mr. Gravesend?"

"I met Quinn for the first time in 1955, when he was nineteen. He was already a brilliant musician. He loved to perform, but he would be very secretive about what he composed. When he was young, he would only let his mother hear a composition in the rough while he perfected it. Later, Julia heard his music first, but never until it was complete. They built that big house, but even so, Quinn put a lock on that second floor studio, and no one could go in while he was writing a piece of music, not even Julia. And that could take up to a year in the doing! She used to tell me that by the time she could get in there and clean the place, the dust on the exposed surfaces was so thick that she sneezed for days afterward."

"So they were a good couple?"

"They adored each other. They belonged to each other, if I am making myself clear. Two halves of a whole."

"Then his wife's death is the reason he stopped composing?" Autumn winced even as she asked the question, hearing the words shoot out of her mouth like knives: pointed and invasive, two things that Mary Gravesend would not approve of. All expression dropped from the woman's face, and her tone became steely.

"That would not be my place to say. Quinn's music is his own province. Julia respected that, as do I, and others should too."

"I'm very sorry. I didn't mean to sound like I was prying. It's just that he wrote such beautiful pieces that students are perplexed about why he doesn't compose anymore."

"I understand, and you are forgiven, Miss Malloy. I am sure that you would never speculate — in print — as to why Quinn has not composed, as others have done over the years. I find that distasteful. The man is free to compose or not to compose. His reasons are his own."

"I understand completely," said Autumn, closing up her notebook. The last sips of tea had turned cold in her cup, but she drank them anyway. Mary Gravesend sat as she had throughout the conversation, straight-backed and attentive, but her face hadn't regained the degree of openness it had shown while recounting the story of Gravesend's secret name. Autumn sensed, as she was sure Mary Gravesend intended, that the interview was over.

Instead of going back to the car parked along Lavellette's main street, she walked up a narrow lane between two beachfront properties and out onto the sand. The wind drove the surf against the shore, and Autumn buttoned her jacket up to the neck. The solitude of the beach in winter created a naturally serene space: The sky between the houses was pink with sunset, and all the air before her stood gray with mist. Down the beach, the mist collected around the lights in white and amber halos. Autumn sat on a dune and looked out at the rolling sea. Even the water looked thick. The empty beach was just the kind of quiet place she needed to sort out all the conflicting thoughts streaming through her head. She sat still, deliberately trying to calm her racing mind, thinking of nothing, concentrating on the ebb and flow of the water.

"Life is what you make it, the ultimate work of art," said a voice in her head. "But everything is created in pairs. An artist spends her life creating art and the rest of the time looking for the other who will pair with her to create a full life. Her Split-Apart."

Autumn repeated the words aloud, "Split-Apart." Gaston had told her about that: a theory or belief that souls progress through many lives together, and in the physical life each person looks for the other soul or souls who belong to that person. But then, Gaston talked about so many strange things. Why did this one stick?

"You may not realize you are looking for anything on the surface," the voice continued. "People may not understand why you do what you do, and you may not realize or understand either. But you are being directed by more powerful forces deep inside. And since your Split-Apart is searching also, the two draw together. Nothing physical or conscious can stop or control that search."

The thoughts trailed away.

"Then Quinn Gravesend is my Split-Apart?" she thought. "Am I in love with a sixty-three-year-old man? Or am I putting too many conditions on all of this? And how can Quinn and I be Split-Aparts if he and Julia were? Do souls detach? God, you're going crazy, Gilhain."

Mary Gravesend's name popped into her head. In the time she'd spent at the Gravesend cottage, what had she learned? She went to inquire about Quinn and ended up talking to his sister-in-law about his dead wife and a secret name. What good did the visit do? She had nothing more than what she started with except the cold from the spray of the ocean, the long drive back over unfamiliar roads to her motel, and the link she wanted to believe existed with Quinn Gravesend.

∾ 4 ∾

Gravesend watched the snowy earth coming toward him as the plane began its descent toward Montreal. There was a thrill to be felt in cheating the northern winter by spending some time where snow is a word with no corporeal form; but, upon return, snow had a comforting effect on the northern mind. It lay like an affirmation that all remained right with the world.

Instinctively he reached for his bag under the seat in front of him and felt the hard outline of the tape case holding the reel of music recorded at Papaté's villa. He couldn't wait to get to his car, get on the road, and get home. He wanted to touch his piano again. He wanted to hear the sounds on the tape and in his head bounding around the Great Room and the studio. And he wanted to see Autumn's face. He thought about the moment back in November when Autumn pleaded with him to see his house and how he thought that moment was a crossroad. He had chosen his path when he told her to come along. Now, as much as he would continue to try and keep his life at school and life at home separate, as far as Autumn was concerned, they were intersecting. The mute piano coming to life and his mute emotions about this strange young woman coming to life. She was like the voodoo men. What he saw and heard of her intrigued him, but there was more he did not know. The thought thrilled and frightened him at the same time.

The time had come to give sound to those contradictory feelings. The tape he recorded in Jamaica was as rough as sandpaper. It was rougher than any of his first attempts given the length of time that had passed since he had last tried to compose a piece of music. But the artist allowed his creative self the moment to dream about the limitless possibilities the music contained. Even his critic self, with standards much harsher than all of the other music critics combined, knew that what lay in the box was a seed of genius. But it would need work to blossom. A lot of work.

He rose to join the file of people disembarking from the plane. There would be other changes. Of that he had no doubt. A new recording would reopen a long-closed world. Life would be different. His relationship to Autumn would be different. She dipped her hand into his life the moment she asked him to compose again. For now, he would keep the composition a secret until it was nearly complete, but it wouldn't be too long before he could call her into the Great Room to hear the fruits of her request. He dreamed of that day, longed for it, and those dreams and longings swept him up the ramp and into the airport's main terminal.

"Quinn?"

Autumn's voice, followed by her body, moved out of his reverie and into the real world of fluorescent light. She came toward him as his senses began to function again. Normally, Autumn had an unusually strong presence: rousing, strident chords underscored by gentle fibrous ones. But now, she was surrounded by a vacuum. Her expression, like her presence, was suspended in a sad and heavy silence. He watched her struggle to find the right words, then she shrugged off the search and simply said what she came to say: "Lyle's dead. He's killed himself."

֍ 5 ֍

Autumn looked up from her musical history text and stared into the quiet of the apartment. The *quiet* apartment. As if to accent the thought, Gaston passed by the kitchen doorway without his guitar.

She went back to her studying, vaguely hearing him go out and come back in. She looked up again, and he was sitting across from her, slack-faced, the unopened mail off to the side, and a large padded envelope in front of him. Wordlessly, he handed the manila envelope across the table to her. The words "TO BE READ TO *SOCIÉTÉ DE L'ESPRIT ARTISTIQUE* " ran across the bottom of the envelope. The return address was Lyle's. The Canadian airmail postmark was stamped two days ago, three days after Lyle's body was found hanging in Mount Royal Park.

"Who do you think sent it?" Autumn asked.

Gaston shrugged. "Lyle knew people in Montreal. One of them, I suppose."

"Do you want to open it now? First?" she asked. "To be sure of what it — "

"No. Not until we're all together."

He called Lyle's landlord to ask for permission to hold a final meeting there that night. From the time he got off the phone, he kept the package near him. They decided to walk rather than drive to Lyle's apartment, and Gaston moved smoothly and seemingly without care, his head up and sunglasses thrust forward in a way impossible for anyone else but natural for Gaston. However, his tell was his guitar; Autumn noticed the neck drooping, the pegboard bouncing only a foot above the sidewalk. Also, he held the package tightly in his other hand. Autumn was used to his silences but not his being a million miles away because of pain. She was glad to see Chet bobbing down the sidewalk from the opposite direction, his travelling easel and drawing case in hand. They met at the steps to Lyle's apartment, and Gaston led the way up. Inside, he flicked on the light.

The first thing to catch Autumn's eye was the mural that Chet and Mary had created during the first meeting, which felt like years ago.

> *Through this shifting world's maze*
> *we race, but stop—.*
> *The sound of the horn delays*
> *the chase. To crops*
> *we're called, our dreams to raise.*

For Autumn, the poem floating around the window had changed in tone. In September, the words were entering their lives. They were green, both with her jealousy of Mary and with the newness of a first step of the Society on a great journey that would be all of their artistic lives. Now, the words looked like they were gathering to fly out the window, and their color matched the deeper, more mature gold of transition and sacrifice: the end of one part of the journey and the beginning of the next stage, with all the doubt and intangibles that went with any beginning born from loss rather than a determined act of creation. Nothing would be the same. Of all the things that spoke of Lyle in the room, it was those words that made her want to cry, for the loss of him and the loss to them all. That thought brought its own stabbing guilt. She could lie with the best of them, and she used to be able to lie to herself, but that skill, too, was disappearing. The truth was that she wanted to cry for herself, for her loss of this group, for what she saw coming, for being set adrift once more. This group wasn't going to be the permanent place she had hoped to land but a brief stopover on the solo trip her choices, and the choices of a few others, set into motion. It was her entire life that made her want to cry, but the cause didn't matter. No tears would come.

"Looks the same," said Chet strolling about the room, "only a good deal smaller."

He brought out his art materials. Gaston laid aside his guitar and sat quietly behind the piano gazing into the keys. Autumn wished she had asked Quinn to come; she felt the need to lean. Instead, she tried to think of the others who were still here in the room with her. She walked past Gaston, running her hand lightly across the upper part of his back, and dropped into a sitting position on the bed nudging Chet's shoulder with her head. He kissed the top of her head, and she heard him whisper something unintelligible before beginning to draw.

"What'd you say?" she asked.

"Just a word to Lyle, should he be stopping by."

The pencil moved in Chet's hand, herding short, gray lines into an outline of a face. She could see Gaston's head moving in time to the piece *Some Children See Him*, which he was playing in pianissimo. She closed her eyes, and the sound of the piano and the

196 | JOSEPH KENYON

sound of the brush blended into a harmony, and she drew some comfort from the two sounds working in concert.

Then the door of the apartment opened, and Patrick and Mary stepped inside. Patrick offered a soft "Greetings, all." Mary nodded. Chet laid down his brush. Gaston finished with a quiet flourish. Autumn sat upright. The five of them looked at each other in silence until Gaston stood and lifted the envelope from the top of the piano. He carefully tore open one edge and peered inside before carrying it over to Autumn. With a shaking hand, he held it out for her to take.

She pulled a sheaf of paper from the envelope with a folded letter clipped to the front. "It's a musical score," she said riffling through the sheaf. She unfolded the letter.

Dear Friends:

I know you're probably wondering why I did this, why I died. But I'm not sure that there are any explanations that would sound as clear on paper as they do in my mind and heart. Or maybe, the thought of admitting the reason to you scares me much more than dying. But I owe you that much. What it all boils down to is weakness.

Autumn took a deep, shaky breath and continued.

Poets say that pain enhances art and vice-versa. I always believed that idea until I found myself in a well of pleasure and pain with Jacques-Yves. For three glorious weeks in the fall, pleasure enhanced the art, and I thought the poets had it wrong. You witness the product of that enhancement, which accompanies this letter. It's a great piece. I'd call it a masterpiece, but I'm biased especially about my own work.

"Bullshit," Gaston said to himself, but in such a quiet room, the word nearly echoed. The skin between his beard and sunglasses reddened. He waved a limp hand. "I mean, Lyle was his own harshest critic."

Chet leaned over and patted Gaston's arm, then nodded with his head toward the letter. "Carry on, Autumn-Girl."

After I found out those weeks were a lie and a trap, there was nothing.

"What's this about a trap now?" Patrick said. He, Mary and Chet stared at Autumn. Gaston looked away as Autumn filled them in on what Lyle had told her the night of the party.

"Good God," Chet said. "You didn't think to tell us any of this before now? Before Lyle went and did this awful thing?"

"She told me," Gaston said quietly. "I told her not to say anything else. I talked with Lyle about it, and he asked that I not say anything to the group. There was nothing we could have said to prevent, you know, what happened. What he did."

"I, for one, would have liked the chance," Chet said. Patrick nodded. Mary shook her head and looked at the ceiling.

Autumn waited through a ten-second silence before turning back to the letter.

> *Dribbles and pieces came, but not anything with any cohesion or substance. Throughout December I tried to work, but I was drained and empty of all music. Only the fear remained. I had been so careful for so long, but then I put my own dream in front of someone else's, someone who has loved and cared for me for as long as I can remember. I know Dad will forgive me and understand, but that wouldn't give him back his dream or my creativity. I looked ahead at my life, and what I saw was denying my true self, a black hole without love and music. Maybe I could live with the guilt replacing one of those, but not both. With my death, the information about me can't be used against my father. The people behind it would look like monsters impugning the reputation of his dead son. And maybe both music and love wait somewhere ahead. To make this situation right, I have to go there. And if nothing exists after death, then all I've done is trade one dead life for another.*

Mary let out a sob. Autumn took another breath, pressing down on her own urge to cry. She felt Chet's arm go around her and tighten his grip on her shoulder. She found her place and continued reading:

So, to you my friends and Society fellows who will not judge I give my legacy, a rich piece where love and music play in harmony. I leave it to you with a last request: as a Society, perform the piece in public once. There is something in the score for all of you, and there are gaps for you to add your own compositional pieces and bridges to it, so it will truly be a Society work of art. It breaks for a verse that Mary can read. Mary, make it anything you feel fits. Autumn can handle the piano, Gaston and Patrick the guitars, and there is a percussion part in there for Chet.

Lyle

Autumn laid the letter on the bed. Gaston leaned against the piano, motionless, but tears ran down from under his sunglasses. Mary and Patrick had their heads bowed. She felt Chet's head touch hers. After a moment, Patrick whispered, "Hand me the score, please."

Autumn gave him the sheaf of papers.

"How's it look?" asked Gaston, shaking his head to clear his eyes.

"He was right. This is a good piece of work to be sure. We'll be pressed to learn it quickly and add our parts, but we should be able to give it a good performance. We know each other well enough."

"He didn't give us a timetable," Chet said.

"No," said Gaston, "but it should be played as soon as possible."

Chet waved in agreement. "Okay, when?"

"And where?" Autumn asked.

Gaston and Patrick traded glances.

"March?" suggested Gaston.

"That's a fair amount of time," Patrick agreed. The others nodded.

"We should play it at the Lick and Poke," said Gaston.

"Will the owner go for it?" Autumn asked.

"I'll speak with him," Patrick said. "He shouldn't mind a bit. It's a great draw for him."

Mary said, "I can make copies of the score on the Writing Department Xerox."

Gaston took the score from Patrick. "Then we're set. I'd like to start working out the piece now."

"I'll open the champagne," Chet said.

Autumn wandered over to the corner where she sat following the initiation. In September, they had been six artists fueling each other's projects and art; now an air of industry pervaded the room. That the Society had transformed into some sort of band with a common work was both exciting and depressing. Despite the intellectual label of "Société," she wondered if they had not always been just a band, a unit, a whole. Now they were filling in the pieces of a missing part. Gaston played the piano with intensity but without his signature flair. He was working, not playing. The same went for Patrick. Mary just listened, and Chet ambled around the room, drinking and staring.

She knew these people. She really knew them. And what she knew told her that the performance they would mount would be marvelous, perhaps dazzling. But she also knew that that performance would be the end. Whether the Society itself would end or just the piece of it that Lyle inhabited, she didn't know, but they would change. Adapt perhaps, but change. She felt the words emblazoned on the window reaching out from the wall and holding a hand over each of them, literally and figuratively. She shivered and turned away.

February

❧ 1 ❧

G ravesend sat with the Society members in the third pew of the University's chapel feeling self-consciously stiff wrapped in a double-breasted suit and silence. He glanced to his left where Messrs. Kunzler and Mallard sat with Ms. Han, whom Mallard introduced as his girlfriend. All three appeared to be at ease. To his right, Autumn and Gunn whispered back and forth, and, to his horror, they both began to chuckle. This was a memorial service, not a funeral, but it felt the same. As long as he could remember, long before Julia died, death had a way of warping his world, making familiar emotional landscapes scarped and uneven. He could try to navigate them, but he wouldn't get anywhere. Only time could smooth the rough terrain.

A door opened and closed and a short, slight man moved toward the pulpit with an earnest look on his face.

"Shhhh!" Gravesend hissed near Autumn's ear. "The Rector's coming in."

His name was Stephen Calles, and Gravesend knew him from some committee work over the years and by reputation. Calles doubled as a philosophy lecturer, and he took both his preaching and his teaching seriously. He didn't water down beliefs to suit the distrust a lot of artists bear clergy, and he didn't back down from the challenges he sometimes faced from those on campus who regarded art itself to be a religion and therefore looked down on the institutional belief that Calles represented. He fancied himself an amateur painter, and every summer he submitted work in the school's open exhibit, the only non-juried show held at NAUFA. The general feeling among the students and art faculty was that the Rector didn't paint well, but he was genuine, a trait all artists respect. The general consensus held Calles to be a good Rector for the non-denominational chapel, a good teacher in an adjunct but important field, and a possessor of the good sense to keep the two vocations separate and distinct.

Calles tapped the fingers of one hand against the edge of the pulpit, eyes closed. Gravesend had never heard him preach, but the word on him as a teacher stated that Calles went straight for the bone at the beginning of a class, without any preliminaries or opening pleasantries, so Gravesend was not surprised when Calles opened his sermon in the same vein.

"In the days and weeks ahead, all of us who knew Lyle Glasser will find private ways to remember him. However, doing so may not prove to be an easy task. Lyle wasn't sick. He wasn't old. He didn't suffer from any visible wounds or infirmities. To the contrary, Lyle, as I have been told, was an excellent student, a promising pianist with a brilliant future. He was dedicated to his art, and he cherished and nurtured the talents that God gave him. It would seem that he had everything to live for. So, don't be surprised, as you reflect upon Lyle and the role he played in your life, if you find yourself asking the question 'Why?' repeatedly in your mind.

It's a natural question and a valid one. What is it inside a man that falls away and leaves him with such little hope that he chooses to end his life? Suicide is a sin against God, not because of the act itself, but because of those things that drive a man to the act: Hopelessness and despair. A man without hope, a man in true despair, is a man without God. Now, I know that term 'Godless' is a tag applied to many of you here, and one that may be applied with even more force when you leave this university. The world is full of people outside of our enclosed pasture of learning who believe that all artists are Godless, that they put themselves before God and say, 'Look at what great works I do.' Some artists may do that, but I have not found that to be the rule of the artists I know in general or what I have heard about Lyle in particular. I have spoken to many people in the past few weeks who assure me that Lyle was a humble man, a good man, one who gave freely to friends and strangers alike. He was not an egoist. He was not self-important. He shared himself and his music with others generously and found in that sharing a great amount of joy."

Calles paused and looked down, as if studying notes. When he looked up again, he swept the room with his eyes before continuing.

"Lyle was also described as a passionate young man, and passionate young men often make mistakes. Passion sometimes leads youth down paths that are best left unexplored. I am not talking about the general, hyperbaric rumors that were mentioned about

Lyle: that he was a homosexual, that he took drugs, and that he was involved in some secret, satanic society."

The Société members exchanged surprised glances, and Autumn covered her mouth to stifle a giggle. Gravesend nudged her back into seriousness.

"I will not dignify such rumors with comment, for they are more of the rubbish people heap upon artists. However, I also heard about Lyle's sudden and rather precipitous drop in classroom performance and his withdrawal deep inside himself. These things tell me that Lyle may have felt something was missing from his life, something profound and important that had come to a climax during the fall term. As I said, suicide is an act of hopelessness and despair. If Lyle became convinced that some crucial part of him were deficient in some way, then that could have led him to draw an evil conclusion."

Calles leaned forward, in full lecture mode now. "I don't use the term 'evil' lightly. Nor do I use it to shock you. You may ask 'Aren't all artists trying to explore the soul?' Yes, artists must tap their own souls and their own voices in order to further their art. But the danger, the evil, comes when one is convinced that what one needs to be an artist, to be a whole person, isn't there. And that is evil because how each of us is equipped when we come to this earth is the province of God, and the plan we know of as our lives is only understood fully by God. There is a romance, perhaps, in the idea of the dark-browed, tragic artist struggling with his own demons, but in real life, that is not only a futile way to live but a dangerous one as well. By focusing on what we don't have, or perhaps on the human limits of our talents, we begin to become obsessed, and obsession with ourselves draws us away from what God created us to do. And that, my students and colleagues, is evil. I have been told that Lyle was a sensitive, brilliant musician. However, if Lyle lost track of his brilliance and focused only on what he perceived he lacked, then he would have become trapped. Too naïve and perhaps too Romantic, he would eventually find no way back and no way forward. That is when despair sets in and the result is the evil conclusion that death is the only way out."

A rustle beside Autumn drew Gravesend's attention away from the Rector. Gunn had shifted in his seat with his arms folded. Behind his sunglasses his eyes were a mystery, but the rest of his body said that he wasn't appreciating the direction of the Rector's sermon. Autumn had mentioned that Gunn felt the most responsible for not picking up on Mr. Glasser's mood and intentions, and for a moment, Gravesend was afraid Gunn was going to stand up and take on Calles. Then Gravesend saw Autumn reach over and squeeze Gunn's left thigh. Gunn responded to the gesture with a faint nod, but he remained stiff, his jaw locked.

"I do not mean to make conclusive assumptions, and I do understand the nature of our unique institution and its aims. I firmly believe in those aims. Indeed, a university of this sort will and should encourage artistic experimentation. Humans are curious creatures, and as curiosity, too, is a gift from God, then we must explore ourselves and find within us that which we need to progress in life artistically, spiritually and physically. But learning about our art also means we need to learn about our limitations. Even with the great collection of talent and genius, on this campus, not all possibilities are open to us. We have to know that and we have to be prepared in order to screen out the unwanted influences that can snare any of us. Lyle, perhaps, was not prepared."

Calles looked down again, and when he faced the congregation, his expression hung somewhere between resolve and sadness.

"However," Calles went on, "years in the classroom have taught me that students can sometimes be the best teachers. Lyle can teach us now. He can teach us how to enrich our lives, how to tend to our art, and he can teach us about the limitations of being human. None of us can know the mind or will of God. For none of us is God. And our quest to be like Him, with Him, must be tempered with the wisdom that we are limited in our approach toward Him. For those who may be asking themselves if there were signs, words, actions that you could have seen and acted upon to prevent this tragedy, again I remind you: you are not God. You cannot know the full mind of even your closest friend, and as so often happens with artists, you may not know the full reaches of your own mind. Who among us claims to completely understand the creative process? So if we can't plumb our own depths, none of us should expect to be able to plumb the depths of another. If you feel a sense of guilt about Lyle's death, absolve yourself. Being our brother's keeper does not mean being his mental jailer. We are free to make choices, and Lyle chose to end his life. Unless you encouraged him to do so, you cannot be blamed for his choice. Worse, if you concentrate only on his death and feel only a sense of guilt, you won't be able to hold the memory of Lyle in your heart without pain, and that would be the worst sin against Lyle that any of us could commit."

Calles drew a pair of reading glasses out from under the top of the pulpit. "Now, if you would all please turn to page 47 in your hymnal, we will ask for blessings on Lyle's soul and remember him through that which he loved best — music."

Gunn's reservations aside, Gravesend thought that Calles had made a good job of the sermon. His point about not knowing the minds of others was a sound one. How well did Gravesend know the mind of Autumn who was currently taking up such a large chunk of his life? What did he know about her four friends beside him and the one they were now singing for? He glanced again at Gaston Gunn. Was the young man soothed by Calles's ending? Gunn stood holding a hymnal, but he wasn't singing. Gravesend wouldn't have described Gunn as lost per se, but he certainly was absent from the world. For Gunn, there was music and then everything else, but Gravesend got the impression that Gunn preferred it that way. Who could blame him? He obviously had a special bond with Mr. Glasser, and now Glasser's suicide cast him back out into the opaque regions of life. While that thought sent a stab of sadness through Gravesend, he also couldn't deny the notion that maybe Gaston Gunn got on better living outside the real world than in it.

Gravesend turned his mind to Autumn. She sang in a muted tone, but there were no tears. Who could doubt that when he first met her in September that she was a lost soul? Now she gave off the vibe of a person growing stronger, not weaker. She wasn't the same young woman. He and NAUFA couldn't take credit for that; Autumn's rebound didn't seem tied to her success at the college as much as outside of it. Could she, too, be finding the penumbral existence of Gaston Gunn more fitting for her? No. Autumn was too gregarious to ever exist well in such alone-ness. She was taking an as-yet-unseen third path.

When the service ended, Gravesend waited for Autumn to retrieve the urn containing Lyle's ashes from the chapel altar. Outside, the six of them gathered for a few minutes before Kunzler, Mallard, and Han wished them a safe trip and wandered off to the Liquor and Poker. Gunn climbed into the back seat of Gravesend's car and picked up his guitar. As Gravesend climbed in the front with Autumn, he asked, "How are Lyle's parents doing?"

"Okay. The last time we spoke to Lyle's mother was after the Montreal police completed the investigation, and she asked us to get the urn and take care of spreading the ashes. They had a private service in Pittsburgh."

"I see. And the other thing? Any threats being made?"

Autumn shrugged. "Kroft came in second in both Iowa and New Hampshire. They're in South Carolina, now. Lyle's mother said he's all torn up, but I'm starting to have doubts."

Gravesend started the car and pulled out into the street. "People grieve in many different ways, Autumn."

"Sure. But I can't help wondering if some politicos are telling Kroft that Lyle's suicide could turn out really well for him. The assholes who paid Jacques-Yves can't use what they got for political advantage, but maybe Kroft is using Lyle's suicide to *his* advantage."

"You're laying a serious charge against the man based on circumstantial evidence and discounting Mr. Glasser's own opinion of his step-father."

Autumn shrugged again. "He had a higher opinion of fathers than I do."

Gravesend glanced in the rearview mirror. Gunn sat sprawled across the seat playing a soft guitar with an impassive expression. He played in that vein all the way to the Syracuse-Hancock Airport. After they boarded the plane, he fell into a window seat and stared out at whichever aspect the turn of the plane presented to him. Autumn took the aisle seat next to him. Gravesend, sitting across the aisle from Autumn, found Gunn still wandering around in his mind emitting vibrations of a muted classical guitar: perpetual and self-willed but unobtrusive. What was going on in that mind, a mind Autumn continually called "genius." The tag was applied like something out of Homer: Flashing-eyed Athene ... Genius-minded Gunn. That tag had been applied to himself for as long as he could remember, and at times it stuck like glue on the skin. Gravesend did know what was awaiting Mr. Gunn. Was he prepared? Was he ready to accept a life in which everybody expects the sky and the stars? "What? You only delivered a planet or two? ...

Sorry, you haven't lived up to your potential." In that way, an artist faced more pressure than a business executive. If the profit margin of a business came up a bit short, it could be made up in the next quarter. But if an artist's work were to fall short of expectations, such a fall became part of his permanent critical record to be cited by every critic for years. Did Gaston Gunn recognize that? Gravesend wanted to ask Autumn to switch places, so he could have a good talk with Gunn and reassure both of them that Gunn had his feet on the ground.

But Gravesend checked the impulse. Maybe Gunn's genius went beyond his musical ability and was grounded in the fact that he just didn't give a damn about any outside examination of his work or his actions. Autumn may be a special case in her awe of Gunn, but as Gravesend searched his mind, he couldn't recall anyone inside or outside the group who had a critical word to say about the young man. True, he hadn't made a record and really put himself out there, but maybe that wasn't his path. Perhaps Gravesend was putting his own fears and shortcomings on the lad. After all, as hard as he tried, Gravesend never could let critical opinion roll off his back, while Gunn had a way of blocking out the world most of the time. The thought of some stuffed-shirt critic asking a pompous question and getting only that shaded, expressionless stare in return made Gravesend smile. Yes, perhaps he was truly a genius and not just musically. Maybe Gunn could teach him how to deal with critical probes and questions that Gravesend found invasive, such as a reporter showing up at the door of his sister-in-law in New Jersey claiming to be from the University's student newspaper. The paper's editor promised Gravesend that no reporter was sent on any such assignment, that a Jeanette Malloy was not even on the paper's staff. Gravesend thought he had kept a tight lid on the composition brewing in his studio, yet apparently that wasn't the case; someone got wind of it. Are you prepared for the critics and invaders, Mr. Gunn? They're sharper, you know, than a preacher/philosopher like Calles, sharper than a *femme fatale* like Autumn. If some music reviewer did sniff out his budding composition, then they were getting even sharper. Beware, Mr. Gunn. Keep your shades on, your head up.

They disembarked at the airport in Pittsburgh and picked up the rental car. Gravesend drove while Autumn navigated him along the highways around the city and out to the Pennsylvania Turnpike, heading east into the rolling foothills of the Allegheny mountains. Nearly an hour passed before Autumn pointed to a hillside on the other side of the road.

"There it is, see?"

Gravesend nodded, proceeding to the next exit, before swinging the car back onto the Turnpike, heading west.

"It's just up at the top of the next hill," said Autumn. "Easy. Pull off on the shoulder there."

Gravesend followed her finger to the side of the road, parking the rental car as close as he could to the hillock of grass. A ditch ran down the hillock connecting with a cement culvert that extended down into the trees and scrub below the Turnpike.

They climbed the hillock with Autumn in the lead carrying the urn, Gravesend following, and Gunn bringing up the rear with his guitar. An old wire fence formed a barrier on their right, running along the tree line. The trees came to an end at the edge of a winter-dead field that covered the side of a higher hill, and in the middle of that field was the graveyard. The stones were arranged in three sections on a squared and leveled space, centered by a twin-trunked pine. Three generations of stones marked the graves. The oldest markers stood tilted, rounded and thin. Another group were squat and squared. The newest stones appeared more like monuments: a tall thin block set upon a square base. A weathered, wooden grave house dominated the left side of the plot.

Gravesend let his eyes wander farther up the hill. "There's a house up there, behind the trees."

"Yeah. Lyle's uncle owns it," Autumn said, following his gaze up to the top of the hill. "His mother's brother. Lyle loved that house, this field, this little cemetery. All of it."

She passed through a gap in the fence and made a beeline for the stones. Gravesend followed more cautiously, feeling a heaviness overlaying his senses like layers of wool pressing in on the skin. He stopped walking midway to the graves. Autumn had reached the edge by this time, and Gravesend watched her lay a light hand on the nearest headstone as she stepped up onto the plot. She stood with the wind whipping her hair across her face, wrapped in a long black coat, looking like she belonged in the scene: a dark figure in the midst of white gravestones. Gunn was behind her. He didn't follow her onto the burial plateau, choosing instead to prowl the perimeter and study each stone along the edge, yet he took great care not to touch any of them. Gravesend turned in his place and made a panoramic inspection of the area. The turnpike divided the field from the coal mine on the far side of the road. On the hill above the mine was a boat showroom. At the end of the field in which he stood was a wide, rectangular billboard advertising a Sheraton motel twenty-four miles ahead.

"I wonder what your Mr. Kunzler could have made of all this," Gravesend called to Autumn.

She made no reply. She moved among the graves, touching everything with her free hand. Gravesend started forward again and then stopped at the edge of the leveled ground. Like Mr. Gunn, he could not bring himself to step up onto it. Autumn finished her inspection, standing above him, her head inclined toward the stone that she first touched.

"He's here," she said looking down at Gravesend through strands of blowing hair. "Lyle's here. You certainly can feel him and his music. It's all here."

"I do feel something. Weighty."

She nodded. "Him." Then she called over to Gunn. "What do I do?"

He shrugged. "Let him go."

Autumn opened the urn and gazed down inside. Then, she swung her arm, releasing human ash into the wind. Gunn jumped back out of range of the flying pieces. After several passes of the arm, she upended the urn and shook out the last of the cremains.

Gravesend looked down at the front of his coat and saw several flakes caught in the fibers. With the greatest care he brushed them free and watched one sail away on the wind.

After the ash settled, Gunn stepped up onto the plateau and took a seat under the tree, with the guitar across his thighs. Autumn stepped off in front of Gravesend, touching him on the midriff of his coat as lightly and with the same care she took in touching the stones. She strolled halfway around the plot, before striking out for the tree line. Gravesend watched her poke around between the trees and the grass. Finally, she found a spot and plopped down with her back to a tree facing the mine and the hills in the distance.

Curiosity overcoming his trepidation, Gravesend stepped up onto the plot beside the nearest grave, listening to Gunn play; the style of the melody sounded familiar, but the tune did not.

"12th century?" asked Gravesend when Gunn finished the piece. "Troubadour, perhaps?"

He smiled, and Gravesend could almost see his eyes light up behind the sunglasses. "Original. Composed on the spot, but I wanted that sound. Thanks."

"Commendable. Too few musicians are acquainted with the troubadour style."

"I don't know it too well. Lyle did. He played like that a lot, especially over the last few months." Gunn shrugged. "Maybe he's helping me get it right now."

Gravesend left the plateau to join Autumn. The ground was bare and free from snow, so Gravesend seated himself perpendicular to her, facing the giant billboard that stood as the southern sentry to the memorial in the field.

"I'll never be a musician," she said after several minutes.

"What makes you say such things, Autumn?"

"Truth. I won't ever be one. I'm good. I can play a good guitar, a good piano, and even an organ pretty well. I can compose some melodic stuff. I think I'm very good. But there are a lot of very good people at the University and everywhere else. As good as I am, I'm just not good enough."

"Good enough for what?"

"To be called a musician. You're a musician. You sense the world by rhythms and translate those rhythms so that people can feel and understand them. Gaston, he's one living musical note. He's got talent and a unique perspective on reality that he sends back to us piece-by-piece through his guitar. And Lyle, he was a musician. He lived it, breathed it. All three of you are examples of what it takes. You're all driven by music, even you. Although you hide it, music is still the center of your life, still tied in with who you are. But I've never reached that level. I don't know what it is to exist on that plane, to have music build up inside like milk in a cow. That's the three of you. Not me."

A dried oak leaf fell into her hair, and Gravesend plucked it out, sending it skittering into a clump of bent and brittle grass. He watched it in comfortable silence. His Canadian sensibilities afforded him a strict sense of what was public and what was private, of when talk was called for and when silence should be observed. He was glad of that. In these instances, he preferred listening over talk.

"What secret memories do you have?" Autumn asked after a moment.

"Pardon me?"

"Secret memories? Things, events that happened to you that defined your life or brought it into focus, but you have never told to anyone. I bet you've had several since you've lived so long ... I mean done all you've done."

"Sixty-three years is not all that old in this day and age, I remind you."

"Right. But it's old enough to have built up a few secret memories. Tell me one. Something you've never told anyone before."

"I have none to tell."

"Yes you do. We all do."

"None that are secret. Everything that defined my life for the first forty years I told to Julia. After that, the only events I could consider defining, or redefining, are Julia's death and meeting you and this group of minstrels you introduced me to. And now, of course, you know about that so there are no secrets left in me."

She leaned her head back against the tree trunk. The wind brushed her hair along the curve of her throat, and her hands moved along the line where her clothes touched the ground, but these were distractions. Wherever she was, it wasn't a good place. Her lips shifted from a beguiling smile to a hard snarl. She came back, but in agitation, tearing a clump of winter grass out of the ground and tossing it away.

"The night before my eighteenth birthday," she said, "my dad told me that his present to me would be to take me on an adventure that summer. When I was little, I spent a lot of time with my dad doing boy things: learning to throw and catch a football, fishing, chopping wood. I was the son he never had. Even the slightest mention of doing anything girlish made him angry, and then he would just stomp away. Girl things were up to Mom. So, when he told me about taking me on an adventure, I got excited. I was more feminine by this time. I had a boyfriend, David Brendanin. Dad hated him, or maybe he hated the female idea of a boyfriend. Either way, I could tell by the look on his face and the sound of his voice that he just despised David. But I didn't think anything of it. I mean, don't all fathers hate the first boys their daughters get involved with?"

"That's the stereotype, but I wouldn't know."

Autumn nodded. "So, I was excited about Dad wanting to spend some time with me. We couldn't go until after I graduated in June, but when the day arrived, he got me up at six that morning, and he and Mom and I all ate a big breakfast. Mom wasn't right the whole time we were eating, but Dad was laughing and acting like a little kid, so I was happy. We were living in the North Hills of Pittsburgh at the time. Right after breakfast, we got into the car and drove off. I asked dad where we were going, but he wouldn't say. He drove north, and five hours later we crossed the border into your Canada and kept on going. All the time he told me about his eighteenth birthday, how it was a rite of passage, the time to become a man. He rambled on about that but never explained what he meant, so he wasn't making a whole lot of sense. But that's the way Dad was when he got excited. We passed through Toronto and kept going north.

"Right around dusk, Dad pulled into this motel off the highway near some godforsaken town. I don't remember the name now. Anyway, he says to me, 'Get into bed and get a good night's sleep because the real adventure starts tomorrow.' So I climbed into bed and went to sleep. When I woke up the next morning, he was gone."

"Gone?"

"Gone. Car and all. On the dresser was a fifty dollar bill and a note that said I was to make my own way home within a month. If I couldn't do it in a month, don't bother coming home at all."

Gravesend studied her face for any sign that this was one of her ploys to dig some information out of him. It was elaborate, he had to give her that. But her face was still hard. "Autumn, that's difficult to believe."

"Difficult for *you* to believe? Imagine what I was thinking. But it's the God's honest truth. He took off. I still have the note if you want proof. He wrote how his father did this to him and his brothers. Said it was how they learned about the world. The ultimate rite of passage for a Gilhain. And I remembered how he and my uncles used to talk about what they called 'their trips' when they were young. But all of it seemed just like stories until that moment."

"Did you go to the police?"

She shook her head. "Once the shock wore off, I was pissed."

"So? Canada has laws, you know. People can't dump their children in a small town and drive back to the States. You were eighteen. Surely you knew this was wrong."

"Maybe, but I didn't think about it. Like I said, I was pissed, and I was young and stupid and cocky. All I could think about was getting back to Pittsburgh and showing up the son-of-a-bitch. I took stock of what I had: a backpack with a change of clothes in it. Since it was summer, I thought we would be hiking or fishing or something, and I brought the backpack because it was easier to carry. So, I psyched myself up and started walking. It took me two days to get back to Toronto. I hooked up with a young Canadian couple from Regina who were on vacation, and they brought me to Niagara Falls. Then a trucker took me back over the border. By the end of the first week, I was in Buffalo and thinking that all of this would be easy as anything. Which was even more stupid because I let my guard down, what little guard I had back then. I hadn't lived a hard life, so I wasn't exactly world-wise, you know? Anyway, I was heading out of Buffalo when an old model Lincoln Continental pulled up beside me on the road. It was some kind of traveling preacher rig with Jesus signs on the doors and two older guys in it. The guy on the passenger side asked me what a girl my age was doing hitching along the road, and didn't I know that it was dangerous, not only for my health but for my soul. He said I was walking a path right into wickedness. So I said, 'Well, then, Reverend, if you'll give me a ride, I'll be back on the straight and narrow, right?'

"'Where you heading?' he asked.

"When I told him near Pittsburgh, he got this big smile on his face, saying they were going back to Kentucky and that they'd be passing right by Pittsburgh. They wouldn't mind going a little bit out of the way to keep me out of hell."

Gravesend said. "And you got in the car."

Autumn nodded. "Yep. The driver was a real nervous guy. He pulled off at the first rest stop and disappeared. The guy in the passenger seat raped me."

"That's incredible," Gravesend said after a moment, "or rather, it's not."

"Yeah, it was. But it also was the turning point of my life, as far as I'd gotten, anyway."

"Did you at least get the police after him?"

"Nope. I set my mind to walking, and I walked, staying on the highway but walking along the edge of the tree line. At night, I just went into the trees and fell asleep. I collected water bottles along the way and filled them at every rest stop I came to, and I figured I could spend a dollar a day on food, which amounted to maybe a hamburger or some crackers from vending machines. I did that all the way from south of Buffalo to Pittsburgh, but really, I wasn't thinking about food, water or being dirty. All I could think about was how my father was responsible for all this. And why hadn't my mother stopped him? And a preacher? I trusted all three and look what I got. But if it killed me, I was going to make it back home under the time limit, and then someone was going to get it. I strolled through the front door with five days to spare, and I took that house by storm. My mother came out of living room, crying, and tried to hug me, but I pushed her aside. I went right up the steps to the tiny little room where my father kept a desk for the bills and things. He was reading some paper, but I tore it out of his hands. I explained that his little adventure had gotten me raped, and told him that I wanted enough money to keep me in housing until I could get a job. I also told him that he was going to give it to me because the New York State Police knew what happened to me, but they couldn't quite figure out why I was strolling around their state's highways in the first place. And if he wanted them to keep wondering, he'd better have the money in hand by the time I was ready to go. So, I showered and packed, and when I went back to that little room, my father started yelling about how *I* cheated. I took the check for five thousand dollars off the desk and left without saying a word. Later, I heard my mother left that day, too."

"Where did you go?"

"To the Southside of Pittsburgh. I got a room of my own, but then I met Gaston and moved in with him. He was playing in clubs, and I accompanied him sometimes, but it was clear even then that he was light-years better than me. There was this sixteen-year-old kid, though, who was very good. He used to hang around the clubs and shadow Gaston. After performances, Gaston would show him some things, and the kid would pick them up almost instantly. Just amazing."

Gravesend smiled. "Let me guess. This kid was Mr. Glasser."

Autumn nodded. "We kept knocking around Pittsburgh while Lyle finished high school. Gaston got pretty big, locally. He would even occasionally open for national acts playing at the Civic Arena. That bet I made with you last fall about Gaston being able to play any request? You remember, that bet you lost and still owe me for?"

"I remember."

"You were set up. We played that game all around Pittsburgh. The only time we lost was one time we let Lyle play the requests." Autumn shook her head. "He wasn't quite up to Gaston's league."

"The two of them stayed very close, I take it," Gravesend said.

"Lyle used to say he was lucky that he lost one father because he picked up two better ones. He considered Gaston his musical father. To Gaston? At first, Lyle was this pain-in-the-ass kid, but soon he became like a little brother. That's why Lyle's death is so hard on him. When Lyle was a senior and it was time to start applying to colleges, he really only wanted to come to NAUFA, but he said he would only go if Gaston and I came along. We were still living together at that time, but the relationship part of it had long since fallen apart. We talked about it, and Gaston said to me, 'What the hell? You should apply too.' I did, and here we are."

"Indeed," Gravesend said.

"The thing is, my parents know about the rape, but you're the only person who's heard the full story. I told both Gaston and Lyle that I didn't get along with my parents, and they never questioned it. So, that's my secret memory."

Gravesend nodded. He was looking past her at Gunn down by the graves, facing away from them and playing to the vista beyond. "Your Mr. Gunn, he—"

"Fascinates you?" Autumn said. "I know the feeling."

Gravesend asked, "Did he ever go to school? What I mean is that he surely did, but it's hard to grasp. He looks like a young man, but he feels so old. Ancient, in a way."

"He's a year older than me, so he's twenty-four. He dropped out of school at fifteen and has lived on his own since then, playing music and doing odd jobs during the day. When he wasn't working, he was studying music." Autumn turned toward Gunn, and Gravesend caught a momentary glimpse of deep pain. "He and Lyle were the only two people I have ever trusted completely since the day I was raped. Now one of them is gone, and I'm worried about the other one. Maybe sitting down there playing is just what he needs. I hope so."

"And what of your soul? What does it need?"

"Just what I'm doing. Talking. Soon to be listening, maybe hearing why Gaston fascinates you?"

"I'm not sure I could explain it clearly."

"Try."

"I think because I understand him in a sense, and that's quite a rare thing for me to say. I spent most of my life not feeling comfortable with the fact that I perceive the world differently from others. And while I have been accused of egoism by some critics for saying that, I really was bothered by the fact that I was alone in my perceptions. I believed I was so congenitally different from everyone else that I was an aberration, isolated by my point of view. Then along comes Mr. Gunn, and, while I do not claim to live in the same world as he, I may have visited there once or twice in my life. He and I may not see music in the same way, but, as you pointed out earlier, we have a similar bent. It's rather like discovering a relative one never knew one had after all these years. That's both heartening and fascinating."

"And that sounds like a secret memory to me."

"Oh no. Perhaps a long-buried thought; however, if you read what some people said about me when I was writing my symphonies and giving interviews, you'll see there's nothing secret about it."

"Well, either bury it again or bring it along. It's almost three, and we have a plane to catch."

"Right. And it's going to take me a minute to get up from this cold ground. Good God! I *am* old."

Autumn offered him her hand. When Gravesend regained his feet, she put her other hand around the one she held and smiled up at him. Then she stretched toward him and gave him a quick kiss on his lips.

"Is that pity for the old man?"

"That's for buying the plane tickets and renting the car to bring us here."

"Good. I despise pity."

"There's no reason for it. You're not old." She tilted her head and a reflective expression crossed her face. Then she raised his hand to her mouth and pressed her lips and cheek to his fingers. "And that's my way of saying that I trust you completely, too."

⇾ 2 ⇽

Autumn didn't know how she came to be where she was, but neither did she care very much; she was enjoying herself, this place. A feeling of contentment and power swelled her. The chair on which she sat was high-backed and throne-like, set between two pillars: one was black, the other white, and both were richly carved. She ran her hand along the blue fabric of her robe that flowed out around her. She touched something that had a raspy surface. She looked down and saw an old scroll of thick paper with ornate silver knobs at both ends.

That's when she heard a tapping at the window. She looked, but the snow fell in blinding swirls, and she could barely make out moving shapes. She laid aside the scroll and left her seat, making her way to the window. Wiping the fog from the glass, she spotted a man on a crutch and a shawled woman. The man turned for an instant just before entering the nether shadows, and the only thing she could see of his face was a beard and a rugged nose.

"Quinn?"

The man disappeared into the snow.

"Quinn! Wait!"

She ran to the door and out onto a stage before a vast, cheering audience. Behind her stood the members of *Société de l'Esprit Artistique*, including Lyle, who rolled his hand as if to say "get on with it." She had no idea what she should say, so she introduced each member of the Society. The cheering grew louder, and the members left the stage through a heavy oak door at the far side.

She followed and found herself in a grove of trees. On each tree hung a Society member by one foot, staring at her with reflective, passive eyes. Then the snow started again, harder than before, falling all around her but not on her. She was standing in a circular patch of dirt surrounded by a thick circle of snow. More fell, but it didn't obscure the open eyes of the hanging Society members. Through it all Autumn remained rooted in her place, afraid to look into those eyes and unable to turn away. Then the voice of a woman she didn't recognize spoke to her.

"Do you really want to stay here?"

Autumn spun around and saw the shawled woman with her head down standing with one foot on the clear dirt and one foot in the mounting snow.

"Where's Quinn?" Autumn asked. "What's going on?"

"Go," she said, "out into the snow, if you like."

"I asked about Quinn?"

"It might be dangerous, but it's a way, you know."

"Where is Quinn?" she shouted.

"Where he needs to be," the woman said, turning away.

"Don't go!" yelled Autumn, as the woman disappeared into the swirling snow. Autumn plunged in after her, calling out for Quinn and then for Gaston, but the snow became so thick, she couldn't see, couldn't breathe. It wrapped around her face and head, smothering her in a strangely warm way. She fell, rolled and shot back up into a sitting position breathing hard. The comforter lay twisted around her on the floor, and the snow was gone, replaced by the shadow the street lamp cast on the far wall of her bedroom. She looked at the clock: 2:24 a.m.

⇾ 3 ⇿

Gravesend woke from a dreamless sleep on Sunday morning with the sun streaming in through his window and a warm feeling all over. He rose quickly, showered and dressed. Heading for the stairs, he stopped at the door to the guest room and opened it a crack. He wanted to go in, but he didn't dare. Even this felt intrusive. So, he closed the door again and went to the kitchen to start cooking breakfast.

Autumn came downstairs an hour later, wrapped in the guest robe, and Gravesend smiled. She was disheveled with waking, without make-up, and worn from very little sleep. She stopped at the threshold of the kitchen and looked around warily.

"Are you waiting for me to carry you across?" he asked.

"Hmmm?"

Gravesend pointed at the line dividing the kitchen from dining room.

"No. I'm … Never mind. Do you have any coffee?"

"Have a seat and I'll get it. Would you like something to eat, perhaps some breakfast?"

"No, just coffee."

He poured her a cup and brought the cream and sugar over to the little side table set in the bay window.

She stirred in the sugar, leaning across the table to see what he had been reading.

"*Société de la Musique du Quebec?*"

"It's their newsletter."

"It's not a society like ours, is it?"

"Not quite, but it is a worthy society nonetheless. Reading the publication helps to keep my French alive."

"Oh." She sipped at the coffee with an appreciative murmur.

"Are you beginning to return to the world of the living?"

"Slowly."

"Enough to explain why you were at my door in the middle of the night? You're lucky I heard you, you know. You could have been out there pounding until I got up this morning."

"I wouldn't've been. I'm not crazy, just stupid."

"The jury is still out on both. It's waiting for your testimony. So?"

"Got anything sugary, like doughnuts or something?"

Gravesend took some sweet rolls out of the refrigerator, along with pumpkin bread and marmalade. He laid the fare on the table and remained standing, leaning against the cupboard.

"Thanks." She bit into a roll and wiped the icing from the sides of her mouth. "I had this dream last night, before I came by."

"A dream?"

"About you. No, that's not right. You were in it, but mostly we just talked about you."

"We?"

Autumn nodded. "A woman in a shawl and me. I thought the woman might be Julia."

"You think you dreamt about my wife?"

"It was one of those dreams where, you know, you don't recognize the person but after you wake up, it hits you who the person could be? The two of you were walking through a snowstorm, and you were hurt, using a crutch. By the time I got outside, I only saw her. She said you were where you had to be, which was with her. So I came by to see, you know."

"No, I don't know. See what?"

Instead of answering, Autumn picked up the newsletter and leafed through it. Gravesend took the seat across the table from her.

"Did you come to my room last night?" he asked.

"You dreamt it."

"You're sure?"

"Positive. If I wanted to be in your room, I would've been there this morning when you woke up." Autumn reached for a slice of the pumpkin bread and dabbed some marmalade on it. Gravesend watched her take a bite and concentrate, not so much on the newsletter but on not making eye contact with him.

"My God! You think you saw Julia in a dream, and she's dead. So, when the woman told you I was with her, you came to see if I had died. That's it, isn't it?"

"Something like that."

"Autumn, what goes on in a dream is not what goes on in reality."

"I know that!" She gazed out the window at the sun-drenched yard, keeping her eyes away from him. "You know, there are things called prophetic dreams. The subconscious picks up stuff that the conscious mind misses."

"Dreams about my death are highly exaggerated," Gravesend said, chuckling.

"Oh, go ahead. Laugh at me."

"Oh, come on. There's no reason to get sensitive on this point. I'm not convinced the best psychiatrists can interpret dreams correctly, let alone you and me. There are too many variables. Suppose, for instance, I had slept right through your knocking. You may have concluded that I died rather than the truth, which is that I am an extraordinarily sound sleeper. By your own admission, you can't be sure you correctly identified Julia. I'm guessing you didn't explain the dream to me as clearly as it appeared in your head. It comes out all muddled. But, for the sake of argument, let's say that the old man and woman in your dream were Julia and me. There's the theory that people in dreams represent aspects of the dreamer, not the people themselves. Julia and I could have been two aspects of your own personality or thoughts or concerns that aren't necessarily even related to me. Do you see how complex all this can get? The fact that Julia said I was where I needed to be has endless connotations."

"But is there anything wrong in checking? In being sure that you were okay? Especially following so close on the heels of Lyle and everything?"

Gravesend reached across the table and took her hand. "There is nothing wrong with what you did. It makes me feel connected, not so isolated, to think you would come all the way over here out of concern for me, or yourself for that matter."

Gravesend felt her squeeze his hand. Immediately, she let go of it and got up from the table. "I better get dressed and leave. I have a test tomorrow that's no dream, and I won't be able to study later on." She fidgeted for a moment, fingering the newsletter again. "Putting aside everything you said about all the possibilities of dream analysis, why do you think I dreamt about Julia?"

"Autumn, please."

"Yeah, yeah. Fine. But I still want to know what you think. I mean, you're the guy who sits in graveyards and talks to his dead wife. A moment ago you sounded like someone who knew something about dream analysis. So use it. What do you think it means?"

"Perhaps," said Gravesend, thinking of the composition-in-progress, "it was you recognizing that I'm being assisted in some way."

"How? In what?"

"I can't say. But that's what I would like to think the dream means. An interpretation that is absolutely subjective, by the way, which is my point."

"So, I'm helping you out?"

"You could be. For what it's worth, and putting the dream aside, I believe you are. In many ways."

免 4 兝

Sunday evening at the Liquor and Poker was known among the students as "Townie night" because students spent Sunday night away from the bar, recovering from too many hours in the place on Friday and Saturday or preparing for Monday's classes. The patrons, then, consisted of the normal, front room townspeople who came without regard to the day of the week. On winter Sundays the emphasis shifted from the stage room to the televisions at both ends of the bar, and entertainment was provided by the Montreal Canadiens, Adirondack Red Wings, or whatever other hockey or college basketball game could be found.

Autumn banked on this Sunday being no different. She went inside and dropped into the shadows of a corner booth, lit by a single, low-hanging lamp and the residual pink glow of a Budweiser sign. She ordered a beer and waited.

Patrick was late, and when he arrived, he stared around the front room blindly before finding Autumn in a booth.

"I've never been in the front of this pub before except to walk through it," he said. "You could die in this booth, and I'll wager no one would discover the body until it began to rot."

"That's the whole idea. I wanted some place private to discuss this. Do you have them?"

Patrick opened a plastic bag and laid three notebooks on the table.

"So?" Autumn asked.

"They're extraordinary. I can't find anything else to say but that. I don't doubt that everyone else will be after your head if they find out what you've done. But my God, it's splendid work. You did more than just record what the Society has done. There are feelings here, an essence or mystique, that you've been able to bring through. I was there for all of our events, but reading your accounts of what went on, I could feel the moment again, as it were. And what you did in bringing out the people was bloody marvelous! You have an uncanny knack for getting inside a person."

"What do you mean?"

He picked up the top notebook and leafed through it to a page near the end. "The entry dated October 17. I was on hand that night, and I remember Gaston improvising that incredible fifteen minutes of music and refusing to play it again. I remember being pissed off and thinking, 'Fine, if that's the way he wants to be about it, I'm not going to bloody beg his majesty for a performance.' But you write:

"Gaston couldn't play the music again. It wasn't that he didn't want to. He couldn't. The music wasn't his to play, and that is a perfect example of Gaston Gunn's relationship to music, his muse, his spirit. He was purging his soul, excommunicating the notes that he could no longer hold inside. It is an incredible thing to watch, this artist whose hands are flying across the instrument in a way that isn't even human. Notes pour out of him that have never been played in that combination and never will be heard again. He doesn't pause, he doesn't miss, and he doesn't remember any more than a person can recall the number and order of the tears she has cried. Nor can she cry again in the exact same way, with the same passion. The music is his tears, his laughter, his words of love, the things he hates, and every other emotion mere mortals express through physical or verbal means."

"I've not known Gaston nearly as long nor as well as you, but the moment I read this I said to myself: 'Right! There it is then, Gaston Gunn!' The difference is I could never have explained it in such clear poetic terms. I don't think the members will be as bothered by the fact that you broke the no-disclosure oath as they will be by seeing their souls bared to the world as they are here. I felt uneasy about some of the things written about me, but they are straight on."

"Poetic? Come on, Patrick."

"The writing's lovely! Yes, some places are raw, but most of the phrases and passages are capsules of poetic prose that sing and paint and write better than the people you're describing. The notebooks have left me with two questions, however."

"Shoot."

"Number one: why is there so little about Autumn Gilhain in these journals?"

"I think there's a lot. The whole thing is laced with my interpretations."

"Perhaps, but there is no tangible Autumn here. I read about the contributions of all the members but you. I read evaluations of their talent, the expressions of their souls, their pursuit of their art, but I didn't read about Autumn's measure of these things."

"Maybe I see other people better than I see myself, but I don't think I contributed very much, except these journals."

"By chance, have you read Thomas Mann's *The Magic Mountain*."

"Never heard of it."

Patrick lit a cigarette and inhaled deeply. "You should read Mann, the German artistic kinsman to the Irish James Joyce. *The Magic Mountain*, you see, is the German soul book. It is the story of a man who makes a visit to his cousin at a health spa in the Alps and ends up experiencing his own regeneration. The book is written after the style of the great German Romantic writers: the soul's unconscious flight to its place of rebirth. Hans Castorp is completely unaware that he needs regeneration, and yet he finds love, life, soul, all the things one needs in the world but which are usually buried by the world."

"What's that got to do with these notebooks?"

"It leads to my second question: what is to be done with the journals?"

"I don't know."

"That's rather an evasive answer, isn't it? What does your heart say, Autumn? You must be listening; otherwise, we wouldn't have these wonderful books. So what's it telling you about what to do with the lovely words you've spread across these pages?"

"Tell me."

"That we need to find the Autumn missing from these notebooks: Autumn Gilhain, the Celt. Now, if I were keeping secret notebooks on my Society fellows, I would write that Autumn is searching for something but she doesn't know what. She is passionate at the formation of the Society, but by Christmas that passion begins to dim. She wanders through the winter searching for something else to ignite that passion, a place where she won't find disappointment. She needs regeneration, a magic mountain."

"That's what you'd write, huh?"

"Yes. It certainly wouldn't be as pretty as your writing. My skill lies with notes and tones, not paper and ink. But the words would be just as sound."

"How can you be so sure you can see that much of me if you say I didn't put myself in the notebooks?"

"Because while you were hiding yourself from view on the pages, your tone is evident throughout, and tone speaks to a musician's ear in a special way. And the tone is that of a seeker. You look for a place to set your spirit moving, a path, or, to use one of Chet's expressions, a place to smack your feet against the solid earth. So I ask you again: what's next?"

Autumn sat back and scowled. "I never thought about what I would do with them, except some vague thing like maybe publish them as a memoir after all of you become famous. An I-knew-them-when sort of thing. But I didn't start writing them with any purpose, and I don't have one now."

"Yes, you had quite a strong purpose in the beginning. These books were born out of jealousy. No, don't look so bloody surprised. You resented Mary's claim on the written word from day one. Well, I'm sure you've heard the platitude 'Be careful what you wish for; you just might get it.' You have it, my love. These notebooks outstrip Mary's best work at every turn. Congratulations. Now, you must carry on with them."

"To where?"

"All the way to bloody here." Patrick leaned across the table and tapped her heart. "Right down into yourself. The magic mountain is inside all of us, and like Mr. Castorp, our paths lead to it, even when we refuse to see that they do. Of course, you can have help on the way. Friends can help. The Society can help. The master can help, although you might find that a bit dicey."

"What do you mean?"

"He's in love with you, isn't he?"

"Patrick, we've had this discussion before. Quinn Gravesend is not in love with me, and I am not in love with him. We're close. I'm a friend to him, and he's a friend to me. That's it. There's nothing more to it."

Patrick gave her a broad smile. "No, love, there is. There's much more to it on both your parts." He shielded his face with his hands. "Now, before you become defensive, know that I'm not accusing you of being in love with each other. I'm only pointing out that the connection is deeper than simply a friendship. Your problem is that you can't admit that anyone can really be in love with you."

"Really? Why Mr. I-know-Autumn?"

"I bloody well do know Autumn! I know her because I'm in love with her. And I've been watching her since September. I've felt her fire, her passion, and I've wanted to warm myself next to it. You remember when I told you that Mary had no passion? That was never more evident than when the two of you were placed side by side. And when I read those notebooks, they nearly burned my hands. I don't claim to be the one who knows you best. I probably know you the least. But what I know of you, I love, and I would like to know more."

"Christ!"

Patrick shook his head. "Is that a positive curse or a negative one? It's rather hard to tell with you."

"That's bewildered, thoughtful cursing."

"Splendid! But while you're thoughtfully cursing, remember, simply because I spotted your search for yourself, doesn't mean I can lead you to yourself. I can't 'bring you' to your soul. Neither can the Society nor the Master. Each person's road to the magic mountain is his own."

Autumn threw up her hands. "Great! What can we do then?"

"Straight off, we could look to see if our roads run parallel."

"I'm not even sure which way to start looking."

"A good start might be made in the direction toward my place."

Autumn smiled. "Are you looking for some luck of the Irish? Or the Celtic?"

"I'm looking for whatever you're willing to give, love, and I'll be lucky for it indeed."

She finished her beer in one long draught. "Sounds to me like you don't give a damn about the mountain; you just want the magic."

"Is that an aye or a nay?"

Autumn rose and scooped the notebooks into the bag, gesturing for him to lead the way out of the bar.

March

❧ 1 ❧

F ew things thrilled Gravesend more than a virgin sound. There was something haunting in its creation, like an unexpected whisper in the darkness. Like loneliness. Like love. It hovered in a disembodied way, its presence looking over the composer's shoulder and growing with every notational change. He knew composers, colleagues and students alike, who complained about being at the beginning of a work, and he couldn't understand the way they felt. If they discussed it at all, they did so usually with downcast eyes and shifting feet, uttering unintelligible phrases like "I'm just starting something" (as if starting was a sin to be atoned for) or "it'll be worth it in the end" (as if there were no intrinsic value in the process). What they were missing! The secret joys of assembling old sounds into new structures in that ovular moment of composition. Didn't they feel the mysterious power at work behind the blind turns and misdirections, the stumbles and the unexpected finds, without which suddenly coming upon the perfect notes or proper links would not happen? The uncharted unknown was where the real work of composition took place: that search for the elusive, unheard chord. Of the hundred rhythms a composer might try, there is one rhythm, the single strand hidden among the multitude of strands, waiting to be plucked out, then nurtured and carved into an expression. That was the law of the art and the craft right there. Those who disliked being at the beginning of a piece usually put their focus on the performance, and Gravesend suspected the reason had to do with ego. No applause came with finding the right note when sitting at the piano alone. But playing the right note before an audience could raise thunder better than Zeus. It only stands to reason. The moment the composer delivers the music back into the air is what the listeners favor. It's then that music can move and inspire others, and, if it's truly great, it can live forever. To deny that rush of adrenaline brought on by a perfectly performed piece and a rousing ovation would also be a lie. But that was the end of the cycle, not the only important stage of it. Birth, growth, and then either immortality or damnation. The latter could not exist without the former, nebulous moment, the empty-handed leap into the void.

For the composers who banked their self-esteem on the judgment of others and who needed the validation and accolades a good performance brings, Gravesend could understand why his own enthusiasm for the long, solo process of composition bedeviled them. Maybe that's why he loved teaching so much. Students were artists without the hardened shells of success at the topmost levels. They bore the brunt of his love for the composing process — the hunt for the mythical beast made flesh — in the hopes that he could imprint that love upon them. Some students did end up adopting his passion. Many went away puzzled or amused. A few became frustrated.

Autumn was certainly of the middle group, or, as he feared, part of the latter. Watching her had brought on this reverie about composition, but now she riffled with exasperation through her notes, growling under her breath at herself, the work, and whatever god or circumstance brought her to this point. He wanted to reach out and bring her hands to a standstill. He would have done so if he thought he had a glimpse of a chance of convincing her that if she funneled all her passion and fury into the task at hand the result could be glorious. But he didn't. The compositional process was as unique and individual as a marriage, and perhaps Autumn's relationship had to be a stormy one.

She dropped her notes on top of the piano, plopped back down on the bench, and banged out a b-flat chord that reverberated around the Great Room. "It's complete shit!"

"Is that word some sort of talisman for you?" Gravesend asked.

"What?"

"Whenever you are working out anything new, inevitably that word springs from your mouth."

"Because it's true. This is shit."

"It's not. It may be rough, but that has to be expected, and with a bit of care and craftsmanship, you can smooth it out. Try ending the first part with an arpeggio. That should set the listener up for the notes that follow."

Autumn looked at the piano like she was looking at an unfaithful friend. "I shouldn't have to be reworking things at this stage of the game."

Gravesend laughed. "Oh no? Tell me, Miss Gilhain, what makes you so special that you should not need to rework your music? You can fiddle about for days to get a passage exactly right and then, once that passage is in place, you discover that you need to change the rest of the movement. Composing is no job for the timid or the impatient. Try the arpeggio."

She started to play again, slowly working through his suggestion. "Hold this moment," Gravesend wanted to tell her. "You are at the beginning of the adventure, working out your first important piece. This is your firstborn. Other pieces will come along, other compositions, and some will be quite good. But no future composition will feel like this one. There will be no work more dear to your heart, more alive in your soul, than this. When you get older and the sense of taste on your creative tongue begins to dull, the moments of this work will spring out of your memory and into your head, transporting you for a glimmer of a second back to this moment, flooding your body, and you'll feel every quiver, every note. And that glimmer will be sharper than anything known to you in reality: the mocking muse. So hold this moment. Revel in it."

She came to another abrupt halt. "Okay, that helps. But will I be able to keep this part if I decide to re-work the opening?"

"How much of the beginning do you want to change?"

"I don't know."

"What is it, exactly, that you want to do?"

"I don't know!" she slammed both hands down on the keyboard, producing a discordant yelp. "This whole thing is so ..."

She waved her hand at the notes on top of the piano. "We all agree on this great idea: we'll compose stuff, and then, as a Society, we'll perform everything in a benefit show for Lyle. A week later, Patrick and Gaston have music written, rehearsed and ready to go. Chet is finishing up the third of three thematic paintings. Even Mary has poetry written and memorized. What am I doing? Still wallowing in this ... this thing that I can't even find a beginning to!"

"Maybe you're trying too hard," said Gravesend rising from his chair and strolling over to the piano.

"Or maybe what I said to you after Lyle's funeral is true. I'm no musician. I'm not a composer."

"Why? Because you encounter obstacles? You have to expect obstacles. That's how anything worthwhile gains value, by working through obstacles. Composing music isn't something you can just do, like the laundry."

"You're not listening! I told you, it has nothing to do with that!" She waved at her notes again. "It's me. I have to force myself to sit here and do it, and I hate every second I'm here! The world stops for Gaston and Patrick and Chet when they're working. Do you realize that Chet hasn't been at the Lick and Poke for two weeks? He's stuck to the walls of his apartment painting. Gaston's said no more than five sentences all the time he was composing. Only the work matters to them, nothing else, not school or people or food even. That's what it takes, and I don't have what it takes. I hate this work. I hate *doing* this work."

"Small wonder. The way you compare yourself to those three, I can hardly believe you ever compose a note. When are you going to realize that you can't place yourself in competition with people you idealize and ever measure up? You'll stop hating the work when you give yourself an opportunity to do some honest work for Autumn Gilhain and develop your own style and habits. And that happens over time."

"Yeah, over time, like twenty-five years, right?"

Gravesend ignored the taunt by picking up her notes and reviewing six pages of scored scrawls. Autumn tinkled at a couple of keys. Then she swung herself off the bench and marched up to the front of the room where she stood with crossed arms staring into the blaze in the hearth. He followed with the papers still in his hands.

"I mean, damn it," she said, "you won't even play the piano anymore."

"I play quite often."

"Not in public. Not in your classes even. I've talked to some of your students. They say you do what you just did with me, make suggestions. But you never show them."

"Students need the experience of working their music out after their own fashion, to find their own way. As you do. This score doesn't look bad, you know; that is ...," he turned the sheet to follow the scrawls up the side, "...what I can make of it."

"Forget that for a minute and talk to me."

He shrugged and eased himself down into the armchair. Autumn sat on the floor.

"I'm going to ask you straight, and I want the truth from you, not the standard line you feed other people. Have you given up playing in public for good?"

"No, I won't say it will never happen."

"What would it take?"

"I'm not sure."

"Would you play for me?"

"That depends on why my playing in public is so important to you."

Autumn looked into the fire, and the flickering light diffused around her, raising an ache in Gravesend's chest. What was it that he loved about her? The question wasn't adolescent pining or an old man's fantasy but the revelation of a quandary: "No, really, Quinn, what was it that you could possibly love about her?" He was a man who valued quiet and soft conversation, and she was raw anger, like the stuff raging in the belly of a star. Because so much of who he was and what he did had its basis in emotion, he valued a person of reason and practicality, yet Autumn had neither quality in any significant measure. She bopped from one emotion to another, one scheme to another, as the whim turned her. She appeared to have a single-minded purpose to what she did. She was tenacious. But her method of achieving that purpose had its roots in chaos. He appreciated directness, a "this-is-what-you-get" attitude, not the video-game quality of emotional tug-of-war he witnessed in so many relationships, especially among his students. Yet, Autumn thrived on competition. Whether intentional or innate, her ruses and ploys all seemed designed to keep him emotionally off-balance. Worse, underneath her anger, he felt darker passageways, dangerous ground. She was a woman of great power who had no idea how to control that power. The person who would eventually become her partner had better have a firm hand, a strong sense of self, and the energy to constantly employ both without letting it devour his own life. With barely enough energy to keep up with his own emotional excesses, Gravesend knew it wouldn't be him. That thought, however, didn't bring the sense of relief he expected, and the desire tumbling about in his chest remained.

Was that the root, then? Were his feelings more akin to the medieval notion of Courtly Love, the kind of love a man feels for a woman but cultivates at a distance because it has no chance of being requited? While he allowed himself the fantasy of trying to imagine a life in which Autumn truly loved him, he never really took that to be a possibility. He was a mystery to her, but once that mystery was revealed, he had no doubt her interest in him would wane. Watching her watch the fire, Gravesend had to admit that maybe he couldn't hold himself above romantic gamesmanship as much as he liked to think. Wasn't he trying his best to remain mysterious to keep Autumn interested in him? To keep her attention? If that were true, Gravesend concluded, then perhaps he was trying to support her musical efforts not because he thought she was talented but because it would keep her attached to him, even in this strange form.

Gravesend laid his head back on the top of the seat and peered into the darkness gathered in the upper reaches of the hall. If that were the case, he told himself, he should stop it right now. He should lean forward in the chair, tell Autumn exactly who he was, what he was doing, what she was doing, reveal everything, and send her on her way with directions not to return. It would be the right thing to do. It would be what Quinn Gravesend would have done six months ago. But not now. He could intellectually know that a future with Autumn wasn't in the cards, but he didn't want to think about a future without her. He was stuck, unrecognizable to himself or to whatever image he had of himself. What did his former colleague, the artist Bosellini, call love? *Il contadino ribelle*. The wayward peasant. How right he was, and how, at this moment, Gravesend wished he, too, could just disappear into the night like Bosellini did, never to be heard from again. Or better yet, if there were gods and they were kind and they really did meddle in the affairs of mortals, he wished they would freeze Autumn and himself here, in this pose, for eternity, like in the poem by Keats. "Heard melodies are sweet but those unheard are sweeter."

"Maybe," Autumn said, plucking and wadding a stray scrap of paper off her jeans and throwing it toward the fire, "I want to know that you have feeling. You're pretty machine-like when it comes to music, you know. I mean, you talk about music with passion, but that passion is still wrapped in, I don't know, a teacher's distance and objectivity. But not in your music. Those symphonies were unrestrained, naked feeling, something like Gaston's music and Chet's painting. It's how Lyle wanted his music to sound. But what you wrote and played went so far beyond all of them, I can only guess how intense your performances must have been. And I'm tired of guessing. I want to see it, feel it, if only once."

"In order to gauge yourself?" Gravesend countered. "Is this another case of putting your own works next to an idealized musician to prove or disprove your artistic worth?"

"Everyone seems to have a way of letting loose their passions, except you and me, and Mary, who has no passion. I thought for a long time that music was the way for me, but it's not. It's sort of like suddenly discovering you're homeless. You have nowhere to go, nowhere to express yourself. And it's scary, you know? You had a way once, and maybe if I could get you to play, you could show me that it's never too late. Then I could find my way someday. If that makes any sense."

"It does. But what you must understand is that each composer, every artist for that matter, has different temperaments and attitudes, and knowing your own soul, becoming comfortable with your own way of doing things, is the path that leads you to fully developing your potential. I have never been able to play on demand. That has nothing to do with my age now or Julia having died or anything that has happened to me in my life. I have always been this way."

Autumn turned around, and her eyes had that animal look, what Gravesend came to think of as the warning. *HC SVNT DRACONES* – Here be dragons.

"You know," she said, "you owe me."

"What do I owe you?"

"A public performance. Last fall at the Lick and Poke when you came to see Gaston play, remember? We bet that you couldn't stump him with a request. And you couldn't. So, you're going to have to pay up and play there at least once. Unless you plan on worming out of it."

"Ah, but forcing me to keep a promise doesn't guarantee that I'll play with an urgency, with feeling. That's what I mean. Throughout my career, I arranged to perform only when I felt the need to perform, when that urge to create my music again became a part of me. I have to be stirred to play, stirred in here." He tapped his chest. "Otherwise, I can play, but I cannot make music."

"I guess I don't stir you enough."

"You do," he said. And that was all. He couldn't get his tongue to move again, to explain the comment or diffuse it. He could see the words as if inside a balloon hanging in the air between them, but he was not quick enough to snatch them back or swipe them away.

"Do I sense a deal being made here?" she said with that chippie smile. "You'd play for me if I promised you ... what? That you could stir me afterwards?"

"Must you always be vulgar?"

"Well, how the hell else am I supposed to take a comment like that. I stir you. What's that mean?"

"I would play for you," he began, measuring each word carefully, "only when I could be certain that I could touch you with my music."

She nodded, the siren smile fading into a pensive and serious face. Such a raw look, Gravesend thought, the way one's face falls when a nerve has been struck. Her head bobbed in time with silent thoughts. When that stopped, she stood and took the score from Gravesend's hands. For a moment, he feared she would pitch it into the fire, but instead, she glanced through it quickly and shrugged.

"The difference between your playing and mine," she said turning back toward the piano, "is you know that you could touch me anytime you felt the urge to try."

◈ 2 ◈

Familiar places and objects tend to blend into a background and form the scenery of life, and, like good scenery, they enhance the play of the players without intruding. But then a place or object suddenly becomes symbolic, surrounding the players' actions in a way that provides a glimpse into their purpose and the purpose of the entire play. Tonight, the Liquor and Poker will become such a symbol. Not the music or the individuals that perform it, but the place, which focuses the meaning of what is performed. Then, when you get up the courage to look, you realize the purpose of life is to celebrate victories and achievements because life itself is so tenuous and changing. Then, you get scared.

Autumn dropped the pen onto the book and looked out from her vantage point in the booth. The bar remained the same: the dim light, the smoky haze, the five elderly mid-afternoon men hunched like question marks over their drinks.

She looked at the corridor, beginning between the rest rooms and stretching beyond her sight past the cellar doorway to the back room. The back room. That was where the scenery became symbolic. She returned to the notebook, her eye falling on the word *scared*. She lifted her beer and doodled around the edges of the paper, around the edges of what she felt and didn't want to write or think about. She let her mind wander with her pen until a voice called out from across the bar.

"What're you doing out here now, Autumn-girl?"

Chet stood at the mouth of the corridor, arms outstretched. The five men stirred in their seats like birds ruffled by an unexpected presence near their nests. When Autumn didn't reply, he called out again, "Go and have a look at what we've done. I've got to see a man about a horse."

Autumn returned to the page, but she couldn't curry her thoughts into an expressible order. She heard the bathroom door slam and a heavy clump of boots coming toward her.

"What's this?" asked Chet, planting himself before the booth. "Does the floor or the beer have your legs? Up with you now and have a look at our handiwork. My handiwork, if I may brag!"

He held out his arm. This would be easier, she thought; she couldn't go in there by herself. She closed the notebook and took his arm, allowing him to escort her down the corridor and across the threshold of the back room. There, he unhooked his arm to sweep it out grandly before her. "'Look on my Works, ye Mighty, and despair!' That's a wedge of Percy Shelley if you don't know; my apologies if you did. So, what do you think?"

A broad cloth painted black and edged in gold hung from the ceiling, stretching across the entire length of the back of the stage, obscuring most of the curtain. Across the middle, in large, gold script, the letters spelled out "LYLE ANDREW GLASSER, IN MEMORIAM." The stage piano stood in the company of a drum kit, two acoustic guitars and microphone stands. Daffodils, Lyle's favorite flower, lined the front of the stage, concealing the footlights that Gaston scrounged from somewhere on campus. Those lights played over Gaston and Patrick, standing at center stage. Mary was off to one side, her lips moving in quiet recital.

"It looks nice, Chet. Really."

He bowed. "Thank you, good lady, but I was aiming for a word like 'fitting' rather than 'nice.'"

"It's very fitting. Lyle would be happy." She gave him a kiss on the cheek and sauntered over to an easel with a covered canvas.

"What's this thing?" she said reaching to lift the cover.

"Aht! Aht! Never you mind. That's not to be seen until tonight."

"You're late," said Gaston.

"I had some things to do."

"This is final rehearsal."

"I know."

She jumped up on the stage and Gaston gestured toward the piano. "The only thing that needs to be worked out is your piece."

"It's fine."

"The bridge is still a little rough, you know? And that's messing up the shift into my section."

She winked at Patrick. "Sounds like a personal problem to me."

"Do you want to run through it again?"

"I just told you it was fine, Gaston."

He nodded. "Okay, then let's pick it up four bars before the bridge."

"That'd be Roland's Pub, if we're going on this side of the bridge, wouldn't it?" Patrick said.

"Ready? One, two, three, and four ..." Gaston nodded at Autumn to start, but she had her hands covering her mouth, laughing.

She waved to Gaston and, when she caught her breath, said, "I'm sorry, but that was so bad."

"So's the bridge," said Gaston. "Are you ready to work it out?"

"What's your problem?"

"We have a show to do in six hours, and things need to be fixed."

"Excuse me, Mr. Director. My part's fine."

"We'll see. Play."

"Don't tell me to play and not to play. I'll play if I want to."

"Ease up everyone," said Chet from behind the drums. "Autumn, play. Gaston, stop ordering people around. Patrick, keep your rotten jokes to yourself."

"On my honor, Sir, I swear it," said Patrick with an upraised hand.

Mary let out a sarcastic snort from the side of the stage.

"Again," said Gaston. "One, two, three, and four ..."

Autumn opened the piece, and the others followed. When the fourth bar was complete, she played the bridge into Gaston's section. But instead of carrying on, Gaston called a halt. "The bridge is still rough."

"I thought it sounded fine," she countered.

"I didn't hear anything the matter with it," said Patrick.

"Oh, so was it good for you too, Patrick?" called Mary.

"What is that supposed to mean?" he asked.

"The bridge has to improve," said Gaston.

Autumn slammed out a chord. "Then why don't you play it yourself? You're so great, play two instruments at once. Better yet, why don't you play all the instruments, that way you can be sure that the music will be so perfectly wonderful everyone will be as enthralled as hell!"

"Just play it right."

Autumn grabbed her left breast. "Play this."

"Oooh, Patrick, does that turn you on?" Mary sang out.

Patrick crossed the stage in four steps. "What are you implying?"

"I'm not *implying* anything."

"Don't play the fool. If you have something to say, then say it."

"Fuck you," Mary said, imitating Autumn's voice.

Autumn shot up from behind the piano. "Are you ripping on me, you little bitch?"

"Sit down and play," Gaston said to Autumn.

"Don't order me around!"

Patrick pointed to Mary, "What's this now? You don't have the bloody courage to say what's on your mind instead of hiding behind sarcasm?"

"Fine. I want your sleazy, cheating face out of my life!"

"Consider it done. And I thank you for sharing this very private moment with our friends."

"She's no friend of mine," yelled Autumn.

Chet put two fingers in his mouth and let out a long shrill whistle. "Enough already, for the love of God! Have you all lost your minds? May I remind you, we are rehearsing Lyle's tribute here? You do remember Lyle, our best friend who died and left a last request asking us to play in public once to honor his memory? He made that request as a toast to our friendship, but damn me if I've never seen people turn champagne to piss as quickly as the four of you!"

The room turned coldly silent.

Gaston shrugged. "I'm ready to play."

"Well, I'm not," said Autumn.

"You have to."

"I told you..."

"Enough!" Chet yelled, kicking the bass drum for emphasis.

"We're not fulfilling a sworn oath here. No one has to play who doesn't want to play, although, Autumn-girl, I can't fathom why you wouldn't want to!"

"Maybe because the whole thing sounds like shit," said Autumn. "Patrick and Gaston are the only real musicians here. The rest of us are just screwing around."

"You're probably right," said Chet. "So why, do you suppose, Lyle made the request of us in the first place since — and forgive me this, Gaston — he was the best musician of us all; he more than anyone knew we wouldn't be perfect players? Hmm? I don't pretend to know the mind of the dead, but perhaps he wanted us to play once more together because he enjoyed playing with *all* of us, no matter how inferior we were to him. However, if he's watching this display, he'd be away doing something else. So, it comes down to this: Lyle asked us for a favor out of love. How are we going to return that love? By putting on one hell of a show or one hell of a fight?" He looked each member in the eye. "I favor the show. Who follows?"

"Let's do it," said Gaston.

Autumn nodded and sat back down on the piano bench. Patrick returned to his spot next to Gaston.

"Blessed be!" said Chet. "Now with a little effort, let's be a Society again and go over the entire piece from the beginning, each minding his or her own corner of the music. And if the performance isn't perfect, piss on it. We'll play it tonight and get roaring drunk then no one'll know the difference or care!"

They ran through the entire piece once more without a stop. When they finished, Chet and Patrick headed for the bar. Mary made a beeline for the door. Gaston sat on one of the empty tables, playing. Autumn went home.

But six hours later, she stood behind Gaston at the side of the room with a hand on his shoulder, looking over the people filing into the back room. About half of the people had instruments of their own at the ready. Others circled the tables, drinking and talking. Several approached the stage and put flowers between the potted daffodils. Chet's covered painting had been moved to the right side of the stage, illuminated by a spotlight of its own.

Chet lumbered in, beer in hand. "A good crowd it's getting to be, isn't it? This night should be a keeper. Where're Patrick and Mary?"

"I don't know," Autumn said. "Patrick swore he'd be here by eight."

Chet glanced at the wall clock. "Five of nine Old Man Time says, and the crowd is waiting. If we don't take the stage, someone else will."

He led the way lifting his glass without breaking stride to acknowledge those who called out to him. Autumn hit several notes to hear how the piano sounded and looked around: Gaston was, as usual, inscrutably calm; Chet looked as happy as a child at Christmas. The clock on the back wall stood at nine o'clock. Autumn glanced at the doorway, and then threw a panicked look at Gaston, who motioned for her to relax. He cleared his throat and approached the microphone.

"Hello, everyone. Before having the open-mike format tonight, we would like to play a tribute piece to Lyle Glasser, a close friend who died a couple of months ago. We thought this'd be the best place for the tribute since Lyle loved playing here, and those of you who come often, I'm sure, remember seeing him on this stage a lot. What we're going to play for you is a piece Lyle wrote just before his death. We call this *The Glasser Concerto*."

Autumn never heard the words Gaston said to the assembled crowd. The fear rose up in her, like rushing water in a flash flood. What did Gaston or Chet know about fear? She couldn't even begin to tell them. She couldn't even tell herself, until now, as Gaston nodded out the introductory beats, and Autumn had no choice but to start into the piece. The absence of Patrick's guitar meant that the void would have to be filled by the piano, and that thought sent her to the edge of panic.

How could she have told them that performing in front of an audience made her heart stop? Who would've believed her? She, Autumn Gilhain, brash and as forward as they come, could never fear people. But they struck terror in her heart. One look at the audience was all it took, and she froze down to the root of her. But she couldn't let that happen now for Lyle's sake. She thought of Lyle. She pressed her eyes tightly shut, pushing down the waves of anxiety breaking in on her. She felt the perspiration beginning to surface and her body begin to quiver, but she was too afraid to take even one hand off the keys for fear everything else would follow, then she would find herself outside the bar, gasping for air and coming up with a hundred excuses she would never use to explain her flight. She could not let go of the keys. She would not let go.

She heard Patrick's guitar slide smoothly into the mix, and the sudden presence of it startled her into opening her eyes. The piano had been turned to face the others and show only her profile to the audience. Patrick stood directly in front of her. Gaston bobbed into view on the other side of Patrick, but beyond Gaston, she saw no one. She signaled Patrick to come closer.

"Where the hell's Mary?" she hissed.

"She's not coming."

"Who's going to do the recital then?"

"I don't know."

Gaston changed keys and tempo, signaling the beginning of part two. This called for a slower pace with each instrument weaving in and out of the others, spiraling down to a soft trilling of the guitars. That was when Mary was supposed to come forward and recite *The Caged Skylark*.

Autumn guessed that they would play right through the passage without the words. Certainly Gaston wouldn't try any changes on the fly. She and Chet were good but neither were skilled at sudden and intense improvisation. But no, Gaston didn't think like that. He believed everyone could do whatever he could do; therefore, he would try to improvise rather than edit the passage. A new surge of panic swept through her. No dice. While she was trapped in this musical hell, she'd be damned if she would let Gaston Gunn lead her through a tour of unknown fiery passages.

She never made a conscious decision; the next sequence of events passed her by like blurring scenery in a speeding car. When the music began its winding descent toward the recital, Autumn faded the piano out of the mix and stepped out from behind the instrument to the first microphone that presented itself.

She pictured Mary. She became Mary, letting her body relax into a pixie-like pose and put forth the sweetly arrogant and self-loving portrait that made up her vision of Mary, only she never opened her eyes. Instead, she focused on Mary's mannerisms and voice, found that voice, and left herself among the others behind her. She didn't give a second thought to the words. Mary had recited the poem aloud at their rehearsals and Autumn was banking on subconscious recall. She opened her mouth and just let the words flow from her brain in an unconscious stream:

> As a dare-glare skylark scanted in a dull cage
> Man's mounting spirit in his bone-house,
> mean house, dwells —
> That bird beyond the remembering his free fells;
> This in drudgery, day-laboring-out life's age.
> Though aloft on turf or perch or poor low stage,
> Both sing sometimes the sweetest, sweetest spells,
> Yet both droop deadly sometimes in their cells
> Or wring their barriers in bursts of fear or rage.

The fear melted away, and a new kind of energy rose inside her. She wasn't aware of it in those terms, but it was as if she were two people: one a poet reciting a work, and the other herself among the crowd listening to her Mary-Poet voice grow stronger and more melodic with each word.

> *Not that the sweet-fowl, song-fowl, needs no rest —*
> *Why, hear him, hear him babble and drop down to*
> *his nest,*
> *But his own nest, wild nest, no prison.*
> *Man's spirit will be flesh-bound when found at best,*
> *But uncumbered: meadow-down is not distressed*
> *For a rainbow footing it nor he for his bones risen.*

She acknowledged the applause with a blind nod, but now that she had to stop being Mary, her anxiety began to seep back into her. She was far out on a very weak limb. Becoming Mary was easy. Leaving Mary to return to Autumn without breaking down was impossible. She took one step backward, and that was all she could manage until she felt a hand touch the small of her back, helping her turn. Still with closed eyes, she groped her way back to the piano with all the grace and steadiness she could muster. Next came finding her way smoothly back into the music. "Don't think," said a voice inside her head. "Just play."

She waded in and immediately knew she hit the wrong notes. But she heard Gaston switch smoothly to match her while keeping her in time for Chet's sake. Patrick took two bars to improvise his way back in sync with them, and then Gaston herded them back to a point in the piece that they all recognized. Even with that security, Autumn refused to open her eyes until the last notes faded. She didn't open her eyes until she stood and walked to the front of the stage to join Patrick, Gaston, and Chet in a bow.

Then Chet drew back the veil from the canvas. Autumn met the painted eyes of Lyle, seated behind a piano in his characteristic pose. His face sent a different kind of chill through her. If he had been alive, Lyle would have been on the piano bench. Seeing the painting, she could almost believe he had been there tonight, beside her, guiding her with a firm gentleness. How else could she have done what she did? Only Lyle was good enough to do that, good enough to have done that for her. The sensation brought tears to her eyes, but she didn't care. The true measure of how much she missed him overcame her, and, for the first time, in front of the entire assembly, she began to cry with hard sobs.

Gaston stepped back up to the microphone. "Thanks. I hope the people who brought instruments will continue the tribute."

Autumn led the way off the stage, tear-blinded, and ran into a young woman with a crewcut and a harp who was coming up the steps. Autumn barreled past her, straight out of the room to the bar. Chet popped out of the corridor a few seconds behind her and stood in front of Autumn with open arms.

"Toss my fat ass right out through the tightest window if I'm not drop-dead amazed!" he yelled before grabbing her in a tight hug and lifting her off the floor. "God be praised, that was absolutely, without a doubt, beautiful."

"Yeah, yeah, fine," she said, wiping her face with her hands and then a towel that Monica, the bartender, supplied. "Someone buy me a beer."

"How'd you remember that poem?" asked Gaston handing her a mug.

"Are you kidding? Mary's been reciting it every day for the past month. I'll be lucky if I ever forget it! Where is that bitch anyway?"

"With Michael Watters," Patrick answered.

"Michael Watters, as in Dr. Watters the English prof?"

"One and the same."

"I'm sorry, man," said Gaston.

"C'est la guerre."

They returned to the room and sat at a table near the back, talking about Lyle and paying only cursory attention to the parade of musicians and poets taking the stage. Around midnight, the crowd began to thin out and by one o'clock only a handful of people remained scattered about the room in the mellow, smoky light. A guitarist finished an acoustic set of George Winston songs, while Autumn and Gaston regaled Patrick and Chet with a story about Lyle before coming to NAUFA. Autumn was the first to notice that the room had grown unusually quiet. She glanced up at the stage, gasped, and grabbing Gaston's forearm, pointed.

Quinn Gravesend sat straight-backed behind the battered piano. From the first note, the music he played swelled, full and golden in tone, but as Gravesend continued to play, Autumn caught undercurrents of wistfulness, of experiencing a special and fleeting place in time.

"Wow!" said Gaston, his eyebrows arching up above the rims of his sunglasses. "Does anyone recognize this?"

"No," said Chet. "Didn't the bet call for him to play something from one of his symphonies?"

The four of them looked at each other.

"Oh my God," Autumn whispered.

The piece leaped and skipped from passage to passage over bridges that were smooth but sounded out of sync with the rest of the melody, as if they were constructed to sew the other parts into a patchwork. To Autumn the music, while rough-hewn, still conjured up images in her mind: pictures of sunsets over harvested fields, armed men walking away from a fight in a swirling wind, and a lover dressing to leave in the morning. The whole thing sounded paradoxical: an ending at the beginning.

Gravesend rounded out the piece and brought it to a close. Still seated, he made a small bow toward the audience in response to the applause. He reached for the microphone stand and dragged it over beside the piano.

"If I may," he said, "I'd like to play one more piece, a song written by Leonard Cohen but, in my opinion, best recorded by John Cale. The lyrics could have been speaking of Mr. Lyle Glasser, in whose memory we are gathered, as well as some other persons in this room tonight."

The tune began at a slow, prancing pace, with Gravesend using only a minimum of notes to tap out the melody line, creating a tense, claustrophobic feeling. When Gravesend began to sing, his voice sounded as constrained and edgy as the music. Autumn felt an eeriness surround the lyrics – "I know this room; I've walked this floor. I used to live alone here before I knew you." An image came into her head of Gravesend being in two places at once, here on the stage and in this room in a former time. Before her. The lyrics were personal, even though he didn't write them. They were words that she had wanted him to say, words that should have thrilled her, but the fact that they were written by another musician made them voyeuristic. She felt like a third person was delivering the message while Gravesend was peeking at her from a hidden place to watch her reaction. She gave an involuntary shudder and looked around. Everyone else was wrapped up in the moment, savoring each note of the performance, realizing the experience for what it was. Only she heard the lyrics like a voice from a distant place, through the static of a short-wave radio; both the sound and the words spooked her. She shook her head and tried to focus on the message. Gravesend was now crying out the repetition of "Hallelujah!" Was he talking about himself, "the baffled king" composing again? Gravesend's voice rose steadily throughout the verses to a throaty growl, and he struck the keys with a ferocity, slowing only during the hallelujah choruses. Then the piano and his voice shifted again, becoming thick and teary. She leaned in, and the full force of the words "But all I ever learned from love was how to shoot at someone who outdrew you" slapped her. Was that a reference to Julia? To her? If the Hallelujah is cold and broken, was Gravesend telling her that this was it? He had had it? With music, with Julia, with her, or with all three? Her eyes stung with the dry heaves of tears that wouldn't come. She heard Gravesend repeat the word "hallelujah" six times, each more like an echo than the last, and the music filtered down as if through a strainer, ending in a series of notes, each growing softer than the last.

Autumn watched Gravesend tap out the final notes, then stand. He made his way off the stage lifting one hand to acknowledge the riotous applause. Gaston, Patrick and Chet stood with the others in the room applauding wildly. Autumn stood with her hands twisting together and a list of questions in her head for when he came to the table. But one-by-one the list dwindled. She wasn't going to be able to ask him any of the questions about *Hallelujah*. They were too personal for the moment, she decided, although deeper down she realized she didn't want to risk what the answers would be. She settled on asking the one question that probably everyone in the room wanted to ask about the first composition. But she formed it as a zinger, a question to draw blood.

But Gravesend kept walking. He passed by their table with a quick nod, and disappeared down the corridor with surprising speed.

Autumn scrambled away from the table and rushed down the hallway after him. Even so, by the time she pushed her way through the outside door and onto the sidewalk, Gravesend was out of reach. She stood in the downpour watching the taillights of the taxi ease away from the curb and make their way out into the rain-blurred street.

❧ 3 ❦

Gravesend waited and listened at the bottom of the stairs. The music came again: a distinct tinkling-twang, resembling the sound produced in the music boxes of his youth, the kind topped by ballerinas or carousels.

His search for the sound led him to the entrance of the Great Room. Pulling open the round door, he heard the sound more clearly, coming from the open space at the far end of the room. He padded along the stone floor but stopped where it met the grass. A thick fog had rolled in, obscuring everything around him except the rough outline of the barn, and yet, he saw the door with great clarity: the wooden brace in the form of an X, the hole that Peter had made with a mattock after Father angered him, the leather thong used to pull the door shut at night. Peter must have forgotten to close it tonight. A thin opening allowed the yellow glow of lamplight to spill out into the grass. Gravesend stepped out onto the grass, going toward that light.

The music grew louder, always looping back on itself to repeat the same melody. Yet the repetition stirred Gravesend because it was so delicately played. He recognized the hand that could play that way, and the recognition made him speed across the grass to the door. He paused at its entrance before pushing through the narrow space. The door groaned, and a woman turned round on a stool. Although her hands left the strings of the harp before her, the music continued to play. She wore the dress of the late Victorian period, a burgundy crinoline skirt filled with pleats and a white silk blouse puffed at the shoulders. A string of pearls hung from her long delicate neck. Her dark hair fell in soft curls onto her shoulders. She had the pale, smooth face of a young woman in her early thirties, and a sparkle of merriment glinted in her brown-green eyes.

"*Mor*?" whispered Gravesend.

His mother held out her hands toward him. "Come stand by me, my darling."

"*Mor*, why are you here? In the barn?" He went forward and stood near the harp. The surprise he felt at first encountering her gave way to a peaceful sensation, the warmth of being home.

"Where else would I be? Do you hear the pretty music?"

"Like a music box."

She shook her head. "Listen, Quinn. Listen like I taught you to listen."

He closed his eyes and absorbed the notes one by one as if recording them on a tape inside his head. They carried a feeling, a sense that was familiar, and suddenly he knew what the notes were.

"Do not look surprised," his mother said laughing. "Of course, they are your notes, but they are my notes too." Her voice took on a teasing tone. "Didn't you know that I would find a way to stand beside your piano and give you my ideas? My, after all this time, you still hate that don't you. But no matter. I do it still."

"No, I don't hate it. I used to, but I don't now. I'm glad. I've felt you there," he waved back toward the house, "beside the piano."

The sound changed from a melody to a single note being struck.

"What's that?"

She cocked her head. The note struck again. She smiled. Gravesend concentrated on that smile in the face of a woman he knew so well, a face from a time when he didn't know her at all. That face remained in his vision while all the background faded. Only that face and the sound of the single note becoming louder with the encroaching darkness stayed with him. He heard a laugh beneath the note, his mother's laugh, elegantly soft but unbridled. Then the face began to fade, and he was left with the darkness and the note. And something else. Coldness. A chilling cold like bare feet on the flagstones of the Great Hall floor. He didn't remember feeling the coldness when he came through the room, but now it pierced him. He opened his eyes, finding himself sitting up on the side of the bed, his feet on the cold hardwood floor. The doorbell rang eight times in quick succession.

"Coming," he yelled throwing his robe around him.

Autumn stood on the other side of the door. "It's about time. I've been ringing that damn bell for hours it seems." She came in, shaking the rain from her hair.

"What are you doing here?"

"Like you don't know! What was that you played tonight at the Lick and Poke?"

"I told you, 'Hallelujah' by Leonard Cohen, although, as I said, the Cale version—"

"Stop it, Quinn. The other piece! Was it original?"

"It was something I tossed together."

"Liar! That's part of a larger piece, isn't it? You're composing, and you didn't tell me! What are you working on?"

Gravesend folded his arms and stared her down. "First, let's pretend that it's any of your business. Second, let's say that *if* I am composing something and *if* I played part of it tonight ..." he paused, drawing every second of juice out of her. "We don't want to talk about it just yet." He never did shut the door completely; now he swung it open and held it for her.

"That's all you're going to say? I come all the way out here..."

"At the earliest of morning hours, waking me up out of one of the most pleasant sleeps I've had in years."

"Fine!" She stormed out to Gaston's car.

"Goodnight!" Gravesend called cheerily after her. He closed the door and found himself facing the Great Room entrance. The memory of the dream came flooding back, especially the passage of music his mother made him listen to. It played in his head in all its fullness. There was no time to even get to the upstairs studio. He repeated the notes in his head, scrambling to find some scored paper, and then he sat at the dining room table transferring the notes from his head onto the page, accompanied by the sound of an intensifying spring rain.

April

❧ 1 ❧

The telephone rang, but Gravesend went on knotting his tie. The phone had been ringing all morning; let the answering machine pick up this call, too. But, when the doorbell sounded, that was another matter. He moved away from the hall mirror to answer the bell, but Papaté stepped between the door and him.

"You're a fool," Papaté said. "No, you're a *damned* fool! They named April Fool's Day in your honor." He waved Gravesend away and turned to answer the bell himself.

Gravesend peeked out through the dining room window. A man stood on the porch and a television truck idled in the driveway. A stranger's voice carried into the dining room. "Good morning. I'm Bob Ollens, entertainment writer for the Albany Courier. I need to speak to Mr. Grave—"

"Mr. Gravesend is not granting interviews at this time. When and if he does, you'll receive a statement. Good day to you, sir."

"But I really need—"

"I said good day to *you*, sir."

"Yes, I know he's probably very busy, but—"

"I said there will be no interview today. Please turn your van around and drive off this property, or I'll have the police come for you."

Gravesend heard his front door slam, but he waited until the man moved away and disappeared inside the van before leaving the window. Then he looked around for his briefcase. Papaté pointed to the corner behind the coat rack.

"Thank you. What time is your flight to New Orleans?"

"One-thirty."

"And when should I expect you to return?"

"If you're still alive, I think I'll come back for the final rehearsals before your performance. You may need a critical eye to help you pull the details together."

Gravesend nodded and headed for the door, but Papaté remained in place, blocking his path.

"Papa, I have a class shortly."

"They'll wait. I called you a fool earlier, but you didn't listen to me. Like you didn't listen when you wanted to follow the voodoo men on Epiphany. That was okay. Angels sometimes guide a fool's footsteps out of danger so the fool gets a second chance to change his ways. But you aren't changing. This plan, this symphony performance that you want to give in less than a month, you won't survive it."

"*You* don't want me to perform? You, who for the past twenty years have been the loudest voice in the Have-Gravesend-Compose-Again choir?"

"Yeah, man. But did you ever once listen to me? No. You never listened to any of the sensible people who suggested you write new music. But now there is fire in your belly, such a fire that you cannot rush this symphony to the stage fast enough because you are so alive with the passion of the music. Why is that, do you suppose?"

"Who can say? The time is right."

"Save that line for the interviews. Papa's not blind. Papa knows you. It's the girl who is behind it. No, that look of confusion will not work with me. You know which girl I mean. You're doing all of this with her in mind, and you are letting her lead you into water much deeper than you know. You're sixty-three, she's twenty-something."

"Of what are you accusing Autumn?"

"I accuse her of nothing; her motives are not my concern. *Your* expectations, ah, that is another matter entirely. Those expectations should not lead your music. Yes, recognize your accomplishment for what it is: an expression of your desire, a hope or dream set to music in order to persuade or convey what you feel. That is grand. But to use that as a vehicle to steer or be steered into the heart of a child? That is foolish even to the fool. Take Papa's advice for once: there is not enough music in any score to close the gap between the two of you."

"You are very wrong, my friend. I write what I feel; I perform what I write. It's as simple as that. Now, may I go, please?"

Papaté stepped aside and opened the door for him. "I pray a good day goes with you."

Gravesend had the same hope, until he pulled out of his driveway and noticed the television truck and another car fall into line behind him. A riot of thoughts and emotions broke out in his mind and traveled downward, stirring up his stomach. After booking the performance with the University Performing Arts Center and telling a friend who played first violin for the Toronto Symphony Orchestra, a friend he hadn't spoken with in years, the media descended in a suffocating volume, wrecking his daily routines and, for the most part, his life. But he couldn't deny that one small quarter within him was thrilled with the interest. Shocked but thrilled. And — Papa be damned — Autumn's newfound awe sat well with him, too. He was not so blind that he failed to note the look on her face, and on the faces of the other members of the Society, as he performed that night in the bar. A parched part of his soul drank long and deep from those looks. His generation remembered Coltrane's performance at the Liquor and Poker, and this generation wished it had been present. Now this generation saw Gravesend perform there. Was it vanity to think at that moment he was the creator of a memory, one to be recalled by members of a generation and to be wished for by future generations? Perhaps. But it was good for the soul to think that way, or at least it was good for the ego. That part of him, too, had gone without food for too long.

But Papaté's words nagged. To imply that the entire composition of the symphony was done in order to snare Autumn's emotional favor, or worse, her sexual favor, cheapened it in a way that Gravesend found disgusting. Papaté was right; the symphony frames and delivers an expression but not something so crude as sex. It was much more personal. It was a howl of admittance, a release of many emotions that had been glued to the inside of him for years. He couldn't remember the last time he cried, so he let the piano do it for him. Each note was a musical tear welling up to produce a cleansing weep of twenty-five years of emotional repression. And if Autumn had a share in that feeling, and if he loved her — both of which he did not deny were absolutely true — then why should she not be a part of the composition? That was hardly a sordid thing, he concluded.

Gravesend smiled as he passed into the faculty parking lot, leaving his posse on the other side of the gate. There was a delicious enjoyment in thwarting those who insist that everything one does should be open to public consumption and comment. And that included Papa who, Gravesend believed, was reading too much into the title Gravesend chose for the symphony. But so be it. Autumn was a catalyst. She provided the push he needed to return to the studio, and she deserved her due for that.

Beside the external issues, Gravesend discovered he had more pressing problems to deal with when he entered his classroom. The morning's lecture was doomed from the start, as his students shot questions at him about his own compositional methods for the symphony, and Gravesend had to walk the tightrope between the musician who ritually refused to talk about an unperformed work, and a teacher who had valuable firsthand information to impart to eager students. He also felt horrible for the thought that one of his students (or perhaps more?) may have accepted money to report on what he said. That truly *was* vain, he told himself, but the thought remained lodged in his head, and he could not remove it.

He returned to his office for some tea. The water had just boiled when Mrs. Bourgione knocked and entered, wearing that murderous look all of the faculty rightly feared. The media must have been hounding her, as well.

"Mr. Parker wants your head, but not necessarily any other part of your body, in his office at eleven, which is in twenty minutes." She closed the door with an extra bit of force.

Gravesend knew nothing about Sam Parker, the director of the Richard LeBlanc Performing Arts Center, but the tone of Mrs. Bourgione's message did not give him warm feelings about their first meeting. He appeared at the director's door and found a tall, lithe man with a melodramatic air, a Texas twang, western boots, and a pained expression on his face.

"Mr. Gravesend, did I run over your dog or have an affair with your wife that I can't seem to recall?"

"Pardon me?"

"Well, Sir, I'm finding it mighty hard to understand why you appear to have gone to great lengths to kill me."

"I'm afraid I still don't understand what you mean."

Parker ran a hand through his hair. "Mr. Gravesend, when you requested the use of the theater, I was more than happy to comply. After all there were no other shows scheduled for the night you wanted, and I've not only understood the duty but also felt honored to showcase the talent we have here on campus. And I did what I always do when we plan a new show: I had my secretary call the local paper to announce it. Do you know my secretary, Elaine Henderson?"

"I haven't had the pleasure."

"She's a lovely lady, sweet as pie, but that poor girl hasn't had the phone off her ear ever since she made that call. Let me show you something, Mr. Gravesend." Parker reached behind him and picked up a stack of papers. "What I'm holding in my hands are three thousand, seven hundred, and twenty-seven requests for tickets to hear you tickle the ivories. And that's just the tally from the first week. Included in these three thousand plus requests are dignitaries from both the United States and Canada: politicians, musicians, artists and other notable people. Mr. Gravesend, there are names of folks in this pile for whom I have done every legal thing — and several illegal things as well — to persuade them to play on my stage, and now they all are beating down the doors to come hear you. Did I mention that the capacity of the theater is one thousand, maybe eleven hundred if you have a good shoehorn and know how to use it properly? So, what this amounts to is a diplomatic rattlesnake in my sleeping bag."

Gravesend felt simultaneous stabs of guilt and joy run through his body.

"In addition," Parker went on, "extra room is going to be needed for the CBC and PRI, both of whom I understand have your permission to broadcast the performance live. So, there'll be tech people, wires, producers, and a whole host of folks running into my people and each other. And to top it off, this morning your request to reserve five front row center seats crossed my desk. Mr. Gravesend, let me ask you, where am I supposed to seat the governor? Because he wants to attend. So does the Premier of Ontario. And the Governor-General, who, if I understand the way Canadian officials line up at the trough, is the representative of the Queen and, therefore, pretty important. Am I right? Now, I've got to ask, Mr. Gravesend, why don't you just shoot me? It'd be a whole hell of a lot easier on everyone, most of all me."

Gravesend felt his face heat up. "Please believe me when I tell you I had no idea this would happen. After twenty-five years, I didn't think anyone would remember my name. I assumed the performance would be a low-key campus affair. In fact, I wasn't even going to send in the request to reserve the seats for my party, that's how ill-attended I believed the concert would be." Gravesend felt himself begin to shake, and guilt winning out over joy forced the next sentence out of his mouth. "If it would save you all these headaches, Mr. Parker, I could postpone the performance and reschedule it at a larger venue and a later date."

"Mr. Gravesend, you don't shoot your dog because it barks. That's what it's supposed to do. I'll be honest with you; if I had gotten the impression you were one of these egomaniacal artists who knew this thing was going to be bigger than Texas but didn't bother or care enough to say so, I was going to let you have a large piece of my mind. But I can see that you're as surprised as I am. So," he ran his hand through his hair, "we'll get by the best we can. I don't deny I wish we had more time and space to deal with, but I also don't deny that this kind of show could turn out real well for our little performance space here. And maybe in return for pulling this off, I can have you help me wrangle a few of those performers into playing here in the future."

"I'll be glad to help," Gravesend said.

Parker nodded. "And I'll try to meet your request, but I can't make promises, understand?"

Gravesend thanked the man and left. He entered the Music building but when he turned the corner, he saw a campus security officer escorting two reporters away from his office complex and down toward the doors at the other end of the hall. Following him were three students Gravesend didn't recognize being herded out by Mrs. Bourgione's fierce look and deadly pointer finger. The guilt that had risen up when he was with Parker crushed any lingering joy. He slipped into his office, grabbed his keys and briefcase and headed out the back way to the parking lot. Driving off the campus, he stopped in town long enough to order a bouquet of flowers for Mrs. Bourgione with an apologetic note. Then, he drove straight out of town, crossing the border, and continuing on until he arrived in Ottawa. He had an early dinner and then strolled about the center of the city until well into the evening. He stopped for a drink in an Irish bar and listened to a folk singer, before returning home to a quiet and, thankfully, empty driveway.

• 2 •

"You're afraid!"

"Not so."

"Are too!"

Autumn danced out from the doorway of the Liquor and Poker straight into the pouring rain, twirled on one foot, and started singing with all the power she could muster. She tossed the rain from her hair in a clumpy spray and called to Patrick, who was hunkering in the shallow space before the door, "Come on! The rain's not going to hurt you!"

"I grew up near London. I'm not afraid of the bloody rain!"

"Then why won't you walk home with me?"

Patrick looked left and right and with a grunt moved out into the downpour. "How much have you had to drink is what I want to know."

"Practically nothing. Two beers. It's what I've had to *think* that's important."

"And that is?"

"I know what I'm going to do."

"Bloody well catch pneumonia. And I will too."

"No! God! I mean with the journals."

She twirled again, grabbing him by the hands and danced several steps before he let go of her and pushed his hands into his pockets.

"What's your problem? I've been talking to you, and you've just gotten, I don't know, mope-ier."

"I'm not 'mope-ier,' whatever the hell that means. Pensive is a better description. Things on my mind that I have to find a way to say"

"Well, get un-pensive for a moment. I'm telling you something that's going to change the way I live, the way I work, the way I create. Don't you understand? This is my liberation from music, from Gaston's shadow and my own sense of failure, you know? Could you at least smile?"

"You haven't told me yet what it is you plan on doing, only that you know what you're going to do with the journals, not *what* you're actually going to do with them."

"If I tell you, will you promise to cheer up for Chrissakes?"

"Here's a smile in good faith."

"Okay, ready for this?" She stopped, and the rain ran down over her face as she held out her arms. "I'm going to take the journals and write a play."

"A play?" he asked, walking on.

"A play." She matched his stride and studied his face. "You don't think I can do it, do you?"

"I didn't say a word!"

"You did with your face."

"Nonsense!"

"You had that look."

"And what did that look say then?"

"That I don't know anything about the stage. You're wrong about that, and I've learned enough to know what I'm up against. The crazy thing is I wasn't even thinking of anything like a play until last night. Gaston was reading this stuff to me about the search for the grail and its symbolic meaning in modern society, and I said,

'Wow! Isn't that like what this whole society's about, a search for the musical grail?' There it was. He laid the idea in my lap, and I immediately thought, 'A play!' I made him tell me the legends and then we stayed up most of the night talking about them. It's perfect. Here we all are questing after the things we want, like success, which is really whatever we make it out to be in our minds, our own idea of achievement. God, I'm not explaining it right, but it's clear in my mind. What a dramatic tale it will make!"

She lifted her face up to the sky and screamed. Then, she turned around to face Patrick and, while walking backward, poked a finger in his chest. "But you don't think I can do it, do you?"

"There you go, putting words in my mouth again. I said nothing of the sort."

"Your tone says it."

"First my face, then my tone tells you the truth behind my words, is that it? I fancy your chances with anything you have a mind to do, all right? Leave off the bloody psychoanalysis!"

"You're crying!"

"I am not."

"Don't tell me you're not; I can see the tears mixed with the rain. What's up with you?"

He looked away from her.

"What's going on?"

"Nothing."

"Bullshit, nothing."

"Well, I'm not discussing it standing in a flood!"

Autumn grabbed his hand and pulled him onto the porch of the nearest house. Inside the house, a dog began to bark.

"Who lives here?" asked Patrick.

"I don't know."

"Are you mad? You can't—" He made a move to get off the porch, but she blocked his way.

"You're not going anywhere until you either push me off this porch or tell me what's going on."

"We're bloody well trespassing, you know!"

"Start talking."

"Autumn—"

"I mean it, Patrick. I'm not fooling around. You're starting to scare me. I want to know here and now what's happening." Autumn put her hands on her hips, planted her feet, looked into his eyes, and regretted it. Patrick returned her stare with a fury of tears and the look of a man who was about to either knock her off the porch and disappear or collapse in a pitiful heap. Instead, he pulled an envelope out of his pocket and tossed it to her.

She removed the paper out of the envelope and looked at the signature first. "Who's Richard?"

"My brother."

She scanned the letter. "He wants to hire you as a session musician? Is this serious?"

"Of course it is. Richard's been with EMI for ten years. Now he's in the London office, providing musicians to staff various European studios. I told him I'd love to have a go at working in a studio, so he put my name in as soon as a position became available. As a session man, I'd be recording a great range of music, learning the studio from the inside, getting to know the up-and-coming artists, all the while still having the time to write and play my own music. And the topper is I'll be working wherever I'm needed but mainly in Copenhagen, which is one of Europe's loveliest and most artistic cities."

"Well, what're you getting so uptight about? This sounds perfect! What more could you ask for?"

"Only one thing: I want you to come with me."

Autumn laughed. Patrick was gazing straight into her eyes, his hands folded behind his back, and she regretted laughing, but she couldn't stop. He never moved his gaze away from her, but he said in an almost inaudible tone, "I see."

She waved her hands and caught her breath. "I'm not laughing at you, Patrick. It's just, well, unexpected."

"Quite. And your answer is equally unexpected, but not surprising." He pushed past her, down the steps and back out into the rain.

Autumn caught up with him, trotting to keep pace. "And what's that supposed to mean?"

"Simply put, you're not capable of going to Copenhagen with me."

"Why not?"

"For the same reason you won't ever write that play."

"What?"

"No, to make a proper job of sharing your life with someone or writing a play, you'd have to open up, not be so dammed self-absorbed. And you'd have to lose that dammed bloody, immature Gilhain-centric view of the world you have: that magical view where everything exists for your pleasure and your system of evaluation, and, until judged, by you, nothing has value in its own right. If you write with that attitude, you'll turn out a piece of nonsensical drivel and be alone in doing it. Then let's see who you turn to in order to cry and whine about things! Well, it won't be Patrick Stuart Mallard, you can be bloody well sure of that!"

Autumn got ahead of him, turned and landed an open-handed slap on the right side of his face, stopping him cold. He drew back his own hand.

"Go for it," she said.

He shook his head, lowering his hand. "It's not worth it." He started on again, but she got in his way, bumping him to a halt.

"Self-absorbed? Me? Okay, maybe I am. But let's talk about you for a second. What did you expect me to say? You don't mind screwing me, but you don't give me any indication, ever, that anything like this is coming. No. You say you're in love with me, but all I hear about is how beautiful Asian women are, how they're so exotic, so sexy, so irresistible." She stepped back and spread her arms, yelling, "Do I look Asian to you?"

"Of course not."

"Then tell me how the hell I'm supposed to know or guess or intuit that you want me to run off to Denmark? You sat in that bar for half an hour with me this afternoon not saying one thing. You never break in and say 'Gee, Autumn, I really have something important to ask you.' I have to pull you up on some stranger's porch to get you to talk to me, and when you finally do, you propose that we run away to Europe together? Going there might not be a big deal to you since that's your home, but it seems like the other side of the world to me. Then you're looking at me, just waiting for an answer, and I know we look like two drowned rats. So, I laughed because the situation was funny. Not at you, Mr. I'm-sensitive-not-like-that-selfish-Autumn-chick. So, I'm very sorry for not having your English sense of decorum and coming up with some romantic Emily Bronte answer on the spot. Oh, I forgot. I couldn't do that because I'm far too self-absorbed to write as well as her. Fuck you!"

She turned and marched ahead. Her apartment was only a block away, and she could hear Patrick following her, but she didn't turn around or acknowledge him, and he made no move to reach out to her. So be it. She climbed the steps and barged through the door. Chet, who was talking to Gaston, barely got a syllable of greeting out before she crashed past him into her room and slammed the door shut.

She spent ten minutes pacing in the room trying not to listen to the murmuring voices of Patrick and Chet, overlaid by the acoustic strumming of Gaston, on the other side of the door. She focused instead on the layers of emotion sifting and settling like sediment in her brain. On top was pure, white-hot anger. How dare he call her self-absorbed when he didn't even wait to hear what she had to say, never even gave the question any chance of discussion? Then, he has the nerve to deliberately take a shot at her because of a split-second human reaction. This from the only person she trusted with the whole story of the journals in the first place. Trusted. Yes, she trusted him. She wanted to trust him. Well, he blew it big time.

The second layer agreed with him. She *was* selfish and arrogant, judging the world with her — what did he call it? — Gilhain-centric point of view. But she had a right to be that way for the same reason she had a right to be angry. There wasn't anyone in this world looking out for her, and yet people expected her to be soft and demure, to throw herself open to the world and let everyone in to inspect and toy with her heart and soul. The only person who proved worthy of that trust was Quinn. So, yes, Patrick was right. What was he going to do about it? She had simple requirements: one person who cares enough about her to break through her facade and discover Autumn Gilhain for who she truly is. She would not accept anything less, even if that meant being selfish.

The third layer simply hurt. It sucked her down and mired her in the thought that there might never be anyone who cared enough to reach her. Why should there be? Look at how the barrier was raised in the first place: her parents, the preacher in Buffalo, Gerry and Lyle dying, Gaston's solitude. Patrick. His falling short hurt the worst not just because it was the most recent but because he alone had read the journals. He saw the woman behind the wall. And still, he could do something like this. "You'll never write the play, never share your life." The cruelty in those words. She wouldn't forgive it and trusting him was unforgivable of herself. If he felt that way, fine, he could just crawl off to Copenhagen.

She leaned her forehead against the window glass. Her thoughts went to Gravesend. Here was this genius, this sad, intriguing genius. What did he feel for her? Love? He never came right out and said those words, but his actions gave him away, the manner in which he reacted to her. Yes, he loved her. And she felt that he genuinely thought highly of her. So, she concluded, she couldn't be all that bad, could she? There had to be some hope. Maybe reason could balance on that slim limb, but she felt like her heart and soul had already fallen.

She left the window for the haven of her bed, going prone on top of the covers, her forehead resting on her forearm. The comforter smelled of her scent mixed with nylon, and both smells grew denser as her damp clothes slowly soaked into the dry material. The school year was coming to an end, and she had no idea what was waiting around the bend of summer. She only knew she could not go through another year in the Music school. Where does a third-year music student who is marginally talented and who has limited interest in music find work? "Hi, I'm an artist; are you ready to order? The meatloaf (or beer on tap, or custard-filled doughnut) is really good." Perhaps a summer — or a lifetime — of that. She didn't want to know the future, the plan of her life. She did want to feel some indication that she would find a path worth pursuing and that, at least, she would be comfortable pursuing it by herself.

A knock sounded on the door. She heard the door latch click open and saw a wedge of light shining on the wall next to her bed. Footsteps approached, but she didn't roll over. A body sat down on the bed beside her and a hand gently ran up her back to her sopping hair and through it. The person continued to brush her hair in long strokes, until she turned over on her side. Patrick touched her cheek and leaned in and kissed her, gently at first, then with more passion and warmth. She pulled away, rolling back onto her stomach and turning away.

"I do love you, Autumn," he said getting off the bed. "More so now than before."

She didn't respond, didn't breathe, until she heard the door close, cutting off the light. Maybe that was symbolic too: the severing of the light, the severing of their two-month affair and what had grown between them. How wonderful it would be to sever everything, not to feel the pain, not to love him, too.

৯ 3 ৩

The ending to the symphony's third movement should have conveyed a paradox. Instead, Gravesend thought while searching for the correct combination of notes, the entire movement was a paradox. What he had was a composition that got stuck trying to relate the fact that the motion of feelings around which the piece was composed had ground to a halt. He knew what sounds he wanted, they had been playing in echoes and shadows in his head for weeks, but he could not bring it into form, not even a rough form.

"You're fighting it," said Papaté, stepping over to the front of the piano and resting his thick arms on the top. "You can't ever find what you need that way, man. All you'll get is frustration."

"Six hours, and I'm only three, four bars ahead of where I started."

"With hardly a break to visit the *pissoir*. It's almost eleven, my friend. I must go soon."

"Was it always this hard, Papa?"

"Things change. There are elements missing."

"Julia?"

"Yes, but I meant other things. You've forgotten, maybe, how it used to be when you composed? For instance, this is the first time I've seen you at the piano without a snifter of brandy. And I remember when six of us were in the Great Room one night while you worked, and after we had gone, Julia told me that you grumbled about how no one ever stopped by anymore. You never knew we were there."

"So what you're saying is that I need a drink and a party to get going?"

"You tell Papa what you need. You drank to cut the intensity. You never noticed the constant stream of people wandering in and out at all hours because you were so enveloped in the work that nothing else existed. You worked like a man dancing for the very first time with the woman he loves. Only you and the music were in the world."

"I think I got into the music very well tonight."

"You yelled for me to be quiet an hour ago when I was singing softly to myself. That tells Papa that you aren't getting deep enough. Is the problem with the composition itself? Is it too vague for you to interpret? What do you hear playing in here?" He tapped his own head.

"The problem isn't with what I hear in my head. The problem is transferring what I hear into physical sounds. The theme focuses on the outlier emotions rather than the common emotions we feel when we connect intimately and intensely with another person. It's not about emotions or feelings per se, but the deep, primal bonds that exist even at the first meeting, as if there were a force that draws two people or a group of people together. The end of the third movement is the key to this theme because this is the point where the bond has been made, the mysterious drawing force has completed its work, and now the individuals involved must take over to carry on the relationship. But at that point of transition, there is a stoppage or void. That's what I'm trying to convey: the paradox of a relationship that stops progressing because what the relationship needs to progress has in and of itself reached an impasse. Do you understand?"

"I understand perfectly. I understand that you have no need for brandy. You're high enough, man. Where's the fourth movement go?"

Gravesend stood and circled the piano rubbing at his beard. He stopped behind Papaté. "It's starting forward again, after the pregnant pause. The slow, thawing rise in temperature from absolute zero."

"If you want to convey movement, fine: then why not write of wheels? Perhaps a special kind of wheel?"

"You want me to compose a tire jingle?"

"No, no. Sweet Baby Jesus! Is it any wonder you can't compose with such a closed mind? Expand. A paradox is a special kind of metaphor. You want to move forward, as if on wheels. What kind of wheels? Make a metaphor."

"Wheels of motion, wheels of time. Movement forward." Gravesend flipped his right hand in continuous motion. "Rolling; not just in a body sense but the rolling of the hills, the rolling of emotions."

"Ah! And what emotions would these be?"

"Wheels that grind to a start, like a mill wheel or ... something that breaks out to begin again with great effort. Something painfully slow ... Like a baby's first steps but with more resistance ... breaking out ... much like – YES!" Gravesend clapped so sharply that Papaté jumped. "Breaking out, like a dog sled driver breaks out the frozen runners of a sled. That moving forward. Moving forward ... into a cold so frigid that it impedes movement. The emotions of the people take over and slowly break out onto their own road against outside impediments. So it's ..."

Gravesend sat behind the keys again, fiddling for the right combination from which to begin, working note by note, jumping from the keys to the pen and scored paper on a sideboard. Finally, he had the bridge he had been looking for: an ending to the third movement and a beginning to the fourth, which worked smoothly into the meat of that part of the symphony. Gravesend let out a long sigh and slowly moved his back in order to work out the kinks. The sound of a single pair of slow, clapping hands greeted him. With an air of dignity, he stood and gave Papaté a deep bow.

"Hey, don't get too carried away; it wasn't that good."

Gravesend snapped back into place. Autumn sprawled across the chair that Papaté had occupied all evening, her back against one arm rest and her feet dangling over the other.

"What are you doing here? Where's Papa?"

"There wasn't anyone here when I came in. I couldn't sleep so I decided to take a walk. I saw the firelight flickering and the door was unlocked so I came in."

"What time is it?"

"Two-oh-seven. I made some comment but you were so engrossed, I decided to watch and listen to Gravesend-in-progress."

"And now that you have heard one of my first efforts with a piece of music, do you think it to be, in your own inimitable word, 'shit'?"

"Not at all. You played some brilliant music."

"There's no need to patronize the old man, Autumn. I am perfectly aware of how rough a first draft composition is."

"I didn't say it was perfect, just brilliant. Brilliance doesn't have to be perfect. Sometimes it's raw, naked expression. Brilliance is watching you open and listening to the creativity pour out of you. It's amazing, and a little awing, to see you in that sort of zone. I just sat here listening to the music being created and thinking, 'I'm the first person to ever hear this.' And you never stopped. You must be exhausted."

"Strangely, no. On the contrary, I was thinking that I would like to hear the third and fourth movements in their entirety in order to evaluate how the new music sounds."

"Do it!"

"So I will." He gathered the papers from the sideboard and moved out from behind the piano. As Gravesend walked by Autumn, he took her hand. "Come on."

"Where are we going?"

"To hear the music," said Gravesend, leading her into the main part of the house. He paused in the kitchen long enough to pour them both a snifter of brandy before leading her up the stairs to the closed double doors of the studio beside his bedroom.

Autumn paused. "Was Julia the last person to go into this room with you?"

"Julia or Papaté. I'm not sure."

"What the hell do I say to that?"

"Say nothing." He turned an ornate key, snapping the lock, and stepped inside, twisting a knob on the wall next to the door.

Lights came up bringing into view the grand Steinway in the middle of the room, topped by a framed photograph. A hundred year gap lay between the Victorian style and décor of the room and the modern recording equipment. The walls were papered in thick, alternating strips of cranberry and blush pink. Paintings hung on two of the walls, one showing a cliff scene in rugged strokes of reds, blacks and silvers, the other showing a moonlit tor and lake in olive, brown, and stark white. A row of windows opened onto the river.

The piano itself was surrounded by acoustic sound panels. A recording and mixing console sat to one side of the room with cables running forward and ending at three thick microphones set around the piano at various heights.

Autumn walked over to the piano and stared at the picture. "Julia," she said reaching for it, but she stopped herself.

"You may pick it up," said Gravesend.

"No," she replied, staring at the face of the woman staring back at her from behind the glass. Then she shook her head and poked around the other side of the piano. Finding a stool near the far wall, she pulled it out and perched herself on it, saying, "So, let's hear it. And do you have a title for it yet?"

"The title can wait until the end," replied Gravesend, laying out his notes. He put a finger to his lips for silence and then went to the console and arranged the levels. Slipping back over to the piano, he sipped from the snifter, studied the score, and began. He listened as he played, glancing at Autumn between references to the score, and assessing the music through both its sound and her shifting reaction. Her posture, her expression, her movements; her nods and sways, as well as her utter stillness during several passages, gave him as many impressions of the effect of the music as the sound he was hearing. Both thrilled him. The music was good, quite good. There were places he noted where it needed to be smoothed and reworked, but the core was there, and then some. Autumn's reactions were also good. The music and the woman began to draw together in his mind, like two instruments that begin playing different chords but slowly draw together in harmony. There were moments when it appeared to Gravesend that Autumn and the music were engaged in some form of subconscious communication. Several times Gravesend felt like a voyeur in his own home, a man watching a movie about a beautiful woman and beautiful music.

He watched and listened as his hands moved through the final sequence, shrinking the room like a closing bag, everything drawing together. His hands skipped lightly down the scale and ended the fourth movement with a sprightly flourish.

Autumn opened her eyes and laughed. "You're blushing!"

Gravesend put a finger to his lips again, getting up to turn off the console's recording function. He stood with his hands on the console, his back to her, leaning forward over the levers so she couldn't see his face.

"Why were you blushing?" Autumn asked.

"It's because ..." he turned back to her and felt his smile gape across his face. "It's because the music is so bloody good. My God, I can hardly believe I said those words, and, mind you, I realize certain passages will need brushing up, but what is here is very, very ... well, simply good."

"It's one of the most beautiful works I've ever heard. What's it called?"

"*Symphony Number 2000 – The Autumn Suite.*"

The room went silent, and the silence went deeper than just the absence of noise. Gravesend couldn't follow it. He felt a charge in the silence as well as a wall. Autumn leaving the stool and stepping over to the piano broke the veneer of the silence but didn't dent its depth. He saw her eyes drop to the keys, her pointer finger brushing several of them. Then she picked up the score sheets and began to read them. Gravesend stepped up beside her. He wanted to say something important, something meaningful, but the only sentence that came into his head – "I decided to title the piece the way I did because I find you to be one of the most beautiful works that I have ever heard or seen" – was so mawkishly teenaged that he felt himself blush again.

Autumn finished reading. She placed the score on top of the piano and let out a long breath that sounded to Gravesend like a combination of sigh and nerve. He turned his head toward her and saw her face rising toward his, felt her lips press against his mouth. The kiss was quick, and she drew back from it, repositioned herself as if she had been off balance, and rose to meet his lips again. This time, she stayed. Gravesend felt her arms go around his neck and her lips work on his mouth like a key on a recalcitrant lock. He breathed in the smell of her and raised his hand to feel the touch of her hair, her denim collar, the skin of her neck.

Autumn broke off the kiss, slipping off her jean jacket and looking around until she spotted the door to the adjoining room. Lowering her head and taking his hand, she indicated the door with a nod of her head, and he nodded in return. They walked through the door and undressed in silence and in darkness. He had one moment's embarrassment when she pressed against him, touching her smooth, fair skin and wondering how rough his must be to her. She whispered something he didn't catch, but the sound was so gentle, so un-Autumn, that it soothed him. She pressed herself against him, length-to-length and held them in that position before swinging him around and prodding him toward the bed.

What came next was a rush of sensation and thought such as he had not had in years. He felt more than a small degree of fear. But to his surprise, she was patient, gentle, and tender. The urge to tell her that the true symphonic music was her touch rose in his throat, but he couldn't get the words any further than that so he settled for repeating it over and over in his mind, hoping to communicate it to her silently.

When they had finished, he moved onto his side and felt her lay her face against his chest, raising such a sensation of warmth and protectiveness he put his arms around her but had to consciously stop himself from pressing her against him with all his strength. For the briefest moment, Julia intruded on his thoughts. However Gravesend settled for listening to the metronomic sound of Autumn's breathing, falling into the rhythm of those breaths himself, and then feeling himself fall further on into an undiscovered darkness and sleep.

ș 4 ș

What do I do?

Autumn re-read the words, repeated the phrase in her head and wrote it one more time: *What do I do?*

"Talk to me," she said. "On one side, there's Quinn, and all I've ever wanted. Another soul to see <u>me</u>, and in an original way. At least I can inspire great art, if I can't create it. Quinn has been my teacher and friend. And yes, I love him."

What do those words even mean? "I love you." They look so strange to me, like the face of a person you've known all your life but suddenly don't recognize. I've felt so many different emotions for Quinn over this past year. Some were awe. Some were anger. Some were déjà vu, like I was repeating with Quinn what I went through with Gaston, hero-worship and the need to be bathed in someone else's light because I had none of my own. What were the words of that song he sang in the Lick and Poke? "All I ever learned from love was how to shoot at someone who out-drew you?" God, anything I write on this subject sounds so teeny-bopperish. I'm in the middle of great things, hearing the birth of a masterpiece, working with a bunch of fantastic musicians, and it's like I'm picking daisies and pulling petals off them saying, "He loves me. He loves me not." Am I "in love" with Quinn? I know I'm in love with the man's genius, his music, his power to command emotions with a single touch of a piano key. But am I in love with the man?

"Does that even make a difference? Come on Lyle; give me a hand here. I mean, people talk about being in love and loving someone like they talk about birthdays: one day you're one age and the next day you're a year older. Really? They're false boundaries. Not like being alive and being dead, right? I loved Quinn yesterday. I love him today. Has anything changed just because in between, Quinn and I found the emotional moment to allow us to do what we've both wanted to do for a long time?"

Then there's Patrick, whom I also love. Why? Because he backed me into a corner and made me see that he loved me. Well that's a crappie reason to love someone. If I love him, it has to be for something more. Or maybe because he's crazy. Good. So is that enough to make me take off to Europe with him? Because he's crazy enough to love me? Then again, life hasn't been so hot in the U.S. or Canada, so why not try Europe? Hasn't my life been played out on worse stages? But am I ready to go to a foreign country, learn a new language and new customs? I mean, I can't name one thing about Denmark other than it's in Europe and its capital is the name of a brand of chewing tobacco.

"Look at this. I'm writing about going to Denmark, like it's totally up to me. Like Patrick still wants me to go after I reacted the way I did and bruised whatever part of his male ego was sensitive that day. And why am I writing about Quinn's emotions? Is it because I love Quinn and just love the adventure of Patrick? Or is it because love isn't a question with Patrick, just what to do about it, but it's not settled with Quinn yet? Or is it because I've screwed it up with both of them, and this is just a waste of time?

"Fuck!"

Autumn threw the notebook which Frisbee-ed across the living room. The pen flew in another direction, bouncing off the floor and landing near the door. She fell back against the arm of the couch, stretched out her legs and stared out the window into the dark night. Thank God Gaston had a four-day gig in Montreal; she needed the alone time. She looked out the window and figured it was after 5 a.m. It would be light soon. A gray light.

Autumn stood and slowly paced around the room. She leaned over and picked up the pen and the notebook, flicked the pen back and forth, and continued her pacing.

"With Patrick, everything's different. I don't feel a cosmic connection. Maybe, I'm too afraid of him to think that. Don't get me wrong; I'm not afraid of him in the sense that he would beat me or anything. I could kick his ass any day. What I'm afraid of is what he does to me inside. There are no bumps there at all, only a naturalness about being with him, an easiness. So, can I trust the next phase of my life to 'easiness'? Or is that just a by-product of the newness of all this feeling? What happens when that newness fades? Does the easiness fade? I really don't know. I haven't had much experience with easy. I think that's what scares me."

She tapped the pen against her leg. "Let's put all this other shit aside and get to the real dilemma. Here it is: Quinn could hate me for running off to Denmark with Patrick, and Patrick could hate me for staying here with Quinn. I don't want to break either bond. But how do I avoid that?"

Autumn flopped back down on the couch, letting the notebook and pen drop to the floor. "This is stupid shit, too, but I have to ask the question. Julia, how did you die and let Quinn go on like he did? You just died. You left him, but he hasn't left you. I always felt someone or something else in the Great Hall, and I know it came from Quinn. When we were in bed, I know he was thinking about you. How could he not? And long before you left Quinn, you let go of the other men and had the nerve to walk off with Quinn into some unknown future. Where does that courage come from? I know how to hurt someone with anger. I just don't know how to hurt someone with love."

Slowly the tears started to fall. Autumn hugged a pillow tightly as she rocked back and forth. Eventually her body lurched with a convulsive sob, and she pressed her face deep into the pillow. The sobs rose to wails. She pounded the pillow, slid off the couch onto her knees and finally let the pillow sail across the room. Then the jag subsided. Her heart was still pounding and her head began to throb. But something calmer and more soothing had moved in to replace the spent anger and frustration. She brushed the tangled hair out of her face and got back onto the couch, reaching for the notebook and pen.

I'm not lost. I know what I want to do. Maybe I've known it all along.

She turned her attention to the window for a moment to think.

Just because it's what I want to do doesn't mean it's right. And it doesn't mean that I'll do it right. It also doesn't mean that I won't screw it up and lose everything. But that can't stop the doing. Still, if all I'm left with is a notebook, I couldn't bear that. I'm not going screw up this time. Not again.

May

❧ 1 ❧

G enius.

A genius, people say. The possessor of a gift that few, if any, other composers ever possessed: the ability to perceive and translate the musical signature of every facet of life. To be able to comprehend the musical arrangement of love, a tree, a snowstorm, a universe, and then craft that comprehension into a coherent composition that carried those sounds to the common listener. It defied imagination and, therefore, was genius.

It defied imagination, thought Gravesend, pacing the small dressing room. So did knowledge of the burden of such genius. Let them try to turn their minds off to a natural sense so that an unwanted emotion won't rise up and intrude into a concert, ruining it. The performance of *Symphony Number 1970,* for instance, with the London Symphony Orchestra conducted by Eliot Strom. The morning of the concert, Peter called to tell him that Julia, who was six months pregnant, had miscarried. He was younger then, cock-sure and confident that he could hide the pain, but it splashed out through his fingers, then poured out. All the clashing emotions mixed in with the music, wrecking the score and sending his playing spinning out into a different orbit. Strom came to his dressing room after the concert to make a point of calling him a bastard, and has continued to do so every time their paths have crossed since.

Being older, Gravesend thought, didn't mean he was better able to control those emotions. It only meant he was better aware of what they could do. He stood in the center of the dressing room, right hand to right temple, trying to count the beats of his pulse. It was a bit like counting what was nearby to get rid of an unwanted song from the mind. Beneath the throb, he could feel the tug-of-war between the various emotions moving inside him, thrusting their way into his consciousness like a fish breaking the surface of water. He was about to open himself up before a real audience. If he couldn't curb his emotions during a concert when he was in his prime, how could he do so now that he was in his sixties? Add to that fact that *Symphony Number 2000: The Autumn Suite* was the most personal composition he had ever created. Not even *The Julia Suite* contained the layered complexity of feeling that he had woven into this composition. What if something goes awry?

"Stop it," he said aloud. "Stop acting like a novice with stage-fright. Focus. Concentrate. Breathe."

A rapping on the door startled him. It swung open, and Papaté stood in its frame. "You are summoned to the stage, Quinn Gravesend. Are you all right?"

"I will be once I start."

The big man smiled and raised a clenched fist. "Papa knows everything will be splendid."

Gravesend checked himself in the mirror one final time, and followed his friend down the corridor to the wings of the stage. What if Autumn arrived late? That's truly what he feared. He would go out on that stage, see the empty chair, and the emotional Furies would be on him. Even if he wrestled them away, the performance would be in disarray. *Then* she'd show up. Genius. At the moment, he'd trade it in for mere concentration.

Papaté stepped aside before entering the wing. Gravesend went on. The piano came into view first, center-stage. Next, he saw the conductor of the Toronto Symphony Orchestra at the top of the pit, then the players. That was as far as he would allow his eye to go. He made it to the piano amidst warm applause from the crowd, nodded to the conductor, and sat.

An anticipatory crackle filled the room in that pause between his sitting and the first notes. It settled and dissipated when he began. The performance version of the piece called for him to introduce the main theme with the piano alone, and he wrote it that way solely to allow himself time to get into the rhythm. It was a hedge against a wrong note or an early entrance. He wanted to control everything until he had settled. He finished the introduction, and the strings came on-board in perfect time with the harp following. The launch was successful; Gravesend felt the music rise and swell, moving out from the stage and pit over the crowd in the way he crafted it to flow.

He kept his eyes away from the audience, not relying on the stage lights to blind him. Better not to know of Autumn's presence than to risk knowing of her absence. However, she was there, in the music, and each bar tantalized him like Orpheus ascending from Hades presumably with the soul of his wife behind him. Gravesend listened for any sound that might betray her presence, any feeling that she was only yards away. He focused on channeling the urge to look into his playing, but that resolve melted away. He looked up.

The lights were bright, but he could make out Gaston Gunn, uncharacteristically *sans* sunglasses, peering back at him with wide-eyed intensity. Papa sat to Gunn's right, Chet Kunzler to his left. The other two seats were empty ... or were they? A hazy shape filled the seat next to Kunzler. It wasn't Autumn; he could tell that for sure, and his scenario of her coming in late helped him to not panic now. But the figure in that seat looked almost to be in shadow. Had Parker moved some dignitary to the open seat? The stage lights played havoc with his view, and he could not see a face, but the strange personage remained, seeming to be both in the seat and not there at all. A chill went through him, and he recognized it: the same chill that had pierced him so powerfully the night of the Solstice party, coming from the shadows of the Great Room; the one that descended over him in the form of a great heaviness in the private cemetery near Pittsburgh in February; the feeling that both times came via the person or spirit of Lyle Glasser. Gravesend looked away and back again until Gunn, puzzled, glanced at the empty chair. The apparition had faded but not the chill. Misinterpreting Gravesend's interest, Gunn pointed to the empty seat and shook his head.

Gravesend bent to the task. He would not lose control, he told himself, even as the passion rose up to take command of his playing. He struggled against himself through the rest of the first movement, but early in the second he shifted the tempo to allegro before it was scheduled. The conductor threw a look of surprise over his shoulder, and Gravesend returned it with a stern face, saying in his head, "Don't be fixed on the score, old man. Follow me."

The piece pounded through the auditorium, running on and away from Gravesend. He was caught in a destructive cycle of being the producer and the recipient of the raw energy of the music looping back on him, causing him to produce more energy. He could see its effect in the faces of the three in the front row. Gunn leaned forward, clenching his fists, restraining the impulse to leap onto the stage and join in. Kunzler appeared pained. And Papa? Musical sense and knowledge of the piece would surely tell him that the performance had popped a joint, but he would be concentrating on what was being played rather than trying to analyze it. However they and the hundreds of others behind them reacted, they were on their own, Gravesend thought. He was powerless to stop his own work, let alone the way it moved through the auditorium, short of stopping the performance altogether.

The third movement fairly vibrated, filled with the memory of Autumn in his studio and afterward. The intensity of the music rose to a towering level, and then, inexplicably, Gravesend found control. "Enough" said a voice in his head. He had no right to hone himself to a blade's edge and thrust his feelings and his pain straight through the audience. Gradually, he reined in the work, easing it into the paradoxical ending of the third movement. The fourth called for him to open softly in adagio and from there the music should grow slowly louder and faster. But he opened the fourth movement at a dirge-like pace. He worked the piece so that it grew in volume but not in tempo. The orchestra hung with him, and the result was the musical equivalent of an abysmal ache. It was music that bled.

Finally, in the fifth movement, he brought the piece back to what the score called for: a moderate tempo, moving through his themes and variations with a tone of slow understanding of what is and what was to be. The ending put forward a face of acceptance, virtually swirling, the orchestra falling off instrument by instrument, finally closing on piano notes that twinkled even more slowly, like star after star going out in the sky. The final note was one of surrender to the total, unrepentant darkness from which there could be no return unchanged.

When Gravesend took his hands away from the keys, the auditorium was silent for several beats before erupting in a paroxysm of applause. Gravesend rose on shaky legs, stepped out from behind the piano, and bowed. The applause was rapturous, spontaneous and overflowing, as if the crowd were attempting to pour back into him some of what he had expended for them. He stepped back and opened his palms toward the orchestra. Then he took his final bow and, quelling the urge to flee, he paced off the stage at a steady, even gait.

Gravesend was hoping for a moment to collect himself in his dressing room, but the production people, the theater workers, and those who could wrangle their way back stage had moved into the corridor to meet him. He worked his way through them as diplomatically as he could, but he wasn't making much headway toward the dressing room until Papaté appeared. His large form drove a wedge between the people, and they started to clear. Gravesend let Papa take his arm and drag him through the throng. When they passed by his dressing room, Gravesend called out for Papaté to stop, to let him go in.

"No time for that," Papaté said. "I am responsible for delivering you to the President's house for the reception."

"But—"

"Do not give me a 'but' or any other contradictory word. You were the one who wanted to be a star this month."

The next two hours at the President's Reception was a blur. Papaté left after the first hour, telling Gravesend not to wait up for his return. Gravesend was roiling on the inside, but he managed to present a calm façade as he met dignitary after dignitary, accepting their congratulations with a smile and making small talk. Finally, he found himself at the door, shaking hands with the University President and her husband. Then he was out in the cool, spring air and freedom.

The house was dark when the taxi pulled up to the door. His final hope was that Autumn would be waiting on the porch, but only the familiar shadows waited there. He went in, made himself a drink, and stepped into the library. Sipping at the drink he moved around the room. What if Autumn had come to the house? No doubt she would be telling him now about some tragic reason that prevented her from attending the concert, or worse, some selfish reason delivered with that stoic, kiss-off pose. Either way, it would have ended with a request for understanding.

"Well, yes, Autumn," he said to the empty room. "I understand very clearly. I should share in your wonders. Not that it matters that you did not think for a second — not one second — how important it was for me to have you share in the performance of a symphony, the first public performance of any symphony in a quarter of a century, a symphony that was named for you, written for you, bloody well meant for you! No. You had to be somewhere else because, of course, any simple idea in the head of Autumn Gilhain is surely the first of its kind in this world, isn't it?"

He punctuated the last word by slamming the glass down on the table and whirling it away across the open surface. It stopped a thumb's width from the edge. He watched the glass stand in its place, and then he fell into a chair. His body heaved, and he caught his breath. It heaved again, and he laid his head down on his arms, letting the sobs come.

❧ 2 ❧

Autumn closed the journal. She placed it on top of the manuscript of her play and slid the entire package into a large padded envelope. She wrote Gaston's name and was halfway through the address when she stopped. Just beyond the envelope was the phone. She felt Patrick's hands on her shoulders.

"Why don't you call The Master, love?" he said.

"Because I couldn't say what I need to say. Because he wouldn't listen. He's got to be pissed as hell, and we'll both say things we don't mean and not say the things that have to be said."

Patrick stopped kneading her shoulders and sat down on the hotel room bed where he could watch her face.

"No," she said, with finality. "The best thing for everyone is to go with the plan."

"You're sure? A call to Prue is cheaper from Montreal than Copenhagen. And there's a long plane ride to consider with plenty of time for brooding."

"I won't be brooding. It's the best way." She finished the address and sealed the envelope.

❧ 3 ❧

The phone rang just after seven-thirty. Gravesend took the call in the kitchen without setting aside his vodka and lime juice. He had no pretenses about the caller on the other end being Papaté or his agent with news about another record company vying for his business. As he reached for the receiver, he wished that the caller would be someone unexpected, even Madame D'Abonne wanting another house party. Anyone other than Autumn.

"Mr. Gravesend," boomed a jovial but nervous male voice. "This is Chet Kunzler."

"Mr. Kunzler? To what do I owe this unexpected pleasure?" He sipped his drink.

"I have a favor to ask of you, Sir. Would you come to the Liquor and Poker tonight, not as a performer but as an honored guest?"

"A guest? Of whom?"

"Of *Société de l'Esprit Artistique*, such as it is. Our ranks have been sorely depleted of late."

"I see." Gravesend paused, gauging his reaction to Kunzler's observation. Part of him would have felt wonderful never talking to Autumn again, but a larger part wanted to see her, to clear the air and set things straight, as painful as that might be.

"Sir," Kunzler continued, "I should tell you that Autumn won't be there."

"I'm not surprised. Her absence at events is becoming routine." Gravesend sensed the tension on the other end of the line rise. "I apologize, Mr. Kunzler. You should not have been the recipient of that remark."

"That's okay. I understand its spirit. Gunn has some materials for you, from her. I don't know if they're intended to be the final word on her behavior over the past month, but my own experience of Autumn tells me that they are more of a first step than a last one. The request to come to the Liquor and Poker is from Gunn and me, for a different purpose. We would truly appreciate your presence. Will you come?"

"What time do you want me to be there?"

"Nine o'clock, if you could."

"Okay, Mr. Kunzler. I'll see you at nine."

"Thank you, Sir. Truly, thank you."

Gravesend made it to the Liquor and Poker at twenty-to-nine and found an open table at the side of the room near the door to the kitchen. Gunn and Kunzler were not in sight. The place was nearly full, and a waitress patrolled the room, indications that the owners expected this to be a big night. Gravesend caught the woman's attention and was set to order another vodka and lime, but checked himself. He asked for scotch on the rocks. Then he waited.

At nine, the two Society members came down the corridor and took the stage. Gunn sat at the piano; Kunzler sat behind the drums. Gunn leaned forward and said into the microphone, "We're only going to play one song. An original by Patrick Mallard. It goes out to Mr. Quinn Gravesend." A cheer went up in the room at the sound of his name, forcing a smile from Gravesend. "From a close friend. It's also from me and Chet to all of you."

Gunn played the chorus melody as an introduction, with Kunzler offering a quiet cymbal roll with mallets at the end. As Gunn moved into the first chorus, Kunzler settled into a soft rhythm behind him, forsaking the snare drum for the toms. Gunn sang.

Où la charité rencontre l'amour, tu es la. Tu es la.

If there is a sense, of sorrow, of longing, from the depths of pain

It comes from loving someone like you'll never love again.
For each sense of truth and love, come like the desert rain.

Où la charité rencontre l'amour, tu es la. Tu es la.

There was a time before you, when darkness was the rule
When laughter was unknown, the soul's unrest at full.
Then you opened up this life, the you who made me whole.

Où la charité rencontre l'amour, tu es la. Tu es la.

No words can take us back, to then, to what we both have missed
And nothing in this world we know sees through the forward mist.
Yet charity and love go on, by these things we exist.

Où la charité rencontre l'amour, tu es la. Tu es la.
Où la charité rencontre l'amour, tu es la. Tu es la.

They brought the song to a close. Kunzler let out a visibly long sigh. Gunn sat at the keyboard for a moment, brushing it with his hand and patting the side. Then he stood and stepped out from behind the instrument, walking slowly to the microphone at the front of the stage. He held up both hands. "I declare *Société de l'Esprit Artistique* defunct."

Kunzler joined him and they both bowed before exiting stage right to a flurry of applause and a couple of sharp, sustained whistles. Gunn paused long enough to lift his guitar case out from the shadows beside the stage, and both men came straight to Gravesend's table. Kunzler looked excited. And Gunn? Gravesend couldn't tell by sight; so much was hidden by the sunglasses. Gunn's smooth and even exterior was real and in place but beneath that the emotion was palpable but mixed. Stirred but not shaken.

"Gentlemen," Gravesend said, "please, join me."

"For a moment," Kunzler said. Gunn sat, leaning both his guitar and the back of his chair against the wall. Kunzler straddled a chair next to him, across the square table from Gravesend. No one said a word.

Gravesend smiled to himself. How like students on the first day of class the three of them seemed to be. Sitting in silence, not knowing what to expect or where to begin. Three eggs to be cracked. He took a deep breath. "Am I to assume that the song you played written by Mr. Mallard had contributions from Autumn?"

"The lyrics," Gunn said. "She didn't want us to announce her name. She said you'd get it."

"Indeed," Gravesend replied. "All the lyrics?"

Gunn shrugged. "I'm sure Patrick translated the chorus into French. The words are what Autumn wanted, but she doesn't know the language very well."

Kunzler opened his arms. "Well could one of you translate it for me? I know I'll have to learn it if I hang around in Montreal, but right now, I'm just some guy from Montana."

Gravesend saw Gunn look at him, but he stayed still.

"*Où la charité rencontre l'amour, tu es la*," Gunn said, "Where charity meets love, you are there."

Kunzler nodded. They lapsed back into silence until Kunzler made a show of looking at his watch. "'Old Time is a-flying,' and old Chet has to go." He stood and offered Gravesend his hand.

"Sir, witnessing the performance of your latest symphony was truly an honor and an experience I'll never forget as long as I live, and I wanted to thank you for the opportunity."

"My pleasure, Mr. Kunzler," Gravesend said, giving the man's hand a firm shake.

Kunzler nodded. He signaled to the waitress, and when she came to the table, he put his hand on Gunn's shoulder. "A beer for this good man here, and one more of whatever the professor is having this evening." He gave her a bill, told her to keep the change, and turned back to Gravesend. "I wish I could stay, but I have other commitments. Thank you again, Sir. Gaston, I'll see you in the north."

"See you, man."

Kunzler gave a general bow and was off. Gunn opened his guitar case and removed a package, which he laid on the table in front of Gravesend: A large, padded envelope addressed in Autumn's hand. Gravesend opened it and pulled out a hardbound journal and a bundle of paper held together by a rubber band. The top sheet was a simple title page: *The Society of Secrets* by Autumn Gilhain. Gravesend laid it aside, opened the journal, read the first line, and closed it.

"Tough stuff, huh?" asked Gunn.

"For you no less than me. The two of you were very close."

"But I let her go a long time ago. I guess now she's just found the nerve to take me up on it. I read the play."

"So that's what it is?"

Gunn nodded. "It's good. I was surprised, but it's really good."

"I'm sure it is. I never doubted that there was some great talent lurking inside her."

They fell silent, and Gravesend took to looking over the crowd, only he didn't see anyone. Impressions came to him, sounds and half-tone photographs crowded into his head forming a swirl of chaotic thoughts, much like dreaming. "Autumn is the beginning," his inner voice said, and Gravesend pricked up his senses to listen. "Then Winter sets in, long, cold notes of acceptance, feeling unrequited but unexposed. The seed that will flower later. Into Spring."

There it was, so clear it could have been written in a neon beer sign. A trilogy. Autumn, the season, was the beginning that marked the end. The paradox. Certainly he, Gravesend, was at an end, never to feel again how he felt about Autumn Gilhain. That was the province of youth. That realization called for a period of reflection and mourning, a period of pain and darkness — a winter — under which the emotions re-order and re-seed, much like winter's snows cover the raw materials of life that are reborn. When? In the spring. There are always other bonds to be formed, but different, like the bulbs of spring sprout the same annual plant but never the same flower.

Gravesend shook his head. Order. He needed to focus those thoughts, and when he did the pattern was complete. *The Autumn Suite*, already composed, portrayed the paradox of the beginning in the end. Now there needed to be *The Winter Suite*: a dark, rough, cold piece covering and nurturing hope and kneading the raw into the new. And then *The Spring Suite*: music of renewed joy that can only come with the acceptance of the present and the letting go of the past. And Julia would always be, had always been, Summer.

"Hey," Gunn said. "You look like you're working over there."

"In a manner of speaking, I am, yes." He sketched out his rough thoughts for Gunn.

"Autumn, winter, and spring," mused Gunn. "A new way of looking at the cycle of the seasons. Decay as a starting point. Cool."

"It's not new at all, actually. The old planting cultures used to see life that way. Growing the new out of the old, with death coming first and then life. If we don't grow beyond the past and find something good in the now and the future, we end up as bitter, old people. That's something I realized after the concert when Autumn didn't show up. I went home and had a terrible time. Later, I came to realize that we both had been rather childish at points, and the root of my childishness was the fact that I tried to recreate the past instead of moving into the future, as we all must. Autumn's purpose in my life may have been to help me shed the day-to-day reliving of the past and get on with the future. Perhaps *The Autumn Suite* and her disappearance form the first step."

"Something like that metaphor you used that fired Lyle up so much, hunting the mythical beast?"

"Mr. Glasser took that to heart? Funny, in class he always looked inattentive, distant."

"You looked like that a second ago. That's how I knew you were working. He had the same look when his mind was turning on to something musical. You had a great influence on him, you know?"

"No, I didn't. And I never would have guessed." Gravesend paused, thinking of the shadowy figure in the seat beside Papaté. "At least, he never told me in so many words. However, Mr. Glasser would not be the only member of your group whom I haven't noticed. I never really gave Autumn her due, either. I never saw her in her true light."

"You influenced both of them more than you know."

"That's something positive, at any rate. I'm looking for positive things now that I have my own mythical beast to hunt."

"Isn't autumn when hunting season begins?"

Gravesend laughed. "You are an intelligent lad, Mr. Gunn."

"Not enough, 'cause I can't figure out what you're going to do about summer? You leaving it out of the cycle?"

"No, not really. If I can compose along the themes that I set out to you, summer would be the time of attainment, of achievement, the rest following the work. What better way to convey that than silence? I might have to end the notation of the Spring symphony with an extended rest."

"That means these will be your last works."

Gravesend smiled and signaled the waitress for another beer for Gunn. After paying her, he stood. "Composition calls. Since Mr. Kunzler left us with a quote, I'll carry on that theme: I have a journey, sir, shortly to go / my master calls me, I must not say no."

"That sounds like something a guy would say before killing himself."

"I've been killing myself for years, Mr. Gunn. It would be pointless to do it again now when I have so much work ahead of me." He offered Gunn his hand. "Good luck. You have a brilliant future ahead of you. I, for one, will be listening."

He tucked the package under one arm and turned to leave, but Gunn's "Mr. Gravesend?" brought him back around to the table. Gunn was standing, his guitar in hand and a permanent ink marker raised with the timidity of a fan who should know better but just can't help himself. Chuckling, Gravesend signed the instrument and left.

The house was dark and silent. Gravesend climbed the stairs to his room. He stood at the windows gazing out over the land and thinking of the river running on its way to where it had to go. Of Autumn somewhere in this world. Of Gunn and Kunzler at the beginning. Of Julia and Lyle Glasser ... where? At the end? The beginning? Something in him understood that Glasser and he were closer in mind and heart than he was to any of the others, save Julia. He went to the desk and sat, opening the journal.

❧ 4 ❧

The only way to come to terms with all that has happened is to see things the way they are. I have spent a year of my life indulging in secrets, and in the end the only person I have been hiding things from is myself. No more.

Since the day my parents betrayed me, I've been searching for someone to love. First, I thought it would be Gaston, so I made him love me in my mind, but that was a deception I couldn't keep up. He so obviously loved his music first and foremost that there was precious little room for a second lover. Then, I thought it would be Quinn. I convinced myself that he was giving me the love I craved, but there was always a nagging doubt to that conviction. However, it wasn't until I went to Ottawa in late April and early May to write the play that the doubt became reality. Quinn never realized I was gone, never even noticed my absence. I was crushed and angry. "Fine," I thought. "I'll disappear from his life forever. Let him forget about everything."

It was while I was licking my immature wounds, feeling sorry for myself, and labeling myself a failure that I came to a realization. Love is not about finding someone to love you. Love is about nurturing and expanding the capacity within yourself to love another. I re-read my play, and found that theme running through it. If that was love I also realized that I have never felt it.

But when I started to view my relationship with Quinn in that light, I saw that I had made my first tentative steps toward loving someone else. I prodded him, showed interest, encouraged him, and got him involved. Did I do all that out of love? No. But I did have a sense that he needed to be involved, awakened, and I went to great lengths to wake him. And it worked. Because of the capacity to recognize what another needed and to act on that recognition, the world has *The Autumn Suite*, and Quinn has a new sense of life. And whether or not I intended it to happen, I took the first steps toward finding a capacity to love. Selfish steps, for sure, but first steps are always awkward.

In acting on that capacity, I find now, ironically, that Quinn made the first tentative offering of what I needed, too. He gave me my first taste of what it meant to be loved, the emotion, the responsibility, and the exchange. In short, he trusted me. He opened up his world and let me in. He gave the best and worst of himself for no other reason than he loved me.

Those gains should not be diminished by the fact that the love we shared was not the committed, life-long love of marriage. Quinn has two great loves in his life: Julia and music. His love of music did not consume his capacity to love another. He committed himself to both and both still fill his soul.

I don't know what I can commit my soul to. I don't know if Patrick and the play are the beginning of such a commitment, but it is time to move on and find out. I owe Quinn Gravesend quite a lot. I only wish I would have come to this sooner and put aside my hurt feelings about his not noticing my absence and gone to his performance. However, I am coming to know my own faults, and while it's too late for Quinn, at least I can look at Patrick and say, "I am ready to try." He has said the same to me. We don't know anything else. We don't know where our relationship will lead. But I am sure that it would never have come this far without what Quinn gave to me.

❧ 5 ❧

Gravesend had no concept of time after he closed the journal. Autumn's words ran through his mind and turned into notes, but he felt no need to reach for paper. The notes danced and floated like puzzle pieces waiting to be fitted into the correct slots to show the big picture. Slowly they started to fall together, but then more notes came, as if jumping through the window to greet him. He enjoyed the mess of sound, confident that they would eventually align in the right order. Not even the ringing of the telephone would stop them, but the ringing needed his attention. He picked up the receiver.

"Hello, Quinn," came Autumn's voice.

"Hello. Are you calling from Copenhagen?"

"No, London. Patrick has business here, and he wants me to meet his family, so we're staying for a few weeks. You know."

"Yes, I do. But my God, the time is well past midnight here. It must be after four in the morning in England."

"Yeah. My sleep is all screwed up. I talked to Gaston earlier. He said you got the package."

"Yes."

"Did you read the journal?"

"I did."

"Good. I have something that I want to say to you, but it won't mean the same thing if you've thrown the journal in the Great Room fireplace." Autumn paused. "You didn't, did you?"

"No, I didn't. I'm thinking more along the lines of putting it on top of my studio piano."

"I'd like that. Thanks."

The line went silent. Gravesend waited, giving her the same thirty-count he gave his students to answer a tough question. He got to fourteen.

"I love you, Quinn. That's what I want to say."

"I love you, too, Autumn."

"And just for the record, the performance was great. You put on quite a show."

Gravesend chuckled. "My improvisation came through over the radio?"

"No, in person. I watched it from the projection room at the top of the theatre; one of the techs I know got me in. You really didn't think I was going to miss the debut of my symphony, did you?"

It was Gravesend's turn to let the line go silent. He doubted Autumn was counting. "Did any of your group know about that?"

"Nope. They all thought I was in Montreal."

"I see."

"Anyway, when Patrick and I get back to the States, we'll drop by."

"I'll hold you to that. Give my best to Mr. Mallard."

"I will. Goodnight, Quinn."

"And I guess that's good morning to you, Autumn."

Gravesend heard her chuckling as they both hung up the

phone. He sat still for a minute and listened. Yes, the notes had waited for him. Then he stood, and with the journal in both hands, he crossed out of the bedroom and into the studio. To begin the long search at the keyboard. To find what he was just beginning to hear.

ACKNOWLEDGEMENTS

Any good work of art features a great team behind the artist. This novel is no exception.

Heartfelt gratitude and kudos to the premier editing team at BookMakers Editing and Submission Services. I came to them with what I thought was a good book, and when they were through, I had a book that was so much better than I ever thought it could be.

Special thanks go out to Dan Snyder. As kids, we harbored the dream of working on an artistic venture together. It isn't a record hitting #1 on the charts, but being able to work with you on this project feels like it to me. Thanks, buddy.

Thanks to Brian Fell who endured numerous suggestions and changes with patience and artistic aplomb. The cover is a book's first impression, and thanks to you, this novel makes a great one. Thanks also to Jennifer Terranella, who tramped through a cold late-autumn day to find the perfect tree.

Thanks to my creative writing colleagues at the Community College of Philadelphia, especially the 17th Street Writers and before them, the members of Prose Writers. Your honesty, support, and encouragement are invaluable.

Long overdue thanks to my family and friends, living and dead, who weave the threads that help make me the person I am today. A line in a book may be poor repayment for all you give, but know I give thanks for each of you every single day of my life.

Thanks to Frank Hoffman for policing my French.

Finally, thanks to the fine publication team at Mill City Press. Your upfront approach to publishing is refreshing.

ABOUT THE AUTHOR

Joseph Kenyon has published numerous short stories and poems in literary magazines and anthologies over the past twenty years. At the same time, he has taught writing at community colleges in New Jersey, Michigan and Pennsylvania. Currently, he is on the English faculty of the Community College of Philadelphia. *All The Living And The Dead* is his first novel.

CPSIA information can be obtained at www.ICGtesting.com
Printed in the USA
BVOW08s1940181016
465379BV00001B/43/P